While she began heating some water the children went outside, and she could hear them murmuring quietly to one another until there was the sound of a gate opening and Rowena changed to her grown-up voice. Out of her mother's range of vision Rowena stood by the wire fence smiling at the tall man walking up his garden path. At first she thought he was going to ignore her, but then Barnaby cleared his throat and the stranger turned to look at the children.

'Hello!' said Rowena carefully. 'I'm Rowena Lorrimer, and this is my brother, Barnaby. We've come to live next door.'

Margaret Bingley has written eighteen novels for both adults and children, many of which have been translated. She is passionate about opera, and lives in Lincolnshire.

Change of Circumstances

Margaret Bingley

Woman's Weekly Fiction

A Woman's Weekly Paperback
CHANGE OF CIRCUMSTANCES

First published in Great Britain 1986
by Severn House Publishers Ltd
This edition published 1995
by Woman's Weekly
in association with Mandarin Paperbacks
an imprint of Reed International Books Ltd
Michelin House, 81 Fulham Road, London SW3 6RB
and Auckland, Melbourne, Singapore and Toronto

A CIP catalogue record for this title
is available from the British Library
ISBN 1 86056 071 7

Printed and bound in Great Britain by
BPC Paperbacks Ltd
A member of
The British Printing Company Ltd

Chapter One

It was Whitsun, and for once the weather was beautiful. Heather and Brian sat in their garden chairs on the patio beneath the shade of the canopy and enjoyed the sight of Rowena and Barnaby playing in the swimming pool.

'Aren't you glad I talked you into it?' laughed Heather. 'They get more pleasure out of their swimming than anything else.'

'So they should – it cost enough!' Brian's voice was tolerant. His wife knew that he would do anything to keep her and the children happy. Even though he had made some token protests at the time, murmuring something about the financial situation of his company and the uncertainty of things picking up, she had never doubted that the pool would be put in.

'I think I'll join them later,' she continued. 'Cook excelled herself today, so perhaps I'd better wait a while to make sure I don't sink like a stone!'

Brian moved uncomfortably in his chair. 'I rather think I ate too much. I've got terrible indigestion.'

'I'll get you some of that medicine Dr Gates prescribed. I really think you ought to go and see him again; it doesn't seem to be doing you any good.'

'There's no point. He'll only tell me to slow down, and that's impossible. This is a bad time for engineering firms.'

Heather stood up. 'You say that every year. Your

trouble is that you're secretly hooked on the pace. I'm sure the business wouldn't collapse if you took things a little easier.'

'That isn't true. If . . .' He glanced at his slender, blonde-haired wife with her wide blue eyes and long curling lashes. She didn't look a day older than when he had married her ten years earlier. He had been forty-two and Heather nineteen. Spring and Autumn his friends had joked, but it had worked out very well.

Brian adored her, and their two children had only added to his contentment. If he could not make her understand about the business it was his own fault as he had never wanted her involved in his work. She was something separate and precious. He had kept her isolated from any problems, not wanting her to grow older, taking pride in her youth and almost child-like naivety. Time had stood still for Heather, because that was how her husband had wanted it, and she had been very happy with the arrangement. Their marriage worked because they each fulfilled a need in their partners. She made him the envy of his contemporaries; he protected and cossetted her as her parents had done before him.

He was just wondering if he had been sensible in his attitude when he heard the light tap of her heels on the slabs.

'Here you are, Mr Lorrimer. Two spoonfuls please, and no arguments!'

He reached out for the bottle, and winced as the pain in his chest increased.

'What's the matter? Is it getting worse?' Heather was momentarily frightened by his pallor.

'Just an extra strong twinge. I'll cut out the Yorkshire puddings from now on!' He poured some of the peppermint-flavoured liquid into the spoon and lifted it to his lips. A wave of nausea swept over him and he felt dizzy. His hand shook and the medicine spilt onto the floor.

Heather ran to his side. 'Darling, what is it? Do you want the doctor?'

He began to shiver, and the dull ache in his chest started to increase. He nodded, tried to stand up so that Heather could help him indoors, then gasped as the pain jabbed agonizingly through him, and his chest tightened so that breathing necessitated a major effort. The garden spun crazily round and the ground seemed to tip beneath his feet. There was a final burst of pain, a pain so great that he was unable to cope, and he blacked out, crashing against the light table and sending it spinning over as he collapsed in a heap at Heather's feet. For a few seconds she stared at Brian in disbelief, then she began to scream. The children stopped their splashing and looked towards her. They had never heard her scream before and glanced at each other in apprehension. They decided to stay in the pool.

Mrs Brice, busy with the washing-up, came running instantly. After one look at her employer she ran to the telephone and rang first for an ambulance and then for Dr Gates. Pausing only to collect a garden rug, she hurried outside again.

Heather was silent now, standing motionless, staring down at Brian. Her eyes were enormous and she looked at Mrs Brice in child-like bewilderment. 'What is it? Why can't he hear me?'

'Because he's unconscious. Come along, put this over him and then take the children indoors. I've sent for an ambulance and the doctor, so it's better that Rowena and Barnaby are out of the way. You don't want them frightened unnecessarily.'

Heather frowned and wrapped her arms round her body. 'He didn't take his medicine,' she said in a flat voice. 'I took too long getting it.' Plainly she was deeply in shock and of no immediate help.

Mrs Brice took over. She fetched the children and took them in through a side entrance, explaining that their father wasn't well. Once they were safely upstairs she returned to Heather. 'Go and put some warmer clothes on, dear. You're shivering. Besides, you can't travel with him wearing only your bikini.'

'Travel with him? Where's he going?' She was in a complete daze, turning to her cook for assistance now that her husband couldn't direct her. There was the sound of an ambulance siren.

'Hurry up!' admonished the older woman. 'He's bound to be taken to hospital, and you want to go as well, don't you?' Heather nodded and made her way indoors like a sleep-walker.

The ambulance men were placing Brian on a stretcher when Dr Gates arrived. He hastily checked his patient. 'Better make it quick,' he advised the two men, 'he's bad.' They nodded, and within minutes were tearing down the road, their siren still screaming.

As Heather walked down the stairs she found the doctor and Mrs Brice in close conference. When they saw her they drew apart. 'I'll look after the children, dear,' said the cook kindly. 'The doctor will run you to the hospital.'

Heather nodded and obediently followed Dr Gates to the front door. All at once she stopped and turned her head. 'Would you ring Amanda for me? We were due there for drinks tonight, and she'll wonder . . .'

'Come along,' said the doctor abruptly, 'there isn't time to rearrange your social diary.' Shocked by his rudeness Heather flushed and went quickly out to his car.

She was silent during the fifteen-minute drive. She didn't ask any questions nor did she cry or give details of what had happened. She seemed to be lost in a world of her own. At the Casualty department she sat down on one of the small, hard chairs and stared blankly ahead of her. She was vaguely aware of Dr Gates conferring quietly with another man but she didn't want to hear her fear voiced aloud. For as long as it remained unspoken it could be pushed away, denied, avoided.

With a professionally calm expression on his face Dr Gates walked back to Heather and looked down at her. He was amazed by her apparent lack of maturity. He had delivered her children himself, yet he still found it impossible to think of her as a mother. She had remained a young girl on the edge of womanhood, trapped in a time warp by her own inclination and her husband's collusion. He cleared his throat and Heather looked up. 'They've moved your husband to another hospital. The facilities here aren't adequate for his condition.'

'His condition? What's wrong with him? Do they know that much?'

'Of course! As, I'm sure, do you. Your husband's suffered a massive coronary. I've been advising him for the last few years to slow down, but he wouldn't listen. Those chest pains were a warning, and you ignore such warnings at your peril, I'm afraid.'

Heather looked directly at him. 'You told him it was indigestion. You gave him medicine for it.'

'I'm afraid not. I gave him some pills for mild angina. He must have bought the medicine over the counter.'

'Why?'

'Probably he didn't want you worried. Is there any way you can get to Charing Cross Hospital? That's where he's gone.'

'Charing Cross?' Her voice rose incredulously, and several people sitting patiently in the room turned their heads. 'Why have they taken him there? It's miles away!'

The doctor guided her into the narrow, gloomy, corridor, away from their silent audience. 'It's a large teaching hospital. If he's to have any chance at all he needs the most advanced treatment there is, and Charing Cross has the required technology.'

Heather shivered, her mind spinning. He'd been so happy that morning; making plans for their summer holiday in Sardinia, helping Rowena with her tables. It was impossible to believe that he was now desperately ill. In fact she didn't believe it. She was sure they were exaggerating. 'If you could take me home I'll drive myself there,' she said softly. The doctor nodded, and wondered what was going on behind her child-like face.

Two hours later, Heather was sitting beside Brian in a small, cheerless room holding his hand in hers as the large heart machine to which he was wired bleeped gently in the background. He gave her a slight smile.

'I was right about the Yorkshire pudding!' His voice was weak, his breathing laboured.

'Dr Gates told me that you'd been warned to take things easy. Why didn't you?'

'He's an old woman, always fussing.'

'How's the pain now?'

'Much better. Don't worry, I'll be fine.'

A nurse put her head round the door. 'Mr Lorrimer should be resting,' she said briskly, and then withdrew.

Brian tightened his grip on Heather's hand. 'You'd better go, darling. Who's looking after the children?'

'Mrs Brice, but I'll ask Amanda to have them tomorrow. They love it there, especially the tree house.'

'I remember putting it up with Clive – about five years ago, wasn't it?'

'Something like that,' she said vaguely, remembering how she and Amanda had sat on the sun loungers beneath the shade of the garden umbrella drinking iced punch and laughing at their husbands' enthusiasm. She remembered how Brian had looked at that time; fit and tanned, full of energy. Discreetly she took in his appearance now. He was grey, and there was a blue tinge to his lips. She realised with a shock that he looked much older than he had then, and wondered how long the change had been taking place unnoticed.

'Heather!'

She jumped. 'Sorry? I was miles away.'

He made an effort to speak, determined to let her know his feelings. 'Before you go, remember that whatever happens these past ten years have been the happiest of my life. All I've ever wanted was to cherish you and the children and make you happy.'

'We are! And we will be again. You're not going to die. Dr Gates said this is a marvellous hospital. That's why they brought you so far, to make sure you made a full recovery.'

He looked at her smiling face and saw the fear lurking behind the mask. 'Of course I will,' he reassured her, his eyes beginning to close with exhaustion. 'Now, you'd better go.'

'I hate leaving you here. I'll be back first thing in the morning.'

'Give my love to the children.'

'I will. I hope you have a comfortable night.' She bent down and kissed his paper-dry lips. He kept his eyes fastened hungrily on her face. When she reached the doorway he spoke again.

'On your way out would you tell the nurse at the desk that I've got a bit of a pain in my chest again? It's only slight, but I'm meant to tell them.'

Heather nodded, gave a final wave, and quickly walked to the desk. She gave the nurse Brian's message and watched as the girl pressed a small button just beneath the top of the desk. 'He was able to talk,' she said optimistically. 'I didn't expect him to be talking so coherently. How long will he have to stay, do you think?'

'We won't know that until we've done quite a lot of tests, Mrs Lorrimer.'

'I suppose not, it's only . . .' she tailed off. It would sound so feeble if she said that she didn't know how to cope. The nurse coped with sickness and death every day of her working life and there was no way that she would understand or sympathise with Heather's feelings. 'I'd better get back to the children, then,' she said reluctantly.

The nurse glanced up. 'Do we have your telephone number, Mrs Lorrimer?'

'What for?'

'Just in case we need to contact you quickly.'

'Is that likely?'

'Your husband's condition is critical. It's a sensible precaution.'

'I see.' With shaking hands Heather wrote the number down on a form. 'I realise he's very ill, nurse, but he was quite bright just now. He isn't going to die, is he?'

Once they were said she wanted the words recalled, but fortunately the nurse was taken aback and slow to react. Most relatives were less forthright in their questions. This woman had blurted her query out like a child seeking reassurance. As she sought for the right reply the telephone rang. She excused herself politely and slowly Heather walked away.

In his room her husband slumped against the pillows, his hands and face clammy and his head spinning after the effort involved in allaying his wife's fears. He closed his eyes to sleep and the machine bleeped steadily on, with only the occasional hiccup which the patient didn't hear.

Heather heard the telephone ringing as she put her key in the door. She thought that it was probably Amanda and quickly picked up the receiver.

'Mrs Lorrimer?'

'Yes.'

'This is Charing Cross Hospital. I'm afraid your husband has suffered a second heart attack. It would be best if you could come as quickly as possible.'

'He's not . . .?'

'His condition is extremely critical.'

'I'll come at once. I've only just got back . . . I thought . . . he seemed . . .'

'If you could come at once, please.'

With a muffled cry Heather crashed the receiver back in its place and then backed away from it, shaking her head in disbelief. It couldn't be true, not after the way he'd been able to talk to her. She stood whimpering for a moment, not noticing Mrs Brice coming out from the kitchen.

'The children wouldn't settle, Mrs Lorrimer. Mr and Mrs Martin collected them in the end. They seemed happier to sleep there.'

'Yes, that's fine . . . thank you . . . I'd better . . .' Her fingers fumbling, she dialled Amanda's number.

Amanda sounded almost as shocked as Heather. She and Clive had known Brian for twenty years. They had helped him over the death of his first wife, Nancy, twelve years earlier; and they had welcomed his second wife into their home with genuine warmth and enthusiasm. 'I'll leave Clive here with the children and drive you back, Heather. I'm sure you'd like some company. I'll be about ten minutes, all right?'

'Yes,' whispered Heather gratefully. It was all like a bad dream.

They drove to the hospital in silence and hurried up the three flights of stairs and through the swing doors marking the entrance to the intensive care ward. The nurse on duty just managed to step round the desk in time, cutting off Heather's path to her husband's room. She glanced at Amanda, relieved that Mrs Lorrimer had brought a friend.

'Mrs Lorrimer, I'm very sorry to have to tell you this

but your husband died some fifteen minutes ago.'

Heather stared at her in stunned horror. 'Dead? Brian's dead? I don't believe you. He can't be. I want to see my husband! Where is he? I want to see him.' Her voice was rising with every sentence.

The ward sister arrived and took hold of Heather's arm. 'Of course you can see him, my dear. He went very peacefully at the end, but I'm sure you'd like to see that for yourself. Come along with me. Perhaps your friend . . .?'

As Heather began to whimper Amanda put an arm round her waist, and together the two women guided her to the small room where her husband was lying. She stopped at the door, her feet unable to respond to her brain's command. 'I can't!' she whispered.

'Would you like me to come with you?' asked Amanda. Heather nodded, and together they walked quietly in.

It was several seconds before Heather could find the courage to look at his face, but when she did she was amazed. He looked like the Brian she had married. The lines of pain had gone from his face, leaving it smooth and peaceful. She was grateful to the sister; this was how she wanted to remember him. For several minutes she studied him, then turned and walked away, leaving him behind her for ever.

She was alone.

All at once the enormity of his death descended upon her. She cried as she sat down. She cried silently, behind her hands, but she longed to scream aloud. To rant and rave, shriek with pain and desolation. She wanted to, but her parents' training, their insistence upon never creating scenes in public, proved too strong a habit to break.

In a daze she went through the formalities, assisted by Amanda who proved invaluable. It all took time, and it was three in the morning before they arrived back at Amanda's. She gave Heather a sleeping pill, settled her in the guest room and then woke her husband, who had fallen asleep on the sofa.

As Heather lay in a drugged sleep, husband and wife

discussed what should be said to the children in the morning if they asked questions before their mother woke up. It was fortunate that they did. At seven a.m. they stood in Amanda's kitchen hand-in-hand. 'Where's Mummy?' asked Rowena.

'Asleep in the spare room,' replied Amanda, thinking how much like her father the child looked.

'Why is she sleeping here? Why didn't we go home last night?' demanded Barnaby, his bottom lip quivering.

'Your Mummy was late getting back and she didn't want to disturb you.'

They glanced at each other. 'Where's Daddy?' asked Rowena at last, her eyes fearful.

Amanda went over to them and crouched down, putting her arms round their shoulders. 'You're both going to have to be very brave about this, I'm afraid. Your Daddy died during the night. He wasn't in any pain, he just fell asleep and didn't wake up.'

Rowena went white round the nose and mouth and her body became rigid. Barnaby started to cry. 'I want him to wake up!' he sobbed. 'I want my Daddy to come home again.'

Amanda gathered the children to her, and tried to offer them comfort. Barnaby collapsed against her, sobbing into her housecoat, but Rowena remained stiff and her tears rolled silently down her face. As she held them Amanda wished that Heather was a more maternal woman. She was so immature herself that Amanda doubted very much if she would be able to handle her own grief, let alone supply the comfort and support the children were going to need.

As the days passed it became more and more obvious how correct this assumption had been. Brian's almost paternal indulgence of his wife, his apparent belief that she was unable to function as an adult but had to be humoured and petted like the children, now reaped disastrous consequences. Abruptly wrenched into the real world where decisions had to be made and responsibilities faced, Heather collapsed. She moved through the days in a trance-like state, apparently unaware of her children's suffering and taking her friends' assistance for granted.

'Thank goodness Brian was well off,' commented a shattered Amanda on the evening before the funeral. 'At least that offers some protection. Simply being alone is traumatic enough for her; if she were alone and penniless I don't think she'd manage.'

'To be fair,' put in Clive mildly, 'she did go straight from life with elderly parents into marriage with Brian. He simply provided a slightly different form of cocoon from reality. Mind you, I think he under-estimated her. Still, you're quite right. She's used to money. I can't envisage her earning her keep!'

'She says they'll all move back into the house after the funeral. I confess I'm relieved. Without us I don't know what would have happened to the children. Heather doesn't seem aware of their presence half the time.'

'She's always had help with them, that's why. They're between au-pairs at the moment, aren't they?'

Amanda nodded. 'I wonder what will happen to the business?' she mused aloud.

'I imagine Heather will sell it, and make quite a tidy little sum out of the transaction too. Briggs & Marshall are her accountants and Oliver Sutton her solicitor; she can't go very far wrong with all of them to help her. In fact, she'll be a very wealthy young woman.'

Amanda sighed. 'I wish she was a little more mature. I can imagine her falling victim to the first fortune-hunter who appears on the scene.'

'Well, there's nothing we can do about it. She is twenty-nine, despite not looking a day over twenty, and if she does take up with a fortune-hunter that's her business. Let's just be grateful she's well provided for.'

'Amen to that!' said Amanda firmly. It wasn't until after the funeral that they both discovered how wrong they had been.

Chapter Two

Heather was ushered into Oliver Sutton's spacious office by a quietly sympathetic secretary, and immediately Oliver was on his feet, hand extended towards the widow of his old schoolfriend.

Her large blue eyes had purple shadows beneath them and she was very pale, but her beauty wasn't in the least diminished. She had always looked fragile, and there had been many occasions when Oliver had envied Brian. His feelings towards the dead man at this precise moment were somewhat different.

'My dear Heather, do take a seat. Before we get down to business I'd like you to know that you and the children have my deepest sympathy.'

She looked blankly at him, the words scarcely registering. For day after endless day people had been talking at her, their words flowing round her, but they were all meaningless. It was like being in a foreign country where every word was unintelligible. This time, however, she forced herself to make an effort. Clive had emphasised the importance of this meeting. Oliver was going to help her cope with all financial matters, and so she attempted to summon up some concentration.

'My deepest sympathy,' repeated Oliver, wondering if she'd heard him the first time or not. She gave a brief nod; the smallest of acknowledgements. He retreated to the chair behind his desk. He felt more in control there, less personally involved.

Heather stared steadily at him, watching as he fiddled with his papers and re-arranged his pens. He was no longer looking at her, indeed he was almost making a point of avoiding eye contact. She felt a flicker of unease.

Oliver cleared his throat. 'This is very difficult for me, my dear; very difficult indeed. I only wish that there was something I could do, but . . .'

'It's all right. I'm not going to cry or anything. It's just that I need to know how I stand. There are so many bills and things and I don't . . .' She tailed off, unable to remember exactly what Clive had told her to ask.

'My dear, it's . . .'

'Financially! That's right. I need to know how I stand financially.'

'Well, unfortunately . . .'

'I do know there's a big mortgage on the house, but presumably if I sell the business I'll be able to pay that off, and some friends of ours said that there were a lot of stocks and shares, and that I should be able to live off the interest, whatever that means. I don't want things to change. The children are settled here and . . .'

'Mrs Lorrimer!'

Heather stopped abruptly. Oliver had never addressed her so formally before. 'Yes?' Her eyes and voice showed her surprise and Oliver had to steel himself to continue.

'There won't be any house. Your husband's business affairs were in a lamentable state. I've been cautioning him for the past three years but he wouldn't listen. He wanted to sell the business and retire at sixty, but of course you know that.'

'No house? What do you mean? I'm Brian's wife – widow. Didn't Brian leave it to me in the will?'

'Mrs Lorrimer – Heather – your husband left you everything in his will, but in this case "everything" amounts to virtually nothing. He had taken out a substantial second mortgage on the house; he had sold his stocks and shares and poured all of that money into the business, and there are a lot of creditors waiting for the business to be wound up so that they can recoup some of their losses.'

'You mean that I will have to sell the house in order to pay people off? How will I live? Where will I take the children? Can't you explain the situation to these people? Surely they'd understand.'

'We aren't talking about personalities, Mrs Lorrimer, we're talking about a building society and two loan companies. Brian borrowed money from loan companies by offering his cars, house contents and art and porcelain collections as security. It will all have to be sold. They have first claim on his money: the law is quite clear on that point.'

Heather shook her head. 'I don't believe it! What am I expected to do? Won't there be any money left? How will we eat? How can I pay the staff wages?'

Very slowly Oliver leant over the desk, his voice soft. 'You won't need the staff, Mrs Lorrimer. After all, there won't be a house for them to look after.'

For the first time Heather's numb grief cleared. She looked at Oliver's smooth round face and thought of his wife, immaculately groomed and holding three dinner parties a week. She felt a tremendous rage building up inside her. 'You're pleased, aren't you?' she said. 'You're thinking that this serves Brian right. If he'd listened to you none of this would have happened, and you're enjoying every moment of it.'

Oliver flushed. 'I assure you I . . .'

'Well, let me tell you this. If you'd been a true friend, or even a reasonably competent solicitor, you wouldn't have allowed him to get into such a mess. Didn't you point out that this could happen? Didn't you . . .?'

Oliver sat back in his chair, stiff with annoyance. 'My dear Mrs Lorrimer, your husband had accountants to advise him too, you know. The truth is that he was a very stubborn man, and he seemed incapable of refusing you anything at all. He started living beyond his means and just got deeper and deeper into debt. Then you must remember that he died at fifty-two; no one could have anticipated that tragedy. Had he lived, then, of course, everything would have worked out as planned.'

'You mean it's my fault? That I pestered him for possessions that he couldn't really afford? Well, I didn't. I never wanted anything but Brian. He was the one who wanted us to have the best of everything. He . . .'

'There was the little matter of the swimming pool,' put in Oliver smoothly.

'Shut up!' shouted Heather, her bitterness suddenly surfacing. 'You've got a swimming pool, haven't you? And a sauna. And a tennis court. It isn't you who uses them though, it's your wife. Don't try and blame me for what's happened. That swimming pool is the only thing I ever asked for, and even then it was for the children.'

'Heather!' Oliver's voice was once more kindly and paternal. Her words had hit home and he didn't want them spread around the entire neighbourhood. 'I wasn't blaming you in the least. Brian did what he did with the best of intentions; building a secure future for you all. He felt that your life had been too secluded, he wanted the time and money to travel the world with you in a few years time. All he wanted was your happiness, and who can blame him for that?'

She slumped back in her seat, her moment of fury had passed leaving her utterly exhausted. 'What can I do?' she whispered. 'I don't know what to do.'

'Naturally you'll have to put the house on the market, and then start looking for something smaller for you and the children. Perhaps in another area where property's cheaper?'

'But how can I buy anything? I don't have any money of my own.'

'I understood that when your parents died they left you a considerable sum. That little nest egg will certainly prove most useful now.'

She stared at him in growing horror. 'I gave it to Brian,' she said, 'he was going to invest it for me. It seemed sensible as I didn't need it for anything.'

'He took it all?' Even Oliver was stunned.

'Not quite. I've got £15,000 in my own deposit account.'

'And how much did you originally inherit?'

'Thirty thousand pounds.'

Oliver stood up and went round his desk so that he could put an arm round Heather's shoulders. 'My dear, I don't know what to say to you. Believe me, if there was anything I could do, anything at all, then I would. Unfortunately, as you mentioned, Grace has a taste for the good things of life and . . .' He stopped for a moment and looked down at Heather's golden hair which hung to her shoulders, turning neatly under at the ends. He wanted to reach out and touch it. It looked soft and silky, like a child's.

'Of course,' he continued, 'there might be one way. I do own a small flat in London. If you and the children lived there, for a very nominal rent, then I could call in and see you from time to time. Advise you on business matters. Talk about old times.' As he spoke, his arm tightened round her.

Incredulously, Heather realised that he was propositioning her. There was nothing she could say, he had been too clever for that. If she complained he would say that she had misunderstood him. She pulled herself free of his grasp and stood up. Oliver waited. He thought that she was going to accept. Her prospects weren't good if she didn't. Not many men would want to take on two small children.

Heather flicked her hair behind her ears and looked him directly in the eyes. 'Thank you for everything, Oliver. I'm sure that Brian would have appreciated the way you've assisted me. As you so correctly pointed out, I'm going to have to move away from this area so I doubt very much if we'll meet again.'

The solicitor flushed and held out his hand, but Heather ignored it. 'Well then,' he said, with an attempt at kindly bonhomie, 'I wish you the very best of luck.' Without another word she turned and left the office, closing the door behind her with exaggerated care.

She drove home, stunned at the revelations that the home wasn't hers at all and that she was virtually penniless. Drawing up at the house she was surprised to find that she was crying. Tears were running down her face without her knowing. She glanced at the wisteria-covered walls of the house, and felt a brief moment's peace, until she remembered that very soon the house would belong to someone else and she would never see it again.

Once inside she collapsed into the mahogany telephone seat and sobbed. 'Brian, come back,' she cried, rocking backwards and forwards as she spoke. 'Please come back. Don't leave me here alone. I can't bear it. I just can't bear it.' She was so immersed in her grief that she didn't notice Mrs Brice approaching her and jumped with surprise as the cook spoke.

'There's a gentleman to see you, Mrs Lorrimer. He's in the living-room.'

Still choking with tears, Heather struggled for composure. 'Who is he?'

'He gave me this card.'

She studied it carefully. 'K L Matthews, Loan Director.' Reluctantly she got to her feet and went to meet him. He didn't hear her arrival and for a few seconds she studied him examining the Meissen porcelain in the cabinet and looking intently at the paintings on the walls. Then a small sound alerted him for he swung round, his sharp face and hard grey eyes trying to soften into an expression of regret.

'I'm Mrs Lorrimer,' she announced, keeping her hands firmly at her sides.

'Ah yes, my condolences. You are probably aware that your late husband owes my firm ten thousand pounds, and your porcelain collection and the paintings in this room and the dining-room were his collateral. I wondered when it would be convenient for us to collect?'

Heather hated him. She hated his greedy expression, his obvious lack of interest in the precious objects as anything but hard cash. With a lump in her throat she remembered Brian's pride every time he added a fresh piece to the cabinet. The times he would buy a painting at a London auction and then they would celebrate in the evening with a bottle of champagne followed by a slow and gentle night of love.

'When it would be convenient?' repeated Mr Matthews.

With a start, Heather came back to the present. 'Never,' she said shortly. 'It will never be convenient.'

'I'm afraid that . . .'

'It's all right, I know that I don't have any choice, but I don't have to like what's happening! These things were my husband's joy; they were his hobby. He loved each figure in that cabinet. They were precious to him, and because of that they're precious to me too.' She was beginning to cry again. 'Don't you understand? You're taking away my memories. This house, our possessions, they were all part of our life together. Surely you can appreciate that?'

The man's face was cold and untouched. 'In that case it's a pity he saw fit to offer them as security. I'm only doing my job.'

'Why don't you take them now? Take everything. Would you like my split-level cooker? The microwave oven? The antique table and chairs in the dining-room? Or perhaps the children's toys? Yes, I'm sure you'd enjoy taking the children's toys.'

She was completely distraught and Mr Matthews backed away from her, relieved at the sight of Mrs Brice entering and moving to comfort the young woman.

'Come along my dear. Let me make you a nice cup of tea.' Heather nodded, walking blindly towards the door.

'Would tomorrow be convenient?' he pressed, determined to get an answer.

Heather turned back to him. 'I'll be moving soon, can't it wait until then?' He shook his head. 'All right, come tomorrow. Come any day you like, but keep out of my sight. I don't want to watch. Do you understand that? I don't want to see it go!'

Immediately the women had left Mr Matthews hurried out of the house. He hated scenes like that one. It wasn't his fault if men were so stupid or wives so greedy that they ended up bankrupt.

Over the cup of tea Heather told Mrs Brice everything. She made sympathetic noises and patted Heather's back, but inside she was as dumbfounded as her employer. 'What am I going to do?' sobbed Heather at the end. 'Where can I find enough money to buy another house? How am I supposed to manage? I can't cope, I know I can't. I wish I were dead too!'

'That's nonsense,' said the cook firmly. 'You've two lovely children to live for, and you've got to think about them. Besides, I'm sure that some of your friends will be able to think of ways you can afford something, even if it is a lot smaller than this.'

'No,' said Heather, remembering Oliver's proposition. 'I don't want their sort of help.'

'As you like, dear,' responded Mrs Brice, secretly thinking such false pride rather foolish.

The very next day two large, virtually silent men collected the porcelain and six paintings and carried the items out while Mr Matthews ticked them off his list. It took them less than an hour, and when Heather heard them drive off she came down from her bedroom and walked through the two rooms.

The empty cabinet and the marks on the walls were the

only signs of Brian's collections. She sat down on the wide window seat and stared out into the garden. Soon she realised the furniture would have to be sold. If she ever did manage to buy a small house there wouldn't be any room for heavy antique furniture.

'They're taking you away, Brian,' she whispered, her face pressed against the glass. 'By the time we go there'll be nothing left to show that you ever lived here.' The lump in her throat grew even larger and hot tears sprang into her eyes. Rusty, the family spaniel, crept close to her and jumped up onto the seat beside her. She put out a hand and stroked his soft coat. 'And what are we going to do with you?' she whispered, then bent her face to the dog, letting her tears fall into his fur. He licked her ear gently, as though in sympathy.

Chapter Three

A week later Heather and Amanda were sitting in Amanda's garden. It was mid-morning, the sun was shining and the children were at school. As soon as Brian's lack of business acumen became apparent, most of his so-called friends had vanished. Heather promptly ceased to exist for everyone except Amanda and Clive, who were her sole source of support and comfort.

'I had a letter this morning,' Heather said, taking it out of her handbag. 'It's from an old schoolfriend, Yvonne. We haven't seen each other since I married, but we write a couple of times a year. She heard about Brian's death and suggests that I move nearer to London from now on. She's living in Croydon and says it's highly convenient for shops, commuting and so on; not that I intend to commute just yet, but I do wonder if perhaps it's a good idea. What do you think?'

'It sounds an excellent idea,' said Amanda firmly, detecting the uncertainty in her voice. She and Clive had spent hours going over Heather's problems, and knew only too well that Berkshire was out of the question for her under her new circumstances. This was the first time that a friend had ever been mentioned, and it was a great relief to Amanda who had terrible visions of a waif-like Heather eternally haunting their house, totally disoriented and incapable of positive action.

Encouraged by this enthusiasm Heather studied the letter again. 'She suggests that I spend a week or so with her in order to have a good look round. I'd like to, but what can I do with the children?'

'Good heavens! Don't worry about that. We'll be delighted to have them. You go, you might not get another chance.'

Reluctantly Heather nodded. She did realise that Amanda and Clive couldn't prop her up for ever and that she really had to go, but she was terrified at the prospect of spending time in a strange house; and the thought of the train journey made her hands go clammy with fright. Suppose she missed her train? Or even worse, caught the wrong one? Abruptly it occurred to her how little she had appreciated the convenience of her own car in the past.

'That's settled then,' said Amanda with scarcely suppressed relief. 'I'll get Clive to sort out a train for you if you like. Then you can ring your friend and tell her your arrival time.'

'You're very kind,' murmured Heather, and Amanda changed the subject before the younger woman could think up any more excuses for not going.

At three-thirty the following Saturday – a hot and sticky day – she finally arrived at Croydon station. Her dress was limp and clung to her stockinged legs as she walked. Her hair was damp with perspiration and had lost its bounce. All in all she felt a complete wreck.

Yvonne was waiting at the station entrance. Heather's relief at seeing her was so enormous that it wasn't until they were speeding along the road in the little Mini that she had time to notice the changes in her friend. When they had last met, at her wedding to Brian, Yvonne had had long raven-black hair and worn a suit in fuschia pink with matching lipstick and nail varnish. She had been an extremely striking girl.

Now her hair was medium brown and almost cropped. She was wearing a long, rather drab skirt with a faded yellow T-shirt, and could easily have been taken for thirty-five instead of twenty-eight.

Sensing Heather's appraisal she turned her head. 'I know, I've let myself go! Well, you haven't. You don't look a day over twenty, it's positively indecent! I suppose having money helps. Incidentally, perhaps I should warn you that you might find Rupert a little difficult. Since Luke and I split up we both spoil him to compensate, and he takes full advantage of it. He's only eight so it's perfectly natural. How old's Barnaby? I get mixed up, the time flies by so fast.'

Heather's head was aching and she desperately needed a toilet, but she tried to follow Yvonne's excitable and rapid speech. She hadn't remembered her as being so highly strung, but perhaps it was only in contrast to the slow pace of her own life in recent years. As she remembered Brian a terrible wave of grief swept through her. 'Yvonne! I think I'm going to be sick!'

The Mini was pulled abruptly onto the grass verge; Heather stumbled out and was immediately very sick. When it was over she slid back onto the hot, plastic-covered seat. Yvonne looked sympathetic. 'You do look bad! Did you eat something doubtful on the train?'

'I think it's a stomach bug. I've spent most of the day rushing from loo to loo!'

'Probably nerves,' said Yvonne casually. 'I remember you were always ill at school when it was exam time. I don't know why. It all came easily to you, didn't it?'

'Did it? I only remember being afraid of letting my parents down.'

'Mmmm. You were always too anxious to please. It doesn't get you anywhere, I can tell you. We're nearly home now, it's just down the end of this road.'

They pulled up outside a neat, modern, semi-detached house in a quiet cul-de-sac. The front lawn, unlike its neighbour's, was badly in need of mowing and the paint was peeling off some of the window frames. Heather hadn't expected it to be so small.

'Don't look at the grass!' cautioned Yvonne. 'Luke's meant to cut it when he visits Rupert, but he never does. He gets hay fever badly. The golf course doesn't affect him, but the lawn does. Typical man!'

Before they were in the front door there was the sound of running footsteps and a short, sturdy boy with ash-blond hair and smokey-grey eyes cannoned into the back of them. 'Mummy! Lee kicked me, and then I hit him, and Muriel's cross because Lee's got a black eye, but he started it. He wouldn't let me have a go on his new bike. I always let him play with my toys. Mummy, Mummy, are you listening?'

'Yes, and so, I imagine, are half the road. Oh, God! Now I'll have Muriel round complaining. Say hello to Heather, she's come for the weekend.'

'Hello!' said Heather, putting out her hand.

'Hi! Mummy, can I have a bike for my birthday?'

'You've already got a perfectly good bike. Put your case down, Heather, and sit in the dining-room. It's cooler there. By the way, I've got loads of brochures from estate agents, and I thought we'd go round looking tomorrow.'

There was nothing Heather felt less like doing but she smiled and nodded, then made her way quickly upstairs to the bathroom. When she came down Yvonne was arguing fiercely with a tall, red-haired woman who, Heather assumed, was Lee's mother, Muriel. She retreated to the coolness of the dining-room.

Eventually Yvonne joined her. 'Feeling better?' Heather nodded. 'Good. I've sent Muriel packing at last. How about a cup of tea? I thought we'd eat at eight, after Rupert's in bed, but we can have some cake now providing there's some left.'

'There isn't!' said Rupert rudely. 'I was starving last night and I finished it up.'

Yvonne shrugged helplessly. 'Boys! What can you do with them?'

Plenty, thought Heather, but she kept silent. It was

very good of Yvonne to put herself out in this way and she would just have to put up with Rupert in silence for the duration of her visit.

When they finally did sit down to eat Heather was unable to manage anything. 'Not even ice-cream?' suggested Yvonne with concern. 'I've got about six different flavours; Rupert adores it.'

'I know. I watched him eat two helpings for his supper.'

Yvonne heard the note of criticism behind the words. 'It's all very well for you, Heather, you've never had to bring up your children. You've always had nannies and au-pairs. I bet you hardly ever ate with them.'

'I did!' protested Heather. 'I often joined them in the nursery for four o'clock tea.'

'Four o'clock tea! Christ, that's priceless! I didn't think there were any people left who took four o'clock tea. We must take great care of you, you're a dying species!'

'No ice cream thank you, and as a matter of fact most of our friends took afternoon tea, and so did my parents.'

Yvonne put some ice cream on her own plate. 'How old are your friends? I mean, I'm not surprised about your parents, they always lived in the Dark Ages, but these days! What kind of circles have you been moving in, Heather? It sounds ghastly. The sooner you join the real world, the better.'

'They're not geriatrics,' said Heather, defensively. 'Why, Amanda and Clive are only in their late forties.'

'You're *twenty-nine,* Heather. What can you possibly have in common with people in their late forties? How did you celebrate your birthdays? A mystery coach tour?'

'I was happy with Brian,' said Heather sharply. 'I don't want to join your real world. I hate all the noise everywhere. The people rushing frantically along platforms; the rude, sniggering teenagers. If that means that I'm a premature geriatric I don't care. I loved Brian and I liked his friends. If all you're going to do is sneer then I'm going home now, late evening or not.'

To Yvonne's consternation Heather collapsed into tears, great sobs tearing at her while she tried ineffectually to cover her face with her hands. 'I'm sorry, Heather. I didn't mean to sneer at Brian. He was a smashing man, I know that. I was only trying . . . Well, it doesn't matter, now probably isn't the time. I'm truly sorry, please don't go home. You know me, once I start I never know when to stop and I see so few adults these days that I can't stop talking when I've got company! It isn't all roses here without Luke. I try to pretend I'm coping, but sometimes I don't manage to convince myself as well as I'd like. I miss Luke, and he's still alive. Every time he comes for Rupert I have to see him and remember that he's no longer anything to do with me, he's only Rupert's father. That hurts, Heather, believe me it hurts.'

Slowly Heather regained control, listening with growing surprise to Yvonne. She realised that her friend had been more hurt by her divorce than her letters had indicated and she was consoled by the thought that at least she and Brian had stayed in love right until the end. Death left you grieving but had, eventually, to be accepted. Divorce was a wound that apparently remained perpetually unhealed, particularly when children were involved. 'I'm sorry too, Yvonne. I'm over-tired and my head's spinning. I'll go to bed now, and hopefully I'll feel ready to start the big house-hunt tomorrow.'

'Sure. Have you any sleeping pills?'

'Yes, thanks. Goodnight, Yvonne.'

Yvonne watched her friend leave the room and sighed. It was already plain that in the next few months Heather was going to have a terrible time adjusting to all the changes in her life, and she only hoped that Heather had sufficient strength of character to carry her through.

Much to Heather's relief the sleeping pill enabled her to have a good night's sleep, and she woke up feeling greatly refreshed. However, her feeling of well-being only lasted for as long as it took her to wash, dress and go downstairs.

Listening to Rupert being insolent had been hard enough, watching – and listening – to him eat was even worse. He piled his spoon high with cereal and then crammed as much as he could into his mouth, allowing the residue to spill out onto the table. When he wanted to speak, which was often, he didn't bother to finish eating but mumbled through a soggy mass in his open mouth. Yvonne did two boiled eggs for her son and Heather, explaining that she never ate breakfast. If Rupert were her son, thought Heather, then neither would she.

By ten o'clock they were ready to go but Luke, who was due to collect Rupert at nine forty-five, was late, and as the delay lengthened Rupert became more and more uncontrollable, running from room to room firing a noisy machine gun and screaming at his mother and Heather to fall down dead.

Unused to such a confined space his noisy behaviour reverberated constantly through Heather's head. There seemed to be no escape from him in such a small house, and just as her stomach started to churn and her head to ache Luke arrived with a dramatic squeal of brakes.

Rupert went dashing out of the front door to meet him. 'Mummy's going to buy me a new bike for my birthday,' he shouted. 'A racing bike with ten different gears.'

'Of course I'm not,' said Yvonne sharply. 'I told you, there's nothing wrong with the bike you've got, and you're far too young for a racing bike.'

Her son pouted and clung to his father's arm. 'Where are we going, Daddy? Can we go to the Zoo?'

Luke's eyes turned towards Heather. She had never met him before, but he was exactly as Yvonne had described, right down to the quick, easy smile. After a few polite words Rupert and his father left. 'Perhaps *I'll* be able to get you a bike,' Luke was saying, as he walked down the path.

Yvonne scowled. 'See what I mean? What's the use of trying to discipline him when Luke ruins everything I do?

Come on, let's get going.'

The first house they looked at was situated in the middle of a large housing development on the outskirts of Croydon. 'This looks quite promising,' said Yvonne cheerfully, rummaging in her handbag for the details. 'Look at this! "Modern town-house" – that means terraced but you won't be able to afford an end one – "with three bedrooms, part central-heating, lounge and large kitchen-diner, and a combined bathroom and toilet." It's what's termed an ideal first-time buy!'

'I'm not a first-time buyer.'

'Yes, you are! Brian owned your present house, didn't he? Besides, that only relates to price. It could be your tenth house for all they care!'

Yvonne laughed, but Heather was regarding the vast development with horror as they drove slowly round looking for Appletree Close. Once found the name seemed highly inappropriate as none of the gardens had enough room for an apple tree to grow, and even the grassed area in front of the row of houses had given up trying and was a trampled brown patch where a few boys were idly kicking a ball.

They both got out of the car. 'Here we are, Heather. Number 8.' Heather didn't reply. 'The one with the red door,' added Yvonne.

'The peeling red door.'

'Sure, but that's why it's relatively cheap. Plenty of room for improvement.'

'Give me the sodding ball!' shrieked a golden-haired boy of about three. Heather turned in astonishment and saw that a brown-haired child a little older had tucked the football under his arm and was running off. All at once he stopped and turned to the smaller boy. 'Bugger off home!' he retaliated. 'You stink!'

Yvonne laughed. 'The age of innocence! Come on, let's go and look inside.' Obediently Heather followed her up the path, but she already knew that she couldn't possibly live on an estate where children spoke to each other like that. She just had time to note the flaking window frames and neglected front lawn before a tired-looking woman opened the front door.

She had a small baby in a sling round her neck and a toddler hanging onto her skirt. Without a word she stepped to one side to let the two women in.

A small girl was lying on the kitchen floor crayoning, her tongue poking out of her mouth as she concentrated. All at once her hand slipped and the crayon skidded across the picture leaving a bright purple line on the paper. 'Bloody hell!' she muttered, screwed the paper into a ball, threw it vaguely in the direction of a pedal bin and stomped out of the back door.

It was quickly apparent that very little work had been done on the interior of the house either. The walls still had their original thin coat of emulsion and the plaster was peeling off in the bathroom. It only took Heather five minutes to realise that she and the children could never live in such a house and she was surprised at the act of enthusiasm Yvonne managed to put on.

'This is a snip, Heather. The carpets stay, which saves about a thousand pounds, and the children can play in safety. I love the kitchen too; that breakfast bar is superb.'

Biting back the retort that nothing on earth would induce her to allow Barnaby and Rowena to play with the children on the estate, Heather followed the owner out of the back door into the back garden which wasn't much larger than Heather's present patio. Once again brown grass and weeds dominated, and there was no wooden fencing, no possibility of privacy from the neighbours. The only division between the gardens was a piece of wire fencing about three feet high.

'We're sorry to be going,' confided the pale woman as they returned to the lounge, Heather trying to ignore the screams of the children floating through the open window.

All at once the walls of the house seemed to be closing in on her and she felt unable to breathe properly. She cast a look of desperation to Yvonne who stared blankly back.

'Well, we must be going,' mumbled Heather, aware that Yvonne wasn't going to help her make a speedy exit. 'I've several more houses to look at, but thank you for your time.'

'It's my pleasure. Do you have any young children?'

'Yes, two. A boy of six and a girl of nine.'

'In that case you'll appreciate the play area out front. It means your children can play outside but within your sight; I find it an absolute godsend.'

The screams from outside intensified. 'Don't you mind the noise?' Heather enquired faintly.

'No, to tell you the truth I don't notice it any more. You quickly get used to it.'

Once in the safety of the car Heather slumped in her seat. 'That was ghastly! It has to be one of the worst houses I'm likely to encounter. That ridiculous little back garden, there wasn't even room for the children's swing and slide. As for these awful wire fences, they don't conceal a thing. The noise, Yvonne! I'd go round the bend. It's so peaceful at home. When I sit in my garden there's never a sound, it's as though I'm in a world of my own.'

'You are,' said Yvonne bluntly, 'only now you've got to leave it. Quite honestly, Heather, you won't do better than this. There's a junior school within easy walking distance, buses to town every twenty minutes, it's marvellously convenient.'

Heather stared at her friend. 'You're not serious? Do you think I'd let my children go to a school where the only thing they're likely to learn is profanity? The house was horrible, the garden hopeless and the area revolting. Let's move on to the next one. I hope that isn't so small as I felt positively claustrophobic in there.'

'For God's sake, Heather! This is Croydon, not

Berkshire. I suppose your two are at private schools now?' Heather nodded. 'You've got to be realistic. That life's over. Now's your chance to show what you can do on your own, and this house is ideal for you. It's got four walls, is basically sound, and only costs £35,000. You won't see anything better.'

'I can't possibly live here. Brian would have been horrified. He was so particular about the children's speech.'

'Brian's dead! He won't have to listen to it any more.'

'Yvonne!'

'I'm sorry, Heather, I know that sounds dreadful, but you've got to face facts. You're on your own, you've virtually no money, and it's a harsh world for single parents. Still, if you won't consider it, we'll try number two.'

The second house was an old terraced one. The brickwork was crumbling and the guttering was hanging loose round the back. The road itself was narrow, with cars and motorbikes on both sides, making it difficult to park the Mini. This time even Yvonne didn't find anything to enthuse over. The lounge had a damp mark running along the middle of one wall, and the entire house smelt musty. There was no garden, only a patch of concrete at the back; a patch that the dog of the house obviously used for his own needs, and his deposits were littered everywhere, covered in flies and giving off a foul smell in the heat of the sun. They left quickly and silently.

'Shall we have a pub lunch before we do any more?' asked Yvonne as they drove away.

Heather shuddered. 'I don't think I could eat. That back yard was revolting.'

'Mmmm. I told you the first house was good.'

'Only by comparison with that slum.'

After a quick lunch they managed to look over two more houses before Yvonne had to get back home for Rupert. Both were badly neglected. In one there was no room in the kitchen for Heather's deep freeze, washing machine and fridge, let alone her tumble drier. Yvonne tried to point out that it was highly probable some of these items would have to be discarded. The cheaper semi-detached and terraced houses weren't designed for such luxuries; but to Heather they weren't luxuries, she considered them necessities and Yvonne knew that anything she said would only cause trouble. She waited for the inescapable truth of her new situation to dawn on her friend, at which point she should hopefully become more amenable to suggestions.

Back at Yvonne's, Luke and Rupert were already waiting, Luke looking as aggrieved as his son. 'It's half-past bloody six. I'm due to pick Zöe up at seven, she'll be livid.'

'Then let her be livid,' snapped Yvonne. 'Heather's got to find herself a house quickly. Don't you think that's possibly marginally more important than taking your ladyfriend out to another boozy dinner? I suppose it's too much to hope that you positively enjoyed having Rupert for an extra forty-five minutes?'

'It certainly is. I'm not a masochist. He's absolutely ruined by you these days. Taking him out holds very little pleasure. It consists of an endless stream of "wants".'

'Really? *I'm* not the one who said "perhaps I'll be able to get you a bike".' Luke flushed and Rupert stood quietly by the door, his eyes darting from one adult to the other and a smile of triumph on his face.

It was the final straw for Heather. She brushed past the arguing family and just managed to get to the bathroom before she was violently sick.

She was lying on her single bed in the guest room when Yvonne came quietly in. 'Sorry about that, Heather, it's how we always finish up these days. Sad, really, when I remember how we used to be. Are you all right? You look a bit pale.'

'I'm afraid I was sick. It *must* be a virus.'

'It's nerves. Stay there for an hour; it will take me that long to get Rupert half-way civilised after Luke's visit. We'll talk later, when he's asleep.'

Rupert proved very good at staying awake, and few words were exchanged between the two friends until nearly midnight. Earlier in the evening Heather telephoned Amanda to check on the children. She could hear them laughing and playing in the background, and heard also the muted sound of adults talking.

'Are you busy, Amanda? If so, I'm sorry to interrupt.'

'Of course not. We've just had a few friends round for drinks. The usual crowd; they'll all be anxious to hear how you've got on.'

Heather pictured the usual crowd. The immaculately dressed women, the steady, dependable husbands exchanging masculine jokes as their wives discussed the latest au-pair or the unreliability of cleaning women. What would they think if they'd been with her today? she wondered. How would they have coped with the dirt and the horrible, vulgar children? She experienced a surge of bitterness that they were all continuing their lives of luxury, luxury they took completely for granted, while she was reduced to poking round neglected houses scarcely bigger than some of the nanny flats her friends had.

'Heather? Are you still there?'

'Yes.'

'How did you get on? I expect Croydon's rather a pleasant place. The shops are good, I'm told.'

'I haven't been shopping, I've been house hunting. If the houses are anything to go by then I don't think I'll get too excited over the shops.'

'Darling! You do sound gloomy! Don't let things get you down. After all, you knew you couldn't afford a mansion.'

'Yes, I did know that, but you've no idea . . .'

'I'll have to go. Clive's run out of ice. Ring again soon. The children are fine, I'll give them your love. Bye for now.'

'Ice!' fumed Heather, banging the phone down. 'He's run out of ice! I hope Amanda can cope with such a major disaster.' Then her fury vanished, and instead she felt the prickle of unshed tears. 'Why me?' she asked herself. 'What did I ever do to deserve this? How could Brian have been so foolish?'

'What was that?' queried Yvonne, carrying coffee cups into the kitchen.

'Nothing, I was talking to myself.' Already she was feeling guilty. She was being self-pitying again, which was pointless. All the same, for a brief moment she pictured Brian standing beside her at one of Amanda's drinks parties, his arm round her shoulders, his eyes continually on her. How proud he'd been of his young wife, and how she'd revelled in his pleasure.

'I expect the children wanted to hear every detail,' laughed Yvonne.

'I didn't speak to them.'

'Were they in bed?'

'No, but Amanda promised to give them my love.'

'Heather! How could you be so thoughtless? They've just lost their father and now you've vanished too.'

'I suppose it does sound bad,' she conceded, 'but they've always had nannies and au-pairs. We aren't close in the way that you and Rupert are.'

'Then perhaps that will be one good thing to come out of Brian's death. Why have children if you scarcely see them?'

'I do see them, I . . .'

'I know, you take tea at four with them! Come on, I think it's time for a nightcap.'

As they drank their whisky and ginger ales Heather dutifully turned over brochures for the next day's viewing. The houses were all depressing to look at, and one even had a roof repair van parked outside when the picture was taken.

Once Rupert had left for school the next morning Yvonne guided Heather into the lounge. 'There's one thing we haven't mentioned so far, Heather, and we really ought to discuss it.'

'What's that?'

'Your mortgage arrangements. Which building society are you with?'

'I'm not. I've never needed a building society. Brian saw to all our finances.'

'But how are you going to get the money to buy a house? Haven't you approached any building society at all?'

'I don't know what you mean. I've got £12,000 to put down; I thought a deposit would be sufficient.'

'Heather, you're buying a £35,000 house, not a new dress! What about legal fees? Removal costs? New furniture and fittings? I take it your present stuff isn't any use?'

'I have exactly £3,000 to cover all that, and my present "stuff" as you put it happens to be antique furniture.'

'Good for you, but it won't fit into a terraced house, will it?'

'No it won't!' shouted Heather and burst into tears.

Yvonne sighed. She was using up precious holiday to help her friend, and it was proving exhausting work. 'You need a mortgage,' she said patiently, and went on to explain the entire system to an increasingly horrified Heather.

'That's no use,' she said tearfully, 'I don't have a job.'

'No job? Good God, Heather! How are you intending to live?'

'I don't know! I don't know anything. I can't manage money; I'm not qualified for any work; I don't even know how to cook or run a house. You'll have to help me, Yvonne. I need your help.'

Yvonne had visions of her already chaotic life being further disturbed by non-stop calls and visits from Heather. She had no time for that. Her life was one long battle to keep herself sane. Much as she pitied her friend she knew that she must be cruel to be kind. Given half a chance Heather would become a clinging vine, her desperate need for someone to lean on was painfully obvious, and any hopes of Yvonne being that person must be gently but firmly put out of her head. 'I can't keep helping you,' she said quietly. 'I've got my own life to live, and that isn't an easy one either. I know it's hard on you, and I understand what you're going through but I've nothing left to give you. I'm stumbling along myself, learning by experience, and you'll have to do the same.'

'But . . .'

'There is just one way in which I might be able to help. My father owns two shops in Croydon. How about me ringing him up and explaining the situation? There's usually a staffing shortage in one of the shops, and with your deposit, and providing you can find a building society willing to advance you the rest, it will at least be a start. You can look for more attractive work later. What do you think?'

'It's very kind, but what would I do?' Heather was genuinely bewildered.

'Sell shoes, of course! What else?'

'You mean I'd be a *shop assistant*?'

'That's right. What did you imagine? A joint partnership?'

'No, of course not, but I couldn't . . .'

Yvonne lost her temper. 'Look, Heather, if you don't want to sell shoes then don't, but there's nothing else that I can get you, and without a job you won't get a mortgage, and without a mortgage you won't get even a tatty little terraced house. To be honest, I've put up with your niggling complaints ever since you arrived and I've just about had it. Now, do I ring my father or not?'

Numbly Heather stared at her friend. She had no choice. In two months' time she and the children would be homeless. She swallowed hard. 'Yes, please. I'd be very grateful.'

'So I should think,' muttered Yvonne to herself as she went to the telephone.

For seven depressing days they continued their relentless search for a house that Heather liked. Finally, exhausted and stunned by all that she'd seen, she conceded that the house in Appletree Close was the best she was likely to get.

Ten days after her arrival she was on her way home to Berkshire. Yvonne had seen her off at the station, but both women were a little awkward, and Heather knew that it would be some time – if ever – before she tried to contact her friend again.

On the train she finally accepted that this was the end of her life as she knew it. She had a house and a job, and in a few weeks she and the children would make the physical move that marked the beginning of their new life. It was up to Heather whether this life was successful or not. As she watched the scenery flash by she wondered how well she would cope with this sudden responsibility after nearly thirty years of being sheltered and adored. The prospect was so daunting that she pushed it away, took out a magazine and tried to read some of the more frivolous articles. Soon there wouldn't be weekly magazines and endless purchases of the latest make-up and clothes. She buried her head more deeply in the magazine, savouring the final days of the old life.

Chapter Four

Ten weeks later Heather and the children moved, helped by Clive and Amanda. The children were silent during the entire journey, apparently unable to believe that they were actually leaving their home and friends behind them for ever.

'It's very cosy!' said Amanda brightly, as the removal men crowded the furniture into the living-room, scarcely leaving space for anyone to move. 'Think how economical it will be to run, and so simple to keep clean. I quite envy you!'

'I don't think Heather will believe that, darling,' said Clive mildly, acutely aware of Heather's shame and confusion.

'But think of the savings on heating and lighting. Heavens, you'll save a fortune!'

'I'm sure I will. In fact, I'll probably be a millionairess by next year.'

Amanda looked pained. 'There's no need for that, darling. I'm only trying to help you look on the bright side.'

'When do you start work?' enquired Clive, wincing as the kitchen table was scraped along the wall of the hall.

'On Monday, at nine a.m. sharp. I'm told the manageress is quite a stickler for punctuality.'

'And what exactly will you be doing?' queried Amanda, drifting towards the front windows.

'Selling shoes.'

'How quaint! Do look at those little children, Clive. The tiny blond boy's adorable.' Clive joined her at the window, and the child, seeing them there, lifted his right hand and made a rude gesture with his fingers. They exchanged a quick glance before turning away.

'Well, if you think you can manage now we'd better be off,' said Amanda. 'Make sure you ring us next weekend; and if there's anything we can do, anything at all, don't hesitate to ask.'

Heather nodded. 'I'll remember, and thank you for all your help today. I don't know how I'd have managed without you both.'

'Take care,' said Amanda brightly, kissing her lightly on both cheeks.

'Where are the children?' asked Clive.

'Out by the removal van. Would you ask them to come in when you leave?'

'Will do. Now, you're quite sure you're all right?'

'Quite sure,' Heather replied, wishing they'd both go and leave her in peace to nurse her pounding headache and churning stomach.

On the way out Clive told Rowena and Barnaby that their mother wanted them and then climbed into his car. 'She's never going to manage,' he remarked to Amanda. 'I think that what Brian did to her is unforgiveable. Petting and cossetting her like an expensive pet and then leaving her penniless and homeless with two children to care for.'

'I don't suppose he wanted to die.'

'I never said he did, but common sense should have told him to make some sort of provision for them all. Trust funds for the children would have made a hell of a difference.'

'Mmmm. Quite honestly, I'd rather starve than live in that tiny little house and go out selling shoes to horrible women every day of the week.'

'Don't be so bloody stupid! What do you know about starving?'

'I only meant . . .'

'I don't care what you meant, it was a ridiculous statement.' They didn't speak again until they reached home.

Unaware of the argument she had unwittingly caused, Heather watched her children walk reluctantly up the front path towards her. Rowena was very pale and the sprinkling of freckles on her nose stood out vividly. Barnaby walked straight into the lounge and stared out at the toddlers playing on the grass. He was sucking the middle fingers of his right hand and clearing his throat every few seconds. Both habits had started after Brian's death, and whilst Heather knew that they were beyond his control the throat-clearing irritated her intensely.

'Is this where we're going to live for ever?' asked Rowena in a small voice.

Her mother forced a smile. 'That's right. Come upstairs and I'll show you your bedroom. You come too, Barnaby. Come and see where you'll be sleeping.'

He kept his eyes on the play area outside. 'I don't want to look.'

'But Barnaby, surely you'd like to come and decide where to put your toys?'

He shook his head. 'I'm not going to unpack them. I'll keep them in their box until we go home again.'

'This is home, stupid!' goaded Rowena, trying to boost her own spirits by turning on her brother. 'We're never going back to our old house. Even a three-year old would understand that! You heard Aunty Amanda, we can go back and stay in her house some time, but never our own. That's got new owners, they're probably sitting down to tea in the kitchen right now.'

Barnaby ignored her. 'We have to go back. I've got James's party to go to, it's a swimming one this year.'

'You're going to a new school, Barnaby,' Heather reminded him gently. 'I told you all about it. It's just down the road, and Rowena will be there too.'

He stared at Heather in disbelief. 'Girls in the same school? That's sissy! I'm not going. I'll stay indoors until we go back home.'

'This *is* home now, Barnaby. Come along, darling. Be a good boy for Mummy.'

He cleared his throat violently and stuck his fingers back in his mouth. Heather longed to put her arms round his thin shoulders but for the moment it seemed more sensible to leave him alone and let him come to terms with things at his own pace.

Rowena's room was at the back of the house, next to the bathroom. She stared out of the window at the garden below. 'Is that all the grass we've got, Mummy? What about our swing and slide? I don't think Marmaduke will like it.'

'I've sold the swing and slide, Rowena. There's plenty of room for you to play out the front. As for Marmaduke, I don't think tortoises mind too much about moving house.'

Rowena scuffed her shoes against the skirting board. 'I wish Daddy hadn't died. Why did he? It wasn't very kind of God to take him away from us. Lucy said it was because he was old, but he wasn't very old. She said that he looked like her Grandad, but I don't think that was true either.'

'It could have been, darling. Daddy was a lot older than Lucy's daddy, but he wasn't very old. I don't know why he had to die. There was something wrong with his heart and the doctors couldn't mend it. Where are you going to keep your dolls?'

'It's probably because he smoked,' persisted Rowena. 'Lucy said smoking kills you. You don't smoke, Mummy, do you?'

'No, and I don't intend to start so there's no need to worry. Come on, sweetheart, where are you going to put your things?'

'When *will* you die? After I've grown up?'

'Rowena, please stop going on about death. I intend to

live to a grand old age so let's get on with sorting out your dolls.'

'I don't like it here,' pouted her daughter. 'Barnaby's right, it isn't nice.' She glanced round the room again and gave a shout. 'My bed's shrunk!'

Heather was hot and tired. 'Don't be silly!' she shouted back. 'I told you that you were getting a new bed. There isn't room here for your old double one. Now, stop behaving like a baby and try to be helpful. If you start making the room look nice Barnaby will probably want to do the same with his. I'm going to find the kettle and make a cup of tea.'

'I'd rather have squash.'

'Have squash then, but for heaven's sake stop moping about!'

Rowena's eyes filled with tears. 'You never shouted when Daddy was alive. If he can see you from heaven he'll think you're horrid. I think you're horrid too, bringing us to this nasty little house where we don't know anyone.'

The knot of tears in her throat threatened to choke Heather and without another word she walked away.

Barnaby was still motionless by the lounge window. 'Squash, Barnaby?'

'I feel sick, I don't want anything. Why couldn't Rusty come? I'd feel better if he was here. I could give him a hug and show him round.'

'Rusty was used to a big garden and long walks. We haven't got a big garden any more and we'll all be out every day. He would have been terribly lonely, and Aunty Amanda will look after him very well.'

'He was *my* dog,' retorted her son. 'Daddy gave him to *me*. I don't think he'd like to know that you'd given him away.'

'Barnaby . . .' He cleared his throat loudly. Defeated, Heather turned away. The gas man was due any time to connect the cooker. She hoped he'd hurry up. They'd all feel better if they had something to eat. Picking her way carefully through the debris she put the kettle on and made Rowena her drink.

By five o'clock the gas man had been, Rowena was resigned to her room and had started to arrange toys, and one of the tea chests had been emptied.

Amanda had kindly filled two carrier bags with food to get them through the first couple of days and Heather took out a cheese and onion flan. Flans were Mrs Brice's specialities, but hopefully the children would enjoy a bought one as much as their ex-cook's. She removed the plastic top, placed the flan carefully on a flat baking tray and closed the oven door. It would take forty minutes, and she decided to use the waiting time by heating the water and prising Barnaby from the lounge window. She opened the bottom of the gas fire and turned the dial on the boiler. Clive had explained how the back boiler heated both water and – in winter – the radiators, and had assured her this was a highly economical method. She expected something to happen, but it didn't; the pilot light simply glowed steadily on. At least it wasn't a noisy process, she thought thankfully.

'Barnaby, I've put a flan in the oven. Let's go upstairs while it's cooking and take a look at your bedroom.'

Suddenly docile, he slipped his hand into hers. 'I don't have to play out the front, do I?'

'Of course not, only if you want to.'

'They're very noisy, and they keep shouting rude words. At school we got order marks for rude words. Doesn't it matter here?'

'I don't know, darling. Come along, up we go.'

Rowena was bustling round full of pride. 'I've nearly finished, Mummy. It looks nice, doesn't it?'

'Lovely! That's made it more like home, hasn't it?'

'No, but it's nice. I'm ravenously hungry.'

'Tea's cooking. We're going to Barnaby's room now. Oh yes, and I've put the hot water on, we'll all need baths tonight.'

Barnaby took one step into his room and turned to his mother in disbelief. 'This isn't a bedroom, it's only a cupboard. I haven't got any room for my Action Man things. There isn't any bookshelf. It's horrid! Horrid!' and he stamped his feet.

'It's lovely and cosy, darling, and my bedroom's next to yours so that you can easily call me if you need to.'

'I don't want to be cosy, I'm hot. Why's Rowena got a bigger room?'

'Because I'm older, stupid,' Rowena shouted.

'It's not fair! Daddy wouldn't like seeing me in this pokey room. I hate you! I want my Daddy back!' and with fists beating ineffectually against Heather, he began to sob so loudly that eventually Rowena joined in as well.

Their confusion and distress was heartbreaking, but Heather was so exhausted that she knew if she started to comfort them she'd soon be crying too. With a monumental effort at self-control she kept her voice level. 'We all miss Daddy, but we've got to try and turn this house into a nice home. I'm sure there are lots of friendly children near and plenty of things to do. It's bound to be strange at first. Let's go and have that flan now, it should be ready.'

'I can smell burning,' said Rowena as she entered the kitchen.

'Well, it can't be the flan. I've cooked it for exactly forty minutes, as per the instructions,' retorted Heather, opening the oven door. The smell of burning promptly increased.

'Ugh! Mummy, that's an awful pong. Mrs Brice's flans didn't smell like that!' cried Rowena. Barnaby stood by the table, his fingers back in his mouth.

Heather stared at the flan. The top looked perfect, a light golden brown. She looked again, and realised that it wasn't the flan which was burning but the plastic wrapper in which it had come. This had melted and there were dark brown pools of melted plastic on the tray, with some of it clinging to the sides of the pastry. With a groan

Heather retrieved the instructions from the pedal bin. 'Remove flan from container' it stated clearly. It was too much. Furious with herself she tried to rescue some of the flan but it all crumbled to pieces as she manouvered a wooden spatula between the pastry and its container. She shared out the resulting pile of cheese and pastry onto the three plates and threw the baking tray into the dustbin.

'I'm not eating that,' said Rowena firmly. 'It's probably poisonous.'

'Of course it isn't poisonous,' retorted her mother equally firmly, but she actually had no idea which of them was right.

Barnaby was so hungry that he quickly picked up his knife and fork and took a large mouthful. 'It's delicious! The nicest flan I've ever tasted!' he said manfully.

'Creep!' jeered Rowena. 'Mrs Brice's flans were real, they didn't come in plastic boxes.'

'That's why she didn't burn them,' laughed Heather.

Rowena glared at her. 'It isn't funny. The cheese will be full of toxic fumes. I'm only eating my beans.'

Barnaby stared at his food. 'I can't see any whatsit fumes.'

'You don't see toxic fumes, dummy, you smell them. They can kill you too. You get terrible pains in your stomach and . . .'

'Rowena, stop it! You're quite at liberty to leave yours but Barnaby and I are hungry.'

Barnaby pushed his flan carefully to one side of the plate. 'I don't think I am *that* hungry after all.'

Regardless of the two pairs of eyes fixed on her Heather finished up every mouthful. 'That tasted fine to me,' she said cheerfully. 'Would either of you like cake?' They shook their heads. 'Right then, washing-up time.'

As she started to run the hot water Heather looked with dismay at the height of the grass at the back. It didn't look as though Mr and Mrs Rose had bothered to cut it once the sale was confirmed, and she wondered if her electric mower would be able to cope.

'What are you doing, Mummy?' asked Rowena.

'Running the washing-up water.'

'You've been standing there for ages.'

'I can't help that, it's still cold.'

'Perhaps there isn't any hot,' Rowena responded cheerfully.

'A proper little ray of sunshine you're turning out to be,' said Heather and went upstairs to feel the tank. It was stone cold. Her heart sank as she realised this necessitated another visit from the gasmen. In the meantime she would have to use saucepans and the kettle for washing-up water. Baths were out of the question.

While she began heating some water the children went outside, and she could hear them murmuring quietly to one another until there was the sound of a gate opening and Rowena changed to her grown-up voice. Out of her mother's range of vision Rowena stood by the wire fence smiling at the tall man walking up his garden path. At first she thought he was going to ignore her, but then Barnaby cleared his throat and the stranger turned to look at the children.

'Hello!' said Rowena carefully. 'I'm Rowena Lorrimer, and this is my brother, Barnaby. We've come to live next door to you.'

'Good. Perhaps your father will cut the grass,' replied the man.

'He can't, he's dead. That's why we're here. He didn't leave us much money. Aunty Amanda called it reduced circum . . . something or other. What's your name?'

'Mr Harrison.'

'Have you any children?' He didn't reply but Rowena pressed on undaunted. She was enjoying herself at last. 'My Mummy cooked our tea inside its plastic case and it all melted. She still ate it, but I didn't. I thought it might be poisonous.'

'I trust she survived?'

'Well, we wouldn't know yet, would we? She's washing up now. The tank won't get warm so she's boiling kettles and things.' As she chattered on Barnaby was glancing covertly at the newcomer.

'What's your brother got there? A hamster?'

'No, that's Marmaduke, our tortoise.'

'I used to have a dog,' said Barnaby, keeping his head down so that his expression was hidden. 'He was called Rusty, but we had to leave him behind.' He cleared his throat and wiped the back of his hand over his mouth.

The man's eyes softened a fraction. 'Tough luck! I'd better go and make myself some supper. I hope your boiler's soon mended.'

'The gasmen are coming out tomorrow.'

'Good.' With a final appraising glance at the two children he continued down his path.

It was nine o'clock before Heather was able to put the children to bed. They were both over-tired and Barnaby was close to tears. 'Suppose I can't sleep, Mummy? May I come in your bed?'

'You'll be able to sleep, Barnaby.'

'Why haven't you got a single bed now that Daddy's gone?' asked Rowena as she slipped her nightgown over her head.

'I never thought of that.'

'We've been talking to our next-door neighbour,' she continued, apparently inconsequentially. 'He didn't say much, and I don't think his eyesight's very good. He thought Marmaduke was a hamster!'

'He couldn't see Marmaduke,' mumbled Barnaby. 'He was guessing.'

'No he wasn't.'

'He was too.'

Heather let them continue their argument as she peeled off Barnaby's jeans and pants before pulling on his pyjamas.

'I told him about the flan,' added Rowena as she

climbed into bed, 'and the boiler, but I don't think he was very interested.'

'You shouldn't have bothered him.'

'He might not have any children of his own. Perhaps he's glad to see us.'

'Yes, and perhaps he isn't! Now, you can both put your lights out when you're ready to sleep.' With a final kiss she left them, turning on the landing light and making a mental note to get a night-light soon to save electricity.

With a sigh of exhaustion she made a cup of coffee and then collapsed into a lounge chair. She tried not to look at all the unpacking that still had to be done, and turned her mind to more practical matters like the back lawn.

She was slowly drifting off to sleep when the sudden sound of heavy rock music filled the air and the bass reverberated through the walls, a loud, monotonous beat that continued to pound in her ears even when she moved to the kitchen. She sat at the table and rested her head in her hands. She had stomach cramps – hopefully not due to the melted plastic she thought in alarm – and her head felt too heavy for her neck to support it. The music was the final straw; she wished that she had the courage to go round and complain.

All her life Heather had been able to have peace and quiet when she wanted it. Her parents' house had been large and isolated. She had gone straight from there to 'The Lawns' where the only noises came from the children, and even they hadn't disturbed her very much. Peace had never been a problem. I've been spoilt, she reminded herself sternly, I'm not used to having people round me, but I've got to learn.

At that moment there was a knock on the back door. Slightly nervous in a strange house at night Heather opened it about half an inch. A tall, well-built woman of between forty and forty-five stood there. She had shoulder-length hair that stuck out in a frizzy mass and was wearing an unflatteringly tight green dress, but her smile was friendly and in her hands she held a pie. 'Hello! I hope you don't mind me calling, I'm Sheila Gray, your next-door neighbour, and I brought this apple pie because I know how ghastly it is eating out of tins for days while you get straight.'

Heather opened the door wider. 'Do come in. I'm afraid it's a dreadful mess. I've got too many things to fit in.'

Sheila glanced discreetly at Heather's expensive linen slacks and white silk blouse and wondered what the rest of her wardrobe was like if those were her working clothes. 'Your other house was larger, I take it?'

'Yes, quite a lot. Was it your husband my children were talking to this evening?'

'Good heavens no! I haven't got a husband these days. I've got a teenage son, you've probably heard his music tonight, and he's quite enough to cope with, I can tell you! Did his records worry you?'

'Well, a little. Our previous house had extensive grounds and I'm not used to having close neighbours.'

'Really? Well, you'll soon learn to adapt. There has to be a lot of give and take when houses are as close as ours. No doubt I'll hear your children quite a lot.'

Heather was surprised, she had expected some form of apology, but she quickly introduced herself and the two women shook hands.

'Where's *your* husband?' asked Sheila, noticing the wedding ring on Heather's left hand.

'He died in the middle of June.'

'I am sorry. Is that why you've moved?'

'Yes. It's all rather complicated but I couldn't afford to keep the other house on.'

'Never mind, you've come to the right place. There are a lot of one-parent families on this estate and we all help each other out. Your other neighbour isn't very popular, but I don't suppose you'll have much contact with him so it doesn't really matter.'

'Why isn't he popular?'

'He's very moody and keeps himself to himself. Rumour has it that his wife ran off a year after their marriage and they sold their house and split the proceeds down the middle. As a result he thinks he's far too good for the rest of us.'

'What does he do?'

'That doesn't help his popularity either, he's a policeman!'

'What's wrong with being a policeman?'

Sheila looked into the innocent blue eyes and knew that Heather would never understand. 'Perhaps we've all got guilty consciences!' she laughed and Heather joined in. 'Well, I won't stop, I can see you're worn out. Just remember, if there's anything you want come round and ask. I work in the mornings, but the rest of the time I'm at home.'

'It's very kind of you. I start work on Monday, at Porters shoe shop in Croydon. I'm dreading it, but at least it's money.'

Privately, listening to the way Heather spoke and seeing the clothes that she wore, Sheila found it difficult to believe that money could be that desperate but she couldn't help feeling sorry for the slight, attractive girl who quite plainly was having to undergo a drop in living standards and who would have trouble fitting in.

'What about your children after school? Why don't they come to me?'

Heather stiffened. Pleasant and friendly as Sheila was, she wasn't the kind of person she wanted her children to mix with. She gave a tight smile. 'It's all right, thank you. I'm sure Rowena will be able to manage. She's a competent little girl.'

Sheila knew at once why her offer had been refused. Heather's emotions had shown clearly on her face, and at once the good-natured woman drew back as though physically touched by the snub. She kept her voice pleasant, but it was definitely cooler. 'That's fortunate,' she replied on her way out, then at the back door she hesitated. Heather looked so lost that she decided to risk one more put-down. 'One other thing, I possess a scythe, and if you want to use it on your back grass you're very welcome.

'Thank you, but I hope my electric mower will cope.'

'OK, but if it can't give me a shout.'

'That's extremely kind of you; and thank you for the pie as well.'

'You're welcome.' As soon as Sheila had let herself out she went hurrying off to a friend's up the road where she could give a detailed account of the newcomer with her high-class speaking voice and aloof manner.

All the next day Heather worked on the unpacking while Barnaby and Rowena explored the estate and lived on drinks, biscuits, sweets and crisps. Their mother doled them out for the sake of peace and quiet and remembered with nostalgia the years when there had always been someone else to deal with the children. It was incredible to her how demanding the children were, and for the first time she wondered if the au-pairs had been under-paid.

When the men from the Gas Board arrived she vented some of her irritation on them. 'I do think your people might have checked the system when they came to connect me. We haven't been able to bath or do any washing. It's most inconvenient.'

'Not our job to check when it's just a connection,' muttered the older man as he went upstairs to the tank. When he came down he was smirking. 'Your switches weren't on in the airing cupboard,' he said with relish. 'I've put on the one for water, don't forget the other when you need your central heating. It's an expensive mistake to make!'

Heather went scarlet with embarrassment and heard the men laughing as they went away. 'I do think you might have checked the system,' one was saying in a high-pitched voice, and they laughed even louder.

That night she dreamt that she was back in 'The Lawns' with Brian. Amanda and Clive were having dinner with them and they were all laughing and talking until suddenly Amanda turned to Brian and said 'you're meant to be dead' and Brian smiled and said 'I am', at which point the dream ended and Heather woke with a start, automatically putting out a hand to her husband's side of the bed for comfort. Then reality dawned and she sobbed and sobbed at the terrible sense of loss that engulfed her. Eventually she cried herself back to sleep.

All Saturday she continued with the unpacking. Her arms and shoulders ached and she had a niggling pain in her back; but she persisted, knowing that if she stopped she would never re-start. Even when empty the tea chests were heavy, and she dragged them through the back door, along the path beneath the kitchen window and then out through the back gate to the brick-built garage at the rear. It felt as though she were taking part in an endurance course for aspiring marine commandoes.

By mid-afternoon she had nearly finished. As she dragged the penultimate chest out of the back gate she was stopped by a tall, gangly boy with shoulder-length hair. 'Mum said I was to help you,' he muttered. He put out an arm to take hold of a corner of the chest and Heather gratefully released it. To her dismay it toppled over and caught the boy on his left foot. He hopped around for a few moments, muttering curses beneath his breath.

'I'm sorry, I thought you'd got it safely,' said Heather, full of concern.

'I said I'd help, not take over. The bloody thing weighs a ton.'

Biting back the retort that she had been coping single-handed for nearly two days now she resumed the struggle and the boy took as little of the weight as possible.

'Any more?' he asked indifferently, already turning away.

'There is one, if you don't mind waiting.' He looked sullen but followed her to the back door. Sweating and straining Heather 'walked' it to where he was waiting and they made the final trip. 'Thank you very much,' she smiled, trying to get some response but the boy merely stared at her.

'Mum told me to,' he repeated.

'You're Sheila's son?'

'Yep. I'm Scott Gray.'

'The one who plays the music!'

'There's no law against it.' His voice was aggressive.

Heather swiftly tried to repair the damage. 'I know that. I was making an observation, not an accusation.'

'You what?'

'It doesn't matter. Thank you again.'

He slouched off down the road, his T-shirt flapping in the wind. Thoroughly exhausted Heather slumped on the settee, trying to ease the ache in her back. She needed a bath, but the children had to be fed first so she opened a tinned steak and kidney pie and heated it up. All thoughts of nutritional value had been abandoned, convenience was her priority for the present.

'There's no goodness in tinned foods,' said Rowena casually as she ate. 'Mrs Brice said that . . .'

'Shut up about Mrs Brice!' screamed an exhausted Heather. The children stared at her in amazement before Rowena put down her knife and fork and ran from the room.

Barnaby quickly finished his meal and then went running out into the garden. He guessed that Rowena was crying in her bedroom and he didn't want to hear. Since his father died he always felt like crying himself. Marmaduke was in a corner of the garden nibbling at a lettuce leaf he'd been given. Barnaby sat down next to him. 'Do you like it here, Marmaduke? No? Neither do I. It was much nicer before, but we can't ever go back.'

'Hello, young man! How's Marmaduke this evening?'

Barnaby looked up at their neighbour. 'Hello, Mr Harrison. He's fine, thank you.'

'Good. Will he eat all the grass, do you think?'

'No,' retorted the little boy and stared solemnly at the man. 'Mummy's going to do it tomorrow,' he added as an afterthought.

'Where's your sister? The quiet one!'

'In her room, crying. She was rude about our tea which made Mummy shout and then Rowena ran off.'

'She'll be hungry then!'

'Not if she's got the sort of lump I've got in my tummy these days. Mummy cried a bit once she'd finished shouting, so she didn't eat much either.'

'Sounds like a lot of fun! Did you eat anything?'

'Oh yes. It wasn't really nasty, it was just different. The pie and the potatoes weren't real, you see.'

'Not real?'

'No, they came out of tins.'

'Ah, now I'm with you. Did your father do the cooking when he was alive?' Guy Harrison was intrigued by the thought of a mother-of-two who couldn't cook.

'No, he earned a lot of money and paid Mrs Brice to cook and Mrs Russell to clean. The money's gone now, so we couldn't bring either of them with us. Or Rusty,' he added wistfully.

'Never mind, things will get better. I've got to go to work now or I'll be late.'

'It's nearly bed-time!'

'I'm a policeman. I work funny hours.'

Barnaby didn't believe him. 'You haven't got a uniform on,' he said suspiciously.

'I'm a plain clothes policeman. Bye for now.'

Barnaby watched him go and went over the conversation in his mind. He decided to keep it a secret, a nice, comforting secret. He loved his mother, but she didn't seem very good at looking after them yet, and men made him feel much safer.

On Sunday morning Heather was so stiff that she could hardly get out of bed. At the thought of the day ahead her spirits sank even lower. She was going to make a start on the back lawn, then she had to make sure the children were ready for their new school the next day. Apart from that there was a pile of washing in the linen basket, and as her washing machine hadn't yet been plumbed in that meant washing by hand, another new and unwanted experience.

When Brian was alive Sunday mornings had been long and lazy. They would read their papers in bed and sometimes, if the children were taken out, they would make love before finally getting up. She didn't really miss the sex, it had always been pleasant but not particularly exciting. What she really missed were the kisses and cuddles, the physical closeness between husband and wife. Brian had been very affectionate and demonstrative and she longed to have him back and snuggle closely by his side feeling safe and loved.

Life had allowed her to stay emotionally immature, far more so than most of her contemporaries. Her parents had been relatively old and exceptionally strict, and since she wasn't a rebellious type of girl she had accepted their restrictions as natural parental care.

At school she had been painfully shy, and had only made two close friends – one of whom was Yvonne – in her entire time at the girls' public school. As a result of her upbringing and personality her one year at Art college was a disaster. Her work was good, the tutors delighted with her ability and diligence, but she hated the mixed classes and was terrified of boys her own age. Everyone else in her class appeared so confident and outgoing that every day had been something of an ordeal. She didn't fit in and knew that she never would.

Brian was one of her father's golfing partners. One Sunday he had been invited to the house for lunch, her own parents feeling sorry for him as a widower, and that had been the beginning. Right from the start Heather was at ease with him. She liked his quietness, his unexpected sense of humour, and slowly they grew closer and closer. Her mother hadn't prepared her for marriage, but Brian was patient and kind and their honeymoon was a great success. She found marriage extremely pleasant and withdrew thankfully from the world of art students to the sedate Berkshire home, 'The Lawns'.

When the children came along Brian made certain that no extra work fell upon his cherished wife, and so she found them adorable and wondered why other women complained about the disruption children caused in their lives.

Her reflective mood was broken by Rowena banging on the bedroom door. 'Mummy, I'm hungry. May I get my own breakfast?'

'You may start the toast. I'll be down in a minute.'

'It's nine o'clock and I'm starving.'

'That's because you didn't eat your tea.' Groaning quietly, she pulled on her jeans. She had already decided not to attempt using the scythe, the very thought of it frightened her.

By ten o'clock she had the mower plugged into the switch beside the sink. There was a lot of lead and Heather wondered what she was meant to do with it. To her annoyance the mower either skidded along tearing the grass or else kept cutting out, which entailed a two minute wait before it could be re-started. Despite the overcast sky and the light breeze she was boiling hot and perspiration dripped from her forehead.

'Why the hell did you buy a mower that size?' enquired a man's voice. She cast a brief glance at her neighbour and then turned back to the mower. 'Didn't you hear what I said? You'd be better off with a machete!'

'This is the only one I've got,' she said coldly.

'It's ridiculously large. Are you intending to extend the garden at a later date?'

'I brought it with me,' she said crossly. 'I didn't realise it wouldn't work here. I thought it was sensible to keep it, but it isn't going to work, is it?'

He looked at her, taking in the finely boned features and trusting blue eyes. 'No, it isn't,' he said gently.

'Should I buy a machete one then? Do most big stores stock them?'

Guy Harrison had a fleeting vision of her marching into a shop and asking for a machete lawnmower and a smile spread over his face.

'It isn't funny,' said Heather. 'I have to get this done before tomorrow.'

He repressed a momentary desire to offer assistance. He knew from bitter experience that women were adept at appearing frail when they didn't want to do something.

'Better stick at it then, and trade it in as soon as you can. Did you get your boiler mended?' He watched with interest as her face and neck turned scarlet.

'There wasn't anything wrong,' she muttered. 'I didn't know about the switches in the airing cupboard.'

He studied her with continued amused interest and Heather felt herself going stiff and awkward under his gaze; determinedly she started up the mower again.

'Look out!' he bellowed.

Alarmed she stopped. 'Is it Marmaduke? I thought he was inside.'

'No it isn't Marmaduke, you stupid woman! It's your lead. If you cut that you'll electrocute yourself.'

'Then we'll be orphans!' called Rowena, strolling out into the garden with Barnaby tagging along behind. He gave Guy a shy smile.

'Good morning, Barnaby. You're a cheerful madam, Rowena!'

She giggled. 'It's true. We'd have to live in a poorhouse then, like Oliver Twist.'

Guy began to laugh but caught sight of Barnaby's

worried face. 'There aren't any poorhouses these days,' he assured the boy.

'Pity, I might get some decent food,' retorted his sister.

This time Guy didn't look at Heather, but he guessed that she was blushing again. 'I mustn't detain your mother any longer,' he said casually, 'she's got a lot of work ahead of her.' With a charming smile he walked away and a thoroughly demoralised and defeated Heather retreated to the kitchen for a cup of coffee.

A few minutes later Sheila walked in. 'Why didn't you collect the scythe? Your mower can't cope with that grass.'

'So the kindly Mr Harrison told me,' retorted Heather. 'He said that I needed a machete. Are they good ones?'

Sheila snorted. 'I didn't know he had a sense of humour. A machete is a knife with a long, curved blade!'

'What an idiot he must have thought me.'

'Look, I'll get Scott to do some scything. He's only lounging around bored to distraction.'

'I really don't think he'll want to.'

'He's going to do it and that's final. You look very pale.'

'I'm always pale.'

As soon as Sheila had gone Heather dashed up to the bathroom. She was becoming increasingly worried about her gastric attacks. She couldn't afford to be ill, and it was going to be awkward coping in a busy shop with customers waiting while she disappeared to the cloakroom. If only she had someone close to confide in. Brian had been very good at listening and would quickly reassure her, holding her close as he did so and murmuring softly in her ear.

She could picture him so clearly that it was hard to believe she would never see him again. How could a person spend fifty-two years on the earth and then disappear without trace, as though he had never existed? 'I can't go on without you, Brian,' she whispered to her reflection in the cabinet mirror. A wave of intense physical longing swept over her and she waited for the tears to follow, but they didn't. Instead her sorrow abruptly turned into a violent, irrational surge of anger at the predicament in which his lack of foresight had landed her and the children.

'Mummy!' called Rowena from downstairs. 'Now that the grass is nice can we make the garden pretty with some flowers?'

Heather thought of Amanda's garden; the flower beds a blaze of colour, the long sloping lawn, without a blemish, and she wished that she could watch Amanda trying to turn this particular garden into something 'pretty' for the children.

'*Mummy*! I'm talking to you. Where are you?'

'I'm just coming.'

Once outside it was surprising how good a job Scott had done. After using the scythe he had run the mower over it to finish it off evenly.

'Flowers,' Rowena reminded her.

'There isn't any room for flowers, darling. Perhaps we could plant some shrubs in the front, beneath the lounge window.'

'What kind of shrubs?'

'I've no idea,' she confessed. 'Do you think it looks better, Barnaby?'

'I suppose so. What will school be like tomorrow? There won't be girls in *my* class, will there?'

'I don't know,' responded Heather wearily, feeling as though she was floundering in a perpetual bog of ignorance. 'Let's get some nourishment!' She had at least learnt that food could always be relied upon to appease them.

Rowena seemed to sense what her mother was doing.

'I'm not hungry,' she grizzled and walked away, her head drooping.

All through the meal she could be heard sobbing in her room, and when Barnaby had finished and went outside her cries still filled the air. Alone he sat quietly in the middle of the lawn, sucking hard on his fingers.

Guy Harrison got out of his car in a bad temper. He had been through a difficult day and now one of his junior officers was on suspension pending a bribery inquiry. He was half-way down his path before he saw Barnaby and the child looked so forlorn that he instinctively stopped and spoke. 'Hello, Barnaby. How's things?'

'All right, thank you.'

'I see Marmaduke ate the grass!'

'No, Scott cut it for Mummy.' There wasn't even the ghost of a smile on the boy's face.

'Where's your cheerful sister? The prophet of doom!'

'Crying in her bedroom.'

'Oh dear! Tell you what, how would you like to come and see my budgerigar? It talks when it's in a good mood.'

'I'd have to ask Mummy. We're not allowed to go off without telling her.'

'Quite right too. You go and ask her.' He had a fleeting vision of Heather as she'd been that morning. Small, frail and entirely out of place as she struggled with her huge mower so obviously intended for a much larger garden.

Barnaby ran out smiling. 'I can come, but only for twenty minutes. It's bath night, because of school tomorrow.'

In the kitchen the budgerigar hopped up and down on its swing. 'What a nice day,' it said clearly.

Barnaby's eyes grew enormous. 'What does he say when it's raining?' he whispered.

'The same, I'm afraid! He's only a mimic, he doesn't

understand what he's saying. We must try and teach him to say "Hello, Barnaby" although Barnaby's a bit of a mouthful.'

The boy stood entranced as Pip went through his entire repertoire. When he said 'Damn it!' Barnaby laughed aloud, and Guy was relieved to discover that the child could laugh after all.

'I've got some fish in a tank in the front room. Do you want a quick look at them?'

'Yes please!'

In the tank angel fish and small goldfish swam around. 'My Daddy used to go deep sea fishing, Mr Harrison. He never took me, but he was going to when I was eight. Of course he's dead now, so I won't go. Do you catch angel fish in the sea?'

'No. I think your twenty minutes are about up now. Perhaps you could come another day?' Barnaby was delighted, Guy surprised. It wasn't what he had intended to say, but he sensed that the boy's quiet love of animals should be nurtured, and he also needed drawing out of himself away from the weeping Rowena's influence.

At the back door Barnaby put out his hand. 'Thank you very much for letting me look. Is your wife out at work? Mummy's going out to work tomorrow, because of the bank balance.'

'I haven't got a wife, Barnaby. I think we'll keep this house for men.'

'Great idea!' Genuine enthusiasm lit up the boy's face and he raced away to boast to Rowena about his new friend.

After he'd gone the house seemed strangely quiet and Guy sighed, then put a record on the music centre. Barnaby had brought back memories that he preferred to forget.

Chapter Five

Monday started badly. When the alarm went at seven Heather waited for Brian to turn it off before realisation dawned. There was no time to give in to the tears that quickly formed in her eyes, but it was with taut nerves that she went to wake the children. None of them wanted breakfast, although Heather insisted on either toast or cereal for the silent children.

'Mummy,' said Rowena as she buttoned up her raincoat – even the weather was against them, the rain coming down in sheets – 'what if I can't make my key work? Suppose Barnaby and me get stuck outside in the rain for hours? We might catch pneumonia.'

'It's not Barnaby and me, it's Barnaby and I.'

'I don't care!' yelled Rowena. 'We'll both get wet however it's said.'

'For heaven's sake, Rowena, you know how to open a door, don't you? I thought you were looking forward to being in charge for a short time each day.'

'She's not going to boss me about,' said Barnaby firmly, struggling with his new, stiff buttons.

'Yes I am. Mummy, tell him he's got to do as I say when you're at work.'

'Will you please both be quiet. I have to go out too, you know. I'm due at the shop at nine.'

'I didn't know a mummy ever worked,' said Rowena angrily. 'All the other mothers in the country look after their children properly.'

'You don't have any idea how other mothers cope. You've both been thoroughly spoilt since you were born, and now you're going to learn that life isn't perfect all the time. Lots and lots of people have to work every day just so that they can afford to keep a roof over their heads and food in their stomachs.'

'Only daddies,' said Barnaby.

'No, mothers too.'

'I wish you'd died,' muttered Rowena. 'Daddy would have looked after us much better.'

'If it weren't for your father's stupidity we wouldn't be in this mess!' snapped Heather, and the children stared at her in shocked disbelief.

'I loved my Daddy,' Barnaby said at last. 'He wasn't stupid, he was nice.'

Heather was aghast at herself, but the clock was ticking relentlessly on and she had to keep them all moving. 'I know, darling,' she said quickly. 'I didn't mean it, I'm nervous myself this morning. I'm sorry. We all loved Daddy, and we've got to try and behave in a way that would have made him proud of us.' There were tears in her eyes but her voice was steady.

The children nodded and moved closer to each other as though seeking comfort, Heather's guilt intensified.

Finally, armed with umbrellas and boots, they set off. At the school gates both children hung back, clinging on to Heather's wet hands and starting to cry. She firmly disentangled herself, gave them a quick kiss on the forehead and turned resolutely away. At the bus stop she allowed herself to look back, and they were walking slowly towards the entrance, hand-in-hand.

It was two minutes past nine when, with much trepidation, she walked into Porters shoe shop. Immediately the middle-aged woman waiting by the sandal display looked pointedly at her watch.

'Mrs Lorrimer? I'm Mrs Winter, the manageress of this branch. Welcome to your new job.'

'Thank you, I . . .'

'I think that I should point out to you that our staff are expected to be in the shop by quarter to nine, so perhaps you'll remember that in the future.'

'I'm sorry, but you see I have to get the children to school and . . .'

'Married women with children still have to obey the rules. I understand that you have no experience of shop work?'

'No, I . . .'

'Mr Simmons is an acquaintance, I believe?'

'Yes, he was kind enough . . .'

'*He* doesn't have to train you! However, hurry along with Rita, she'll show you where to put your wet coat and then you can learn from her for the first hour.'

'I do appreciate it, I . . .'

'Please hurry up!'

Flushing, Heather followed the pale, thin girl named Rita through to the back of the shop. 'She didn't let me finish a single sentence!' she exploded.

Rita gave a sympathetic smile. 'She never does. As you can probably guess, staff turnover's high here! Look, you can hang your raincoat on this peg.' Heather did as she was told and missed the look of surprise on the young girl's face as she saw the powder-blue Jaeger two-piece Heather was wearing. Silently she handed over a blue and white checked overall. 'Come on then, let's brave the customers. You'll soon get the hang of things. The one rule to bear in mind is that the customer is never wrong!'

Five minutes later a middle-aged woman seated herself on one of the plastic-covered chairs and demanded a court shoe in a wide fitting. When she left thirty minutes later no sale had been made and the floor was littered with discarded shoes.

'How many times must I remind you that every customer should find something to satisfy them here?' demanded Mrs Winter.

Rita scowled. 'She never intended to buy. She was only coming in to escape from the rain.'

'Possibly,' conceded the manageress. 'However, a little more persuasion wouldn't come amiss.'

It was fortunate that the day was wet as Heather found everything a nightmare. All the customers seemed querulous and difficult as they tried to force wide, swollen feet into narrow, fashionable shoes before proceeding to complain about the sizing system. By half-past-five her head was pounding, her legs were aching and her calf muscles were trembling with fatigue. She had never imagined that the general public could be so deliberately offensive. They didn't seem to realise that shop assistants had feelings, or if they did they certainly didn't care.

At quarter past six she stumbled wearily off her bus and walked through the estate. Sheila saw her as she entered her back gate. 'How did it go?' she called.

'Not too badly.'

'Better than you'd expected?'

'Oh yes,' she lied.

'That's good. Rowena's been doing a lot of shouting since they got home. If you want them to come here tomorrow just let me know.'

'Probably teething troubles. I'd better go in and check.'

Sheila shook her head and turned away. Obviously Heather didn't want any help. Too proud, she thought to herself. Thinks she's above the rest of us; well, time will tell. There was no malice in the thought, in fact she felt a touch of sadness when she recalled the look of total exhaustion on her neighbour's fine drawn features.

Inside number eight there was chaos. Rowena had tried to make a jam sandwich and there was jam everywhere, with two halves of a side plate stacked neatly in the sink. As Heather stripped off her coat the children came in, leaving the lounge door open so that the television could be heard blaring loudly.

'Turn that thing down!' demanded Heather. 'My

head's aching.'

'So's mine,' grizzled Rowena. 'We were starving and I couldn't make a sandwich because the butter wouldn't spread. The bread kept breaking up.'

'Don't worry; it's going to be margarine from now on, that's cheaper and easier to spread.'

'Hello, Mum,' said Barnaby, coming up for a kiss. She bent down. 'What's that mark on your face, darling?'

'I had a fight, it's a bruise. Can we have fish fingers?'

'Yes. Let me kiss it better.'

'It's all right. Rowena's already done that.' His sister looked smug. Heather sat down and sighed. Taking off her boots and wriggling her toes around was pure bliss.

'Did you enjoy selling shoes?' enquired Rowena.

'It wasn't too bad. A bit frightening at first, but I expect school was too.'

'Not for me. I've made a special friend called Janice. We're going to be best friends.'

'That's nice. How about you, Barnaby?'

He shrugged. 'I don't like any of the boys much. They all shout a lot and say rude words. The teachers shout too.'

'I don't blame them! Come on, let's get tea.'

It was ten-thirty when Heather finally climbed exhausted into her double bed. She hoped that her first day had been a baptism by fire, and that from now on things would get easier.

They didn't. Mrs Winter seemed to have taken a special dislike to the newcomer, as though Mr Simmons had in some way insulted her by taking on an inexperienced girl, and so she took every opportunity to make Heather's life a misery.

On the Friday afternoon, at ten minutes past five, a tall, well-dressed woman entered the shop and started to browse around. Both Rita and Heather cast surreptitious glances at their watches hoping that she wasn't going to delay closing-time. Mrs Winter nodded at Heather who walked over with a pleasant smile.

The customer reminded her of Amanda. She had the same confident manner and even wore the same perfume. She smiled back until Heather spoke, and then her manner changed sharply. It was as though she wanted to remind the assistant of her lowly position. Time after time boxes were brought to her, but nothing proved suitable.

'Are you sure these are real leather?' she demanded as Heather proffered the eighth pair of shoes.

'No, they're not. You've tried on all the leather ones,' retorted Heather. Her smouldering resentment against Amanda had suddenly focused itself onto the customer.

'I don't care for your tone,' the woman said coldly.

'Well, I'm sorry but we don't seem to have anything that will satisfy you – I mean suit you, not in leather.'

'You haven't brought me the white leather pair in the window.'

'No, because you asked for brown shoes. You didn't say brown or white.'

'Are you trying to tell me that I don't know what sort of shoes I want? Where's the manageress?'

Mrs Winter hurried forward. 'Leave this to me, Mrs Lorrimer,' she said with a frigid smile. Ten minutes later the woman left with a pair of cream leather shoes.

Heather was putting on her jacket when the manageress cornered her. 'Mrs Lorrimer, I think that you still have a great deal to learn if you're to keep your job here. Your tone when speaking to our last customer was positively offensive.'

'So was she.'

'Really! I suggest that you think about your attitude very carefully when you get home tonight. If you don't like being a shop assistant there are plenty of girls only too anxious to do the work. Perhaps you should consider that over the weekend.'

Heather pushed past the woman and almost ran from the shop, biting her bottom lip to keep back the tears. As she feared, she'd missed her bus and it was six forty-five before she got home, to find Rowena pacing round like a caged tiger.

'Where were you? We thought you'd been run over. Barnaby feels sick and I don't want to look after the house any more. I want you to be here for us. It's horrible and lonely, and Barnaby won't do what I tell him. Why are you late? Don't you care about us?'

'Darling, of course I care. Do you think I like working this late?'

Rowena shrugged. 'I dunno.'

'Dunno? What sort of word is that? Don't know, please.'

'Everyone at school says dunno.'

'Fine, then keep it for school, Rowena.'

As soon as Barnaby had finished his meal he slid from his chair and raced off. Rowena, who had been sulking all the time, began to cry. 'I want to go too. Why is it only Barnaby?'

'I think it's a man's house, darling. Have you got any homework to do?'

'No.'

'Are you sure?'

'Don't nag!' shouted Rowena. 'I hate you when you nag. I'm going upstairs. Janice gave me some crayons today, she's got hundreds. I'm going to do some colouring.'

'Fine. I hope you thanked her?'

'Of course I did!'

Once she'd gone Heather looked round the kitchen. Not a single work surface was clear or clean, and the sink was full of dirty plates and mugs. She stood up, and put a hand to her aching back. If she didn't make a start now she'd never summon up the energy.

Sighing she picked up the frying pan and then gave a shout as it slipped from her tired fingers. The cooking oil spilt all over the floor and it was the final straw. She sat down, buried her head in her hands and sobbed.

She never even heard the light tap on the back door. The first thing she knew was the feel of a comforting arm round her shoulders, followed by the sound of Sheila's voice urging her to cry it out.

At last she stopped through sheer exhaustion, and immediately a strong cup of tea was put in front of her. 'There you are, Heather. The cure for all ills!'

'I'm so sorry,' muttered Heather. 'Whatever must you think of me?'

'To tell you the truth I'm relieved. I was beginning to think that you were completely without feeling. I didn't know you could cry; it's rather reassuring to find that you're as human as the rest of us!'

'I can certainly cry these days. I'm like a leaking tap!'

'You've every right to feel down. Ooops! What's that?'

'Oh God! That's the oil from the frying pan I dropped. It was too much coming on top of a week working for the sadistic Mrs Winter.'

Sheila looked at the other woman's face. It was pale and puffy from crying and already her hair had lost the shining gloss that Sheila remembered.

'Look,' she said, once more determined to help Heather, 'you stay put and I'll clear up for you. Then, once the children are in bed, you're coming to my house to meet some more neighbours. We always gather on a Friday evening, and they'll be delighted to see a new face.'

'I couldn't possibly. I can't leave the children.'

'Scott will babysit. I'll get him a new tape in recompense! Do come, you need a break.'

Heather didn't want to go. All that she wanted was to creep into a hot bath and then fall into bed, but as she watched Sheila whisking round the kitchen, washing up plates and cleaning the floor she knew that it was impossible to refuse. 'All right then, and I'm very grateful, really I am. I feel so pathetically inadequate.'

'We all have our off days! There, that's about it. Scott will be round about nine, see you then.' With a bright smile she left and reluctantly Heather started to get herself washed and changed.

While she was dressing, the children wandered into her room, Rowena already in her nightdress, Barnaby peeling off his vest. At the sight of her son's legs and arms she gave a stifled cry. 'Barnaby! You're covered in bruises. What happened to you?'

He flushed. 'Nothing.'

'Don't be silly; something must have caused them.'

'It's the other boys,' Rowena chimed in. 'They keep fighting him at playtime.'

'Why are they picking on Barnaby?'

'Because of the way he talks. It's his fault; he should copy the others. I do.'

'I should not!' shouted an incensed Barnaby. 'Daddy wouldn't like it.'

'Daddy won't know, stupid.'

'I'm sure Daddy wouldn't want you hurt, Barnaby. I'll have a word with your teacher.'

'No!' He was panic-stricken. 'You'd make it worse. Don't come to school, Mummy, please. They'll soon get tired of it, Guy told me.'

'You mean he knows about this?' Barnaby nodded. 'Then he should have told me.'

'I made him promise not to.'

'I see.' Heather's voice was grim.

'Don't be cross, Mummy. Guy's my friend.'

'I'm not cross, darling. Come along both of you. I have to go out.' The pair of them made token protests, which Heather ignored, and finally Scott arrived so she went next door.

Sheila had three other visitors: Mary, whose husband had his own business and was never at home; Lynne, a young, unmarried mother whose three-month-old baby never made a sound; and Jane, who had two children at the comprehensive school but didn't go out to work because her husband didn't believe in it.

For most of the time Heather sat listening while the women laughed and joked about their men, or lack of them, and Lynne told of the welfare worker who kept popping in on her unannounced, convinced there was a man hidden somewhere who was avoiding detection because it would cut Lynne's supplementary benefit should he be discovered.

'Chance would be a fine thing!' she laughed. 'I can't think of one single man who'd want a three-month-old baby and an opinionated young mother! Still, I enjoy rushing upstairs and making noises as though I'm hiding shaving things and Y-fronts!' Heather was fascinated by such a carefree attitude to life. It was impossible to imagine Lynne sobbing about an untidy kitchen or a domineering boss.

Mary and Jane both spent a great deal of time complaining about their husbands. 'He's either all over me or else he never touches me,' complained Mary. 'I don't think he's heard about cuddles, chocolates, kisses and flowers. It's sex or nothing.'

'They're all the same,' retorted Jane. 'Right now Mike's so busy that he's the one with the headaches, but heaven help us if I get one!'

'You see!' laughed Lynne, turning to the newcomer, 'you're lucky if you did but know it!'

'But Brian wasn't a bit like that. We'd sit cuddling on the sofa most nights and he bought me . . .' Her voice tailed off as she caught sight of the expressions on the surrounding faces.

For a moment there was an awkward silence. She had sounded too intense, and hadn't realised that most of their moaning was only partly serious. Mary and Jane eyed her thoughtfully. According to Sheila, Heather had fallen on hard times; but they both knew expensive clothes when they saw them, and they didn't care for the way in which she seemed to be sitting back and making a judgement on them.

It was only Lynne who sensed the shyness and lack of

security that lay behind Heather's aloof exterior. 'Lucky you!' she said warmly.

After that the talk turned to other women on the estate, which excluded Heather entirely, and as soon as she could she made her excuses and left. Lynne walked to the front door with her. 'Any time you want some help, just come over. I'm number twenty-four and I get bored stiff talking to fat Daisy here. I'm always delighted to get some adult conversation.'

'Well, I . . .'

'Look, you'll be doing me a favour. Make sure you don't leave it too long or I could get carted away in a straitjacket!' Heather smiled but didn't commit herself.

Half an hour later Sheila came round again. 'I expect you're dying to get to bed but I forgot to mention Saturday week. I'd like you to make up a foursome and come out to dinner. You need something to look forward to in your job!'

'All right,' Heather agreed, resigned to a programme of 'bringing her out'. Rather like the debutantes of old, she thought ruefully. 'I'll come if I can but first I'm going to see a doctor. Do you know a good one?'

'Sure, try Dr Rawle. She's only round the corner and she's a marvellous listener. What's wrong?'

'Only my stomach.'

'Nerves!' said Sheila crisply as she left. It was all right for other people, Heather thought, as she finally got to bed. They didn't know how she felt. Already in her mind she was half-way to the grave with stomach cancer.

However, the following Wednesday evening she took her courage in both hands and went to see Dr Rawle. As Sheila had said she was an excellent listener, and Heather stumbled through a summary of her last few months, confessing to her perpetual feeling of inadequacy and also to her moments of intense anger and bitterness against Brian which left her thoroughly ashamed and even more depressed.

'You're entitled to feel angry,' said the doctor. 'It's a

perfectly natural reaction under the circumstances and there's absolutely nothing to feel ashamed about. In fact, I'd be more worried if you didn't feel anything. As to your physical problems, well, as you've doubtless guessed, they're entirely due to nerves, which doesn't make them any the less inconvenient but isn't anything to worry over.'

'I was afraid it was cancer,' confessed Heather.

'No, Mrs Lorrimer, it isn't cancer. I'm going to give you some mild tranquillisers and some medicine for your stomach, but I want to see you again in two weeks. In the meantime try not to worry over every little problem; save your energy for the major ones!'

Heather managed a small smile. 'They all seem major right now, but I'll try.'

'How are your children coping?'

'Quite well really. They're finding it difficult to settle at their new school.'

'Give it time, children are very resilient. Now, don't forget to make another appointment on your way out!'

'I told you!' said Sheila triumphantly. 'Now you can look forward to next Saturday night. It's all fixed up.'

'Good,' said Heather weakly, and cursed her inability to say no.

By the end of the next week she doubted if she could continue working at the shop unless things improved. Nothing that she did met with Mrs Winter's approval, and every time a smart woman came into the shop she was swamped with such bitter envy that it was hard to be polite and helpful.

At home Rowena began to throw regular, nightly tantrums and Barnaby spent all his spare time at Guy Harrison's rather than listen to her.

Eventually, and to her ever-increasing regret, Saturday evening arrived. She spent a lot of time over her appearance, choosing a powder-blue silk two-piece with pleated skirt and waisted top. She carefully washed and conditioned her hair, which had been badly neglected recently, and then applied discreet make-up to accentuate her already striking eyes.

Scott, seated in front of the television with his feet up on her small coffee-table, gave a low whistle of admiration when she went downstairs.

'You're sure you'll be all right?' Heather asked for the fifth time. He sighed and nodded. 'You've got the telephone number of the restaurant?'

'Yeah! I've got it all. You just have a good time,' and for some unaccountable reason he smirked.

Heather dithered in the doorway. 'I won't be too late.'

'Doesn't bother me. You'll be late right now if you don't shift your . . . get a move on rather.' Reluctantly she left.

'You look fantastic!' enthused Sheila as she let her in. 'The others will soon be here. You'll like them. Graham's something in computers, I've known him six months, and he's bringing along his friend, Roger.' She then smiled a little too brightly at her neighbour.

Heather couldn't believe her ears. 'I thought it was going to be four *women*,' she said in distress. 'I don't want to go out in a mixed foursome.'

'Don't be silly, who ever heard of four women arranging a Saturday night out for dinner! Christ, it would cost a fortune! The food's always good; Graham's very fussy about that, so make the most of it.'

'Sheila, I'm quite content on my own. I don't want another man.'

'I'm not asking you to marry the bloody man, just have a good time.' The two women stared at each other, then abruptly there was the sound of a car horn outside. 'Come on,' said Sheila, taking hold of her friend's arm, 'you can't let me down now. I've been singing your praises all the week.'

Outside Sheila quickly climbed into the front passenger seat and Heather slid into the back, unable to catch more than a glimpse of Graham. Roger was fair and young and eyed her appraisingly with slowly growing appreciation.

Inside the restaurant, tucked away in a secluded corner table, Heather took a closer look at her escort. His fair hair was quite long and his light blue eyes seemed to penetrate her suit, summing up what it concealed.

'You're a widow, aren't you?' he asked after they'd ordered.

'Yes. My husband died in June.'

'You must miss him a lot.' He gave her a glance that she didn't understand.

'I do, every moment of the day. It's hard to realise that he's never coming back.'

'Young, was he?'

'Not really. Fifty-two.'

'That's old! Got any children?'

'Two. Rowena's nine and Barnaby's six.'

'You don't look old enough to have children that age.'

'Well I assure you that I am; and I wasn't exactly a child bride either.' She wished the conversation would become more general, but Sheila and Graham were sitting with their heads close together and Heather could see that Graham had his hand on Sheila's knee. She wished fervently that she hadn't come.

'How about you?' she enquired, turning back to Roger and catching him studying her legs where her skirt had ridden up. Casually she tried to tug it back into place. 'I mean, are you single or what?'

'I'm separated. It's been very uncivilised; in-fighting over access, violent quarrels over the house and contents, nasty letters flying from my solicitor to hers and vice versa. I'll be glad when it's over.'

'How old are your children?'

'Two and five. Both girls; I wanted a boy, but now I'm glad they're girls. I wouldn't fancy a son of mine brought up by a woman.'

'I'm bringing mine up on my own,' she said stiffly.

'Sure, but you'll re-marry. With your looks you're bound to.' The glance that accompanied the compliment was far too personal and Heather felt her hands going hot and clammy.

When the food arrived the strange lump in her throat that plagued her these days seemed to swell, and she knew that she couldn't possibly eat it all or she'd be sick. She picked away at it slowly, hoping the others wouldn't notice. She needn't have worried. Graham and Sheila were too wrapped up in themselves to care and Roger showed complete disinterest in what she left.

On their way home Roger sat very close to Heather, trapping her against the car door, his left hand coming to rest casually on her right knee. She moved her leg, but his hand followed. Rather than endure an undignified scuffle she let it stay there. After all, they were nearly back.

To her horror it was taken for granted that they all went in to Sheila's for a nightcap. Roger put his arm round Heather's shoulders as they walked up the path, and kept it there until Sheila handed them both a brandy glass, each one containing a generous measure of alcohol. Then she and Graham quickly took theirs into the kitchen, leaving the other two alone on the settee.

'Where do you live?' asked Heather quickly.

'Not far away. Near enough to take you out again. You're quite something, you know. When Graham asked me to do him a favour I expected someone middle-aged and repressed, not a dishy girl like you! How have you managed since your old man died?'

'Managed? Well, as best as I could, I suppose. It isn't easy with two children.'

'I suppose not. Who's with them now?'

'Scott.'

'That's OK then. I like your suit.' His hand strayed lightly along her shoulders and rested on top of her left breast. Rigid with shock Heather was frozen to the spot, unable to release herself and hoping desperately for Sheila's return.

Roger turned her towards him and began to kiss her, lightly at first but with increasing passion. She gave a wriggle to free herself which he obviously misinterpreted because he murmured 'It's all right, there's plenty of time,' and continued with increased enthusiasm.

There was the sound of the kitchen door opening and Heather silently thanked Sheila, but she didn't stay grateful for long. 'We're going to look at my etchings!' giggled her friend. 'Enjoy yourselves.'

Roger's hands were everywhere now; he was breathing heavily and trying to fumble with the zip of the back of her suit. It was a situation completely foreign to Heather who had never experimented in the backs of cars, nor indulged in heavy petting.

'I can tell you've missed it,' Roger whispered in her ear. 'Don't worry, I'm good. You'll be surprised what a real man can do for you.' As he talked he managed to unzip the silk top and it slid down Heather's arms and fell into her lap, leaving her in her coffee-coloured half-bra and its lacy edging. Immediately his hands were reaching out, trying to take hold of her breasts as he buried his head in her neck.

All at once she was released from her immobility. She pushed hard at him. 'Stop it! I don't want you touching me. Let me go!'

'Come on, that's the way you women always talk, pretending things get out of hand and that you can't stop your man. Well, if that's your fantasy I'll go along with it. I'll go along with any fantasy you like. You've got a fabulous body, did your old man ever tell you that?'

It was the final straw. Heather wrenched herself free and tumbled to the floor, pulling her jacket up as soon as she hit the carpet. Her face was flushed and her hair dishevelled. 'Don't you dare talk about my husband like that! Who the hell do you think you are to start pawing me about because we've had a meal out?'

His pale eyes grew cold. 'You were keen enough earlier.'

'I was not. I was trying to get free.'

He snorted. 'Don't talk such bloody rubbish!'

'I'm going home,' she cried, tears of shame in her eyes.

'Fair enough. Are you paying for your meal or do I get lumbered with that as well?'

Furiously she opened her purse and flung twelve pounds at him. It was the last of her precious housekeeping but she was determined not to give him any reason to complain. 'There you are!' she shouted, 'keep the change if it matters so much.'

Roger remained sprawled on the settee, his eyes insolent. 'How was I to know you were playing the timid virgin? Graham said you needed a good man, and I'm good so I came along. There's plenty more fish in the sea, and eager ones too. Who are you saving yourself for? Another geriatric?'

She flinched at his cruelty, grabbed up her bag and ran out of the front door, slamming it shut behind her. Roger shrugged and turned on the television. Graham was in for a surprise when Scott arrived home early, he thought with a smile.

Heather unlocked her front door and ran straight up to the bathroom to sponge away the tears and the streaked mascara so carefully applied earlier.

When she went down again Scott looked at her in surprise. 'You're early. Graham still at home?'

'Yes. Now, what do I owe you?'

'Nothing. Mum's getting me two new tapes. I'm off to see a mate as I won't be wanted at home for an hour or so. The kids were no trouble, not a sound from them all the evening.'

'That's good, and thanks, Scott.'

Once in bed she lay awake for hours going over and over

the events of the evening. She still found the whole situation unbelievable and the thought that Sheila fully expected her to make love with a complete stranger was beyond her comprehension.

For the first time she found the thought of men and sex distasteful. She had hated his clumsy fumblings and lack of tenderness. Her thoughts took refuge in the past and her married life. She remembered Brian's gentleness and willingness to settle for kisses and embraces when she was tired or over-tense. She hadn't liked it on the few occasions that their lovemaking had turned into something else, giving her the feeling that she was losing control of her own body. Brian had understood and after a time such incidents ceased.

The entire evening had left her feeling degraded and soiled, and she wondered how she would ever face Sheila again. In her heart she blamed Sheila, because no one else could have misled Roger so badly. It was three a.m. before she fell asleep, and all her dreams were of terrifying, faceless men who pursued her relentlessly throughout the night.

Chapter Six

Heather awoke to the sound of someone knocking at her front door. The bedside clock showed half-past nine, and pulling her dressing-gown round her she went quickly downstairs and cautiously opened the door.

Outside stood Guy Harrison. He was wearing a cream chunky-knit jersey, tight blue cords, and looked as though he had been up and about for hours. There was still a frost on the ground and Heather shivered.

'Perhaps I could come in for a moment?' he queried mildly. She hesitated. 'You're quite safe. I never molest women in the morning, it's far too exhausting!' Flushing, she managed to undo the safety chain. Once inside he dwarfed the tiny hallway and she quickly took him into the lounge where he could sit down. She felt unreasonably threatened by him after the previous night. He was too young, too attractive and far too self-confident. There was no trace of gentleness and sensitivity on his face. It made her long even more for Brian's comforting presence, and it also reminded her of Roger.

Before she could speak, the door from the kitchen opened and Rowena came in. She didn't see the visitor, only her mother, and immediately launched into the attack.

'Barnaby and I were famished! We tried to wake you up, but you were snoring. We've had to get our own breakfast. We've had toast and cereal, but we really wanted boiled eggs. You don't care about us any more, you're only interested in fancy men. If Daddy could see you he'd think . . .'

Heather smacked her daughter hard on the leg and she gave a squeal of surprise.

Before she could start screaming Guy spoke. 'Good morning, Rowena.'

She jumped, and at once her scowl gave way to a smile from beneath lowered lashes. 'I didn't see you, Mr Harrison.'

'So I gathered. Do you often talk to your mother like that?' She shuffled her feet.

'It's only because she hasn't settled down yet,' put in Heather quickly. 'Come along, Rowena, I'll make some tea.'

Then Barnaby came rushing into the lounge at the sound of his friend's voice. He hurled himself into the air and Guy quickly caught him and lifted him above his head.

'Have you come about you-know-what?' whispered the little boy.

'I might have done! Have a good breakfast?'

'Lovely! I had two bowls of cereal and three slices of toast. Mummy never lets us have *two* bowls of cereal.'

'I'm glad to hear you're not starving. Shall I ask your mother now?' Barnaby nodded, flushed with excitement.

'Ask me what?' queried Heather as she brought in a tray of tea.

'I'm going to a local football match next Saturday. I wondered if you'd mind Barnaby coming with me? I've got tickets for seats so you needn't worry about hooliganism on the terraces; he'll be quite safe.'

She looked at her son snuggled up on this stranger's lap, looking as secure as when his father had been alive, and she didn't know whether to be grateful to the aloof, blue-eyed man or resentful that he had so quickly found his way into Barnaby's heart. 'That's very kind of you. Are you sure you don't mind?'

'Quite sure.'

'Hurrah!' shouted Barnaby, running off to tell Rowena.

'I'm grateful for all you've done to help him,' she said stiffly.

'He's a nice lad, and very entertaining company.'

'You've helped him a lot,' she added as she handed him a cup of tea. Her hand trembled slightly at the force of his physical presence, and for one ridiculous moment she wished that he had been her partner the previous evening.

'How are you coping?' he queried, sensing her discomfort and hoping to divert her.

'Not too badly now. I don't like my job, but beggars can't be choosers, and the building society likes prompt payments! The children are finding school difficult. At least, Barnaby is. I think he told you about the bullying?' He nodded. 'I wish you'd told me,' she said resentfully. 'I saw the marks when he was undressing.'

'I made a promise. Besides, sometimes it's easier for children to talk to outsiders.'

'I suppose so. Rowena's coping better than any of us. She's made this best friend who's apparently wealthy and highly popular, so she feels she's made quite a conquest.'

'Really? I thought that perhaps . . .'

'What?'

He shrugged. 'Nothing; it was only a feeling I had, and I'm no expert.'

'I think I know my own daughter well enough to be certain when she's happy.'

'Of course you do. I apologise.'

Abruptly Heather became aware of her unkempt appearance. She also had a terrible headache due to drinking while taking her new pills, and she wished that he'd called at a time when she was looking her best. It would be gratifying to see admiration in those appraising eyes.

Guy stood up. 'I must be off now. I'll call for Barnaby at twelve next week. Did he tell you that Pip, my bird, can say his name?'

'No.'

'Pity. You should try and give him a bit more attention, he needs the security. Perhaps you'd be better off at home on Saturday nights.'

She was furious at the note of contempt in his voice. How dare he criticise her when it was her first outing since Brian had died? What did he know of the pressures to persuade her to make some sort of social life for herself? 'I really don't think that's any of your business,' she said coldly.

'I'm not bothered about you, I'm only concerned for Barnaby.'

'Thank you very much indeed!'

'Your neighbour's reputation concerning men isn't very good, I'm afraid. You might do better to find yourself a different friend.'

'Are you sure you wouldn't like to select my clothes for me!' she snapped, infuriated because she realised that he was probably right. Without deigning to reply he walked out through the front door. She slammed it shut behind him and fumed silently for the rest of the day.

In the evening, once the children were in bed, she settled down in her armchair with a new novel from the library and prepared for an hour's peace and quiet. She was quickly interrupted by a loud knock on the back door. When she opened it Sheila was outside, and she wasn't looking her usual cheerful self.

'Come in,' invited Heather.

'I intend to. What the hell happened to you last night? How do you think Roger felt when you walked out on him like that?'

'How do you think *I* felt when he propositioned me? Did you know what he was like?'

'Like? He's like all normal, red-blooded males. What did you expect, to sit on the sofa holding hands all night?'

'I didn't expect anything like that. If you recall, I

thought it was going to be a women's night out.'

'Like hell you did! You can't be that naive, Heather. Not even a teenager fresh from a convent would behave so stupidly. Besides, even if you weren't that keen on him it wouldn't have hurt to have a good time, would it? Surely to God you want a man again? Or are you planning a life of permanent chastity? If so, count me out.'

Heather was aghast at the ferocity of Sheila's attack. 'I'm afraid that side of things isn't very important to me,' she said awkwardly. 'Brian understood that; he knew there was more to life than sex.'

'At fifty there probably had to be! What about when he was young? And you're young, Heather. You must have gone out with some lads your own age before you entered your gilded cage.'

'As a matter of fact – although it really isn't any of your business – I didn't. I hadn't dated anyone until I met Brian. He was my only boyfriend.'

'Boyfriend! More like a gentleman caller by the sound of it! Do you realise what century you're living in?'

'Leave me alone,' shouted Heather. 'I didn't ask you to fix me up with a blind date. I'm quite happy as I am. I realise you meant well but couldn't you just leave me alone? I'm sure I'm a great disappointment to you, and I'm sorry if I spoilt last night, but that sort of thing isn't me.'

'What exactly do you mean by "that sort of thing"?' asked Sheila dangerously.

'One night stands. Instant sex for instant meals. Casual affairs. All those things.'

'In other words I'm promiscuous, trading my body for food.'

'No! I'm just saying that it isn't the way I want to live. I'm not criticising you.'

'Yes, you bloody well are! Well, sod off then. I'm sick of trying to help you. The others told me I was wasting my time. They said you were stuck-up, but I insisted you were shy. I made a bad mistake, didn't I? You are stuck-up. Still living in the past, sipping iced tea from a long glass while your gardener mows the lawn. Fine, you keep right on pretending. You're a shopgirl with two children, both of whom have problems at school if you did but realise it, but you keep on living in the past. Play the grand lady, but don't come running to me when things go wrong. I'm finished with you, Heather Lorrimer, completely finished!'

As the back door slammed shut behind her Heather stood stunned in the middle of the room. Sheila had misunderstood her. She liked Sheila, and she *was* grateful for all she'd done. Life would be even more lonely without the older woman's cheerful conversations and extrovert personality around the place.

It had hurt to hear what the other women thought of her too. She only hoped that Lynne wasn't one of them, but somehow she didn't think she could be otherwise she wouldn't have issued her invitation to visit, an invitation that Heather vowed there and then to follow up.

On Tuesday night there was trouble at work. After the shop had closed a discrepancy of £17 was discovered in the till. Rita and Heather had to wait while Mrs Winter summoned someone from higher up to deal with the matter, since neither girl was able to give any explanation.

The middle-aged man who finally arrived looked thoroughly annoyed at the incident and brusquely re-questioned the girls. After that he asked if they would mind opening their handbags. Rita began to fiddle with hers but Heather, suddenly sick and tired of the entire business, refused. If they wanted to search her bag, she said, then they could call the police. Mrs Winter's tight-lipped fury was evident, and just as it looked as though they were all going to stand around for the entire night Rita gave a gasp of horror.

'I've just remembered! I had to give that lady with the

faulty court shoes a refund, Mrs Winter. Do you remember?'

'Naturally. That does not, however, explain the error since the shoes cost £27 and not £17.'

'Yes, but she paid £10 for some slippers and then you said that you'd sort out the till because we suddenly had several people come into the shop at once and . . .'

'May I go now?' interjected Heather. 'I've already missed two buses.'

Red-faced the manageress nodded, and Heather knew that from now on life in the shop would be even more difficult.

As soon as she got home Heather hurried upstairs to change. At Rowena's bedroom door she paused, certain that she could hear sounds of crying. When she tapped Rowena quickly opened it. Her eyes looked red and she was very pale.

'What's wrong, darling?'

'I'm missing Daddy.' Heather moved forward to comfort her but Rowena turned away and then held out a letter. 'Mrs Charles told me to give you this. It's about school.'

'Thank you. Would you like to talk about Daddy?'

'No. I want to do some colouring.' Abruptly the bedroom door was closed.

Alone in her room Heather opened the cream-coloured envelope. It was a brief request for her to make an appointment with the headmistress as soon as possible concerning a matter of considerable urgency.

As soon as the children left the next morning, Rowena still very pale, she rang the school and the following Wednesday afternoon found her sitting outside Mrs Charles's office.

The headmistress was a smart, middle-aged woman with her grey hair immaculately permed, and Heather was uncomfortably aware that she should have washed her hair the night before and that two buttons were missing from her coat. Something in Mrs Charles's expression told Heather that the matter was indeed serious.

'I'm sorry to have to ask you along, Mrs Lorrimer, but we're extremely worried about Rowena. As you know, she's a bright little girl, but she's refusing to make the most of her abilities. She spends most of her time tormenting the staff or giggling, thereby disrupting the entire class.'

'Does her new friend have anything to do with this?'

'I haven't been told that any other child is involved. Besides, whilst this is annoying it is something that the staff have to deal with, but last Friday something more serious happened. Your daughter was caught stealing money from another girl's satchel.'

Heather's stomach lurched and she could scarcely find her voice. 'Rowena? Stealing?'

'I'm afraid so. There's been a lot of petty pilfering in her class lately, and now we know why. When she was caught she didn't try to lie her way out of it. She told me that there wasn't enough money at home and she wanted it to buy crisps and fruit.'

Heather had never felt so mortified. The thought of Rowena stealing was bad enough, but to plead hunger was so shocking that she couldn't think of any response. She stared at Mrs Charles in stricken silence.

'I understand that there are difficulties at home?' said Mrs Charles, gently.

Heather swallowed hard. 'My husband died last June and all his money was tied up in his own business. Unfortunately the company had a lot of creditors and so we had to sell up and move away. Things have been difficult, and I know it's hard on the children, but there's no question of them going hungry or needing money to buy fruit. I just can't . . .' She stopped, unable to continue.

'You mustn't distress yourself too much, Mrs Lorrimer. This is obviously a cry for help, and we must all try and give Rowena the support she needs. She tells me that you're out a lot. Presumably because of your work?'

'Well it certainly isn't because I'm socialising!' Heather hid her distress behind as sharp a tone as she could muster.

'I wasn't for one moment suggesting . . .'

'I can't believe it,' said Heather again. 'I just can't believe that Rowena . . .' and then her control broke and she began to cry. Once she had started she was unable to stop as she realised how little she understood either of the children, and how much they were changing.

'I'm sorry,' she apologised, taking a handkerchief out of her handbag. 'It's only that if Brian were here he wouldn't believe it either. She was the apple of his eye and . . .'

'Believe me, Mrs Lorrimer, this isn't the first time children with emotional problems have done this sort of thing. What is important is that we are all aware of the problem and do our best to solve it. I think that in view of all the recent upheavals some family counselling is the best answer.'

'Does that mean Rowena needs a psychiatrist?'

'Not at all. You go along as a family. These people are experts at dealing with problems such as this, and you'll be amazed at the benefit you'll all obtain from a series of consultations. Of course if you refuse to go then . . .' she tailed off.

Heather knew that if she refused then Rowena would be left to carry on until the stealing turned to shoplifting and she would get the blame for turning down the opportunity of help at an early stage. She had no choice. 'Very well,' she conceded reluctantly.

'Excellent. I see from Rowena's form that you all go to Dr Rawle who is a very good GP and will give you any support you need. From now on, leave it to me. I can set the wheels in motion, and sometime in the New Year you should get an appointment card. Thank you for coming and . . .'

'May I just mention one thing?' interjected Heather quickly. 'It's about Barnaby's bruises. He seems to be suffering rather a lot from playground bullying, and I wondered if there was anything you could do about that?'

Mrs Charles's face lost its benevolent expression. 'There's no bullying in *our* school, Mrs Lorrimer, I can assure you. Rough and tumble perhaps, after all boys will be boys, but never bullying. Now, if you'll excuse me?'

Plainly dismissed, Heather shook hands and walked slowly out of the school still stunned by what had happened. She remembered Rowena coming home from school in Berkshire, her face glowing with pleasure over the day's events. Now she was a quiet, sullen little girl who was not only difficult in class but also a thief.

The worst part was that there was no one in whom Heather could confide. It was so shameful that she knew she had to keep the secret to herself, and the burden felt almost like a physical lump lodged in her throat. For the first time she understood why Barnaby kept clearing his when he was under stress. With a sigh she wondered if the old Rowena would ever return, or if she was gone for good.

She turned the problem over and over in her mind and finally came to a decision. She was off work the following Saturday, and with Barnaby going to the football match with Guy it gave her an opportunity to be alone with her daughter for a reasonable length of time.

Rowena was delighted at the prospect of an outing with her mother. By making every possible economy Heather had been saving up her benefit for three weeks in case of emergencies. Feeling that this could be counted as an emergency she took the money with her, and together they chose a pleated tartan skirt and white polo-necked jersey for Rowena.

Already thrilled by her new clothes Rowena was even

more excited when Heather suggested tea in the store's restaurant. As they ate she looked across the table at her daughter, smiling at last, and saw with a terrible wrench the likeness between father and daughter. She wished with all her heart that she could ignore the school interview, but it simply wasn't possible and so she steeled herself for the confrontation.

'Rowena?'

'Yes?'

'I had to see Mrs Charles on Wednesday. Can you guess why?'

Rowena turned red. 'I suppose it was about the money.'

'Yes. Why didn't you tell me?'

'You've got enough to worry about. Besides, I was scared. You get so cross since Daddy died.'

Heather had never felt so guilty in all her life. 'I know, Rowena, and I'm sorry. You see, I'm frightened of all the new things I'm having to do and it makes me nervous and snappy.'

Rowena's eyes widened. 'Are you really frightened?'

'Yes, very. I try to hide it because of you and Barnaby, but inside I'm extremely frightened.'

Rowena traced a pattern on the table cloth with her cake fork. 'I'm not exactly frightened; I'm lonely. I've only got Janice for a friend and the work's boring. I've tried being good and being naughty, but it doesn't make any difference. No one else likes me. Why don't they, Mummy?'

'I think that perhaps it's because you haven't learnt to compromise. Do you understand what I mean?'

'Doing things I don't like.'

'Yes, in a way. You have to give people time to get used to you. You can't expect to go into a new school and immediately have a group of friends round you like before. Just be yourself, that's important, and when the other girls tease or ignore you, try not to let them see that it hurts. They'll soon tire of it. At least you've got Janice.

Why *did* you take the money?'

'To buy sweets. I was going to give them to the girls so that they'd like me.'

'It doesn't work like that. They would have eaten your sweets and then ignored you again.'

Rowena's mouth trembled. 'I miss Daddy terribly,' she whispered as tears rolled down her cheeks.

Heather knew that this was the moment when she should let Rowena bring her grief out into the open, give her a chance to release all her pent-up grief but she simply couldn't. They were in a public place, and Heather knew that if she allowed her daughter to break down then she would as well, thus making a spectacle of them both. She swallowed hard. 'So do I, darling. We'll always miss him, but in time it won't hurt so much. In a way people never die completely because they live on in their family's memory.'

'When Barnaby and I die there won't be anyone left to remember him. He'll be really dead after that.' Her logic was irrefutable and Heather simply kept her eyes fixed on the tablecloth. 'What else did Mrs Charles say?' Rowena asked, realising that her mother wasn't going to say any more.

'She's arranging for us all to attend a special clinic where we can talk about things.'

'What sort of things?'

'Our feelings; the way we miss Daddy; what we think of each other.'

'I'm not telling anyone my private thoughts. They can't make me. I shall invent something.'

'We have to do this properly,' persisted Heather. 'We all need help.'

'Barnaby doesn't. He's got Mr Harrison. I don't think he misses Daddy at all any more.'

'Of course he does. It's only that Mr Harrison helps him. Now come along, we've got a bus to catch.'

Despite a long, cold wait Rowena was extremely

cheerful on the way home and when she went to bed that night Heather realised it had been their happiest Saturday since Brian's death. Perhaps, at last, things were looking up for them.

Sunday morning quickly disillusioned her. It was wet and cold and the children squabbled non-stop. When Barnaby yelled at his sister to 'sod off you stupid cow' Heather gave him a smack on the legs, bundled them both into coats and boots and marched off to Lynne's house.

It was plain that Lynne was delighted to see them. 'Come in! I loathe Sundays, they're twice as long as any other day of the week, at least it seems that way. Look, Daisy, we've got company.' Daisy gurgled happily in her baby-bouncer as Lynne found the two children pencils, crayons, paper, and fizzy drinks. She then pushed a bottle of juice into Daisy's mouth and settled Heather down on a huge red bean bag.

'Right, that should keep them quiet. I'll make some coffee, and while it's percolating you can tell me about your job.'

'It's ghastly,' said Heather, speaking quietly so that the children couldn't hear her. 'The manageress is the pits, and she loathes me. Then there are the customers. They can be incredibly rude, and some of them delight in making my life hell, you can see them getting a kick out of their petty power.'

Lynne gave a peal of laughter. 'It sounds absolutely frightful. I couldn't put up with it; I'd have to answer back or explode.'

'I'd like to, but I daren't. I've got this huge mortgage hanging over my head.'

'Can't you find something better?' Lynne queried, bringing over two large mugs of delicious coffee.

'Not really, I haven't any qualifications. I was an art student before I married, but what use is that? I can't even type.'

'Learn it at evening classes, that will open up loads of

doors for you.'

'Quite honestly, Lynne, I don't have enough money. Evening classes aren't cheap.' She saw Lynne glance at her pure wool pinafore dress. 'I know my clothes are expensive, but they're left over from my marriage. Brian was well off, we had a high standard of living and I always bought good clothes without thinking twice about the cost, but once these are worn out their replacements will be cheap and cheerful.'

'Well, if things are really that bad . . .'

'Believe me, they are.'

'Then I do have a friend who gives private typing lessons at home, but she doesn't declare the money so you'd have to pay cash each week. You'll probably do better on a one-to-one basis as you're not a very social animal, are you?'

'I'm afraid not. Could you really arrange it? I'd be so grateful. At least I won't have to envisage growing old and grey in that horrible shop.'

'I'll do even better. I'll ring her now before you change your mind.' Lynne rose gracefully to her feet and disappeared into the kitchen. She came back beaming. 'There you are, it's all arranged! An hour a week at £1.50 per session as you're a friend of mine and you can start Tuesday evening.'

'But . . .'

'Look, she lives on the estate so there's no hassle over transport and I'll bring Daisy down and babysit for you. Now, any more excuses?'

'No,' laughed Heather. 'You were quite right to force my hand. I would have backed out.'

Just then Daisy dropped her bottle and gave a squeal of annoyance. 'Clumsy,' said her mother affectionately, giving it straight back without even a cursory check for dust.

'Does Daisy ever see her father?' Heather said tentatively.

'Good God no! I knew she never would, especially after I named her Daisy.'

'What do you mean?'

'Well, you see I was a production assistant with a private television company. I met this sophisticated man of the world who swept me off my feet. He was fantastic in bed, you know the sort. We had a great time. Weekends away, stolen evenings in swish surroundings, all the glamour and none of the grot. However, when I found myself pregnant it all changed. Suddenly he had this invalid wife tucked away in the country, totally dependent upon him. I didn't believe a word of it, he'd never mentioned her before, but I got the message. No baby for Mr X. I decided to go ahead and have her anyway, and here we are.'

'But what's that got to do with her name?'

'Oh yes, her name! It so happens that daddy is a well-known gardening personality on the radio; gives weekly lectures on how to keep your lawn looking like a billiard table. I thought Daisy would drive him wild, and it did too!' Heather laughed aloud.

'Don't you worry about her growing up without a father?'

'I might marry some day and then she'll get one. If I don't, I'm quite sure I can raise Daisy on my own without causing her any permanent psychological damage. We're certainly much happier than we would have been with an unwilling Mr X legally bound to us.'

Heather was thoughtful. 'My two are lost without Brian.'

'That's different. What you've never had you can't miss. Besides, I thought Mr Guy Harrison was playing dad to Barnaby.'

'He spends a lot of time with him, and he is a great help, but I don't think he behaves like a father. He just provides much needed masculine company.'

'Lucky Barnaby! I wonder if Mr Harrison would do the

same for me!'

'Do you like him?'

'Well, he is rather dishy with that dark hair and deep blue eyes; he makes me go all soft inside! Don't you fancy him?'

'I never think of him that way! In any case, he wouldn't be interested in me. I look a mess these days. I've put on pounds because I lunch off Mars bars and crisps, and I'm pale but not interesting! My hair's like rats tails, and the women I see going up his path are all slim, immaculate and fresh from the hairdresser.'

Lynne pounced. 'You do fancy him, otherwise you wouldn't have noticed what they looked like!'

'I don't!' insisted a blushing Heather, but she knew there was a spark of truth in Lynne's words.

'Oh yes you do! God, Daisy's crying, look at the time!'

Heather jumped up. 'We'll be going. I'd no idea it was so late. I've really enjoyed chatting to you, you've made me feel human again!'

'It's mutual. Heather, I hope you won't mind me saying this, but couldn't you try and patch things up with Sheila? I don't know what went wrong, but I do know that she's very upset about it all. She wants to get back on friendly terms but doesn't know how.'

'I thought she never wanted to see me again.'

'Sheila's always flying off the handle, but she doesn't mean half the things she says. You pop round there some time and see for yourself.'

'All right, I will; and thanks for everything. Come on you two, time to go home.'

'Oh no!' they chorused, which at least meant they wouldn't mind going again thought Heather, as they walked slowly back through the estate.

After tea, while the children were watching television, Heather tapped on Sheila's back door. She felt a moment of trepidation as it was opened, but this was immediately dispelled by the warmth of her welcome.

'Heather! How lovely! Come in, I've just put the kettle on.'

'I've come to apologise, Sheila,' she said awkwardly, 'I realise now that I over-reacted about Roger. You were trying to help and I made a fool of myself, letting you down at the same time. I'm truly sorry for that.'

'I'm the one who's to blame. I'm always so sure I know what's best for people, and I'm frequently wrong. I honestly didn't realise quite what a sheltered life you'd led or I wouldn't have done it.'

'I hope we can forget it and be friends again,' Heather continued. 'I miss having you popping in and out.'

'Really? In that case be prepared for plenty of popping. Scott's in with a ghastly crowd these days. I'm worried sick about him but at his age what can you do?'

They chatted on, with Heather bringing Sheila up to date on everything, even the typing lessons. 'That's a good idea,' she enthused. 'Trust Lynne to be sensible about things. Did you know she was doing the Open University course of Sociology ready for when Daisy goes to nursery school?'

'No. That makes my typing sound rather pathetic!'

'Nonsense, horses for courses as they say. Besides, from what I can see out of my kitchen window, you've got a potential knight in white armour lined up.'

'What do you mean?'

'Guy Harrison of course. He's a regular caller, and I rather envy you. He might be chauvinistic but he's disgustingly good-looking which tends to compensate!'

'He only comes to collect Barnaby,' said Heather firmly, but she could tell by Sheila's expression that she didn't believe her. It didn't matter; what counted was that they were back on good terms again.

Back home, as she automatically went through the now familiar Sunday night routine of baths and hair washes, she realised that she now had two friends upon whom she could really rely. It didn't change the unpleasantness at work, or the dark cloud of their first Christmas without Brian, but it was something.

At last, she thought, I'm beginning to appreciate the value of good women friends who will listen and help with problems so that, once aired, they no longer seem insurmountable.

Chapter Seven

The typing lessons, coming as they did on top of a day's work in the shop, were exhausting but at least it was a different kind of work. Despite the broken nails and ruined pages Heather drew great satisfaction from the fact that she was on the way towards improving her position.

Due to her exhaustion it was fairly easy to forget that Christmas was creeping inexorably nearer, but when Christmas cards started falling through their letter box she realised that it couldn't be completely ignored. Reluctantly she bought a small box of cheap cards and made out a short list of friends. Despite the cards already received from old acquaintances in Berkshire she decided not to send any in return. She didn't want to think about her old life any more; that part of her life was now far removed from her present existence.

Now and again she did feel guilty about Amanda and Clive. At first they had telephoned her regularly, but when she never phoned back they changed tactics and took to writing letters. Once or twice she had started to put pen to paper, but had abandoned the attempt when she realised how little she and Amanda now had in common. How could she describe the work in the shoe shop? The grinding misery of counting every penny and dreading the sight of bills on the door mat? Then there was the house, and the constant knowledge that all the rooms needed a fresh coat of paint and thorough cleaning.

The prospect of trying to explain this to Amanda was

daunting enough, but in addition Heather found that when she did commence writing she felt bitterly resentful of Amanda's continuing life of ease. She imagined her passing the letter round at a coffee morning, laughing lightly at the thought of Heather – delicate, protected Heather – having to help people choose shoes before going home to a neglected terraced house where even sweet biscuits were a luxury.

The Christmas card from Amanda and Clive was large and beautifully embossed. On the bottom Amanda had written 'Is anything wrong? Please write or phone soon.' Heather put it in the centre of the mantelpiece and ignored the note, hoping they would take the hint and quietly drop out of her life.

In the final two week run-up Heather spent every lunch-hour shopping, then smuggled chocolate bars and crisps back into the shop and munched on them during the afternoons, regardless of her ever-increasing waistline. Finally, work was over and the holiday season had begun.

Christmas Eve fell on a Sunday and so she didn't have to work again until the following Thursday, when the January sales began. Once home she flopped down in the living-room and relished the prospect of a few days off.

On the Sunday morning as she wrapped the children's presents in her room she found herself crying over the small boxed games and annuals. In the past these had been stocking fillers, and she dreaded the next morning and their disappointed faces when the much-longed-for computer and bicycle didn't materialise.

'Mummy!' called Rowena, who was watching television with Barnaby in the lounge, 'there's someone at the door.'

'Who is it?'

'I can't quite see . . . yes I can. Mummy! It's Aunty Amanda and Uncle Clive!'

Heather groaned in horror, and wondered how they

could have been so thoughtless. She wasn't in the least prepared for visitors.

'They've got Rusty with them!' screamed Barnaby. 'Is he coming to stay? Is he? Is he?'

'No, of course not. Let them in, I won't be a minute.' Her heart went out to her son. He had just started to adjust to the loss of his pet, this would set him back months. Without even pulling a brush through her hair she went down to make them as welcome as she could.

'Darling!' exclaimed Amanda, resplendent in a new fur coat. 'Why on earth didn't you send us a Christmas card? We've been out of our minds with worry.'

'Sorry, but things are rather hectic these days and I didn't feel very festive this year.'

Amanda stepped back and studied her friend. She was now a rather overweight woman wearing a skirt that strained round the hips and a jersey that was far too tight. Quickly she looked away, wondering why Heather couldn't at least keep her hair tidy.

'Look who we've brought to see you, young man,' said Clive heartily, aware of the slightly hostile atmosphere. Rusty leapt onto Barnaby's lap and began licking his face and whimpering with pleasure. Barnaby sat absolutely still, his arms tightly round his beloved pet.

'You shouldn't have brought the dog,' whispered Heather as they sat down. 'He's only just learning to live without him.'

'I am going to keep him, Mummy, aren't I?' called a radiant Barnaby.

'No, darling, you can't. You know why, so don't start making a scene. Just enjoy him while he's here.'

Amanda followed her out into the overcrowded kitchen where dirty plates were piled haphazardly on all the working surfaces and the floor needed a good clean. Remembering the gleaming kitchen at 'The Lawns' Amanda wondered how Heather could live in such chaos.

'Actually,' she confided as Heather plugged the kettle in, 'we did wonder if you *could* keep Rusty. He's such a tie when we want to go out, and he's not always clean in the house.'

'He used to be. Besides it's quite out of the question. He'd be alone for nearly ten hours a day.'

'Then I'm afraid we may have to get rid of him.'

'You must do whatever's necessary, but for God's sake don't tell Barnaby.'

'I'm not stupid, Heather!'

Yes you are, thought Heather, stupid *and* tactless. 'Tea's made,' she said aloud, 'I'll take it into the lounge.'

It was obvious that they had come for lunch, and Amanda handed over a carrier bag with tinned meat, rolls and butter. 'We thought you might not have enough since you didn't invite us!'

'No,' responded Heather flatly, 'I didn't.'

'Haven't the children grown? They're rather pale though. Have they been ill?'

'They've had heavy head colds, but I can't keep them home with every sniffle, my employer isn't very sympathetic towards working mothers.'

Amanda glanced round the sparsely furnished room. 'Well, it's all very . . . cosy,' she said brightly. 'How do you children like it here?'

'It's horrible!' said Rowena fiercely. 'School stinks, Mummy's never at home and most of the girls in my class are nasty little shits.'

'Rowena!' Heather was horrified.

'Don't worry,' said Amanda, 'I expect she's showing off for our benefit. It's surprising the things they come out with. Ashley told us the other day that we were middle-class puritans, and all because we wouldn't let his girlfriend stay over for the night in his bed. I said to him, what you do . . .'

'Scarcely on a par with nasty little shits,' said Heather acidly.

Amanda's voice tailed off. 'I suppose not, I was only trying . . .'

'Well, don't bother. I know they're using bad language; I know they don't look well, and I do realise that the house is cramped rather than cosy and it's filthy dirty into the bargain. Is that sofa uncomfortable for you?'

'No, not at all. I'm always fidgety after a long drive. Well, at least Barnaby's pleased to see us.'

'He's pleased to see Rusty,' put in Rowena. Heather glanced at the clock and wondered how long she was going to have to endure their unwanted company.

The rest of the morning and lunch passed without any further awkwardness, mainly due to Clive's efforts and Amanda's gradual withdrawal from the conversation.

When the dishes were stacked by the sink she gave another of her laughs – Heather wondered why she had never noticed its grating falseness before – and looked about her. 'What fun! I haven't washed up by hand for years. Do let me have a go. Have you any rubber gloves? I don't want to ruin my nails!'

'I'm afraid not,' said Heather, biting back a sharp retort. 'Why don't you dry? My hands are ruined already.'

'Very well, but it's a shame to neglect yourself so badly. Are you growing your hair?'

'Yes, it's cheaper than going to the hairdresser.'

'I'm sure things can't be that bad!' Amanda reproved her. 'I always think that when one looks good one feels good as well. It changes my entire outlook on life once I've had my face and hair done.'

'Amanda, things *are* that bad. I am acutely aware that I'm not looking quite as glamorous as before; but since I never see anyone except the children and women customers, who wouldn't really like a fashion plate measuring their feet and running up and down ladders for them, there doesn't seem to be much point.'

'Well, all I can say is that it was wicked of Brian. When you remember that he squandered your own private money as well as his own it's enough to make your blood boil. All because he didn't plan for the future, you're stuck on a nasty estate in a horrid little house with . . .'

'I don't want to hear any more,' said Heather, turning away and drying her hands. 'This "horrid little house" happens to be our home and we're quite fond of it, which is fortunate as we aren't likely to get anything better. I appreciate that you were worried about me, but I don't want to keep in touch any more, and I'm sure that having seen us all you understand why. Perhaps it would be better if you left. There really isn't much for us to talk about these days, is there?'

Amanda raised her eyebrows. 'If that's how you feel, then of course we'll go. Keep the food we brought; I'd hate to think of you starving over the holiday. Clive! We're leaving.'

'Already?' queried Clive as they walked into the lounge.

'Yes.'

He looked from his wife's tight expression to Heather's flushed face and quickly searched for his coat. 'Fine, if that's what you both want. Come on Rusty, old chap, time to say cheerio.'

Barnaby clasped his arms firmly round the dog. 'He's not coming. He's staying here with us.'

'Fine, that's what we . . .'

'He *is* going back,' said Heather firmly. 'Put him down please, darling.'

Barnaby gave her a horrified glance. 'I can't. He likes it here. Look, he doesn't want to go.' Rusty, unsettled by the noise and Barnaby's tight embrace, was trying to hide beneath the boy's shoulder. Heather went over and picked him up.

'No!' shrieked Barnaby. 'Give him back. He's mine, he loves me and I love him. Don't let them take him away, Mummy. Please, please let him stay.'

Clive took hold of the lead and Rusty howled, trying to drag back towards Barnaby. Barnaby's sobs increased and he flung himself forward to embrace the animal again. Heather picked him up, ignoring his flying fists. Rusty continued to howl and Rowena started to cry in sympathy.

Amanda, her face expressionless, put on her coat. 'Happy Christmas,' said Clive lamely. Heather didn't answer him.

'I want my dog!' screamed Barnaby, nearly hysterical in his grief. 'Give me back my dog. I want him! I want Rusty!' Clive tugged hard on the lead, desperate to get away from the appalling scene. Rusty dug his heels in and had to be dragged howling every inch of the way to the car.

'I hope you're satisfied!' shouted Heather above the noise, but neither Amanda nor Clive turned their heads. Within seconds they were off; Rusty in the back, his face pressed to the rear window.

Gently Heather put her distraught son down. 'Barnaby, I'm so, so sorry. Believe me . . .'

'I hate you! I really hate you. You're cruel and wicked. I don't love you any more. Not at all. Not one tiny bit.'

'Darling, it wasn't my fault.'

'They would have let me keep him, they said so.'

'But there isn't . . .'

His sobbing drowned out her words. 'I'm going next door,' he cried. 'I'm going to see my friend Guy. He'll help me even if you won't. Oh, Rusty! Rusty!' Still sobbing he ran blindly out of the house while Heather watched him, helpless in the face of such grief.

'Did they bring us any presents?' queried Rowena.

'Don't be so mercenary. Haven't you any feelings?'

'Sure, but they won't help Barnaby. They're a couple of real dummies doing a daft thing like that. They've probably ruined his Christmas. I wonder if a dog can die of a broken heart?'

'Stop it!' shouted Heather. 'Sometimes I don't understand you at all.'

'No,' mumbled Rowena to herself, 'you don't.'

Barnaby sat on the lounge floor of Guy Harrison's house, tears streaming down his face while Guy kept busy decorating the miniature tree and silently cursing the tactless adults. They must have been out of their minds he thought; and Heather was as bad, allowing them to bring the boy's beloved dog of all things.

The child was trying desperately to recover himself. 'He knew me, Guy. He sat on my lap all the time, and he didn't want to go. They had to drag him on his lead. I wish they'd never come. I want Rusty to live with me again.' He dropped his head to conceal his tears.

Guy sat down next to him and put a comforting arm round his shaking shoulders. 'I can't think of any words to help you, Barnaby. I know it must have been awful, and all I can say is that I hope they're never so stupid again.'

'Mummy was cross with them.'

'Good for mummy. Shall we clean Pip out?'

Barnaby nodded. After working in silence for a few minutes he cleared his throat. 'What happens to people if they're caught stealing, Guy?'

'They get taken to court and a judge decides their punishment.'

'Do they go to prison?'

'Sometimes. Why?' He had a horrible vision of Heather slipping something for the children's stockings into her coat pocket.

Barnaby went red. 'You won't tell? I mean, you are a policeman.'

'I won't tell.'

'It's Rowena. She was stealing at school, but they told Mummy and we've all got to go to some council so she's stopped that. Now she takes things from shops. Last Saturday, while we were shopping with Mummy, she put some rubbers and pencils in her pocket. I saw her, but she said I mustn't tell or she'd kill Marmaduke.'

Guy felt a surge of relief that it wasn't Heather, but this was quickly followed by compassion for Rowena who seemed to be floundering unassisted through all her emotional and physical upheavals. He wished that Heather were a little more aware of her children's feelings. 'Try not to worry, Barnaby. I'll think about what you've told me and see if I can come up with any help. All right?'

'You won't tell her that you know?'

'I won't tell her that you told me. Trust me, Barnaby; I'm your friend, remember?' Relieved Barnaby nodded.

Much to Heather's relief on Christmas morning, both the children were delighted with their presents, and she wondered exactly who she and Brian had been thinking of when they spent so much money every year; perhaps, she thought wryly, they themselves got the most pleasure and the children would have been equally content with less.

She had been deeply touched when both Sheila and Lynne had given her small gifts for the stockings, and late the previous evening had come the greatest surprise of all.

Guy Harrison had called round and handed over two small, square parcels, neatly wrapped with a small piece of holly sellotaped to each one. 'Just a small token of friendship,' he'd said with a smile. 'I'm sorry there isn't anything for you, but Barnaby told me that Father Christmas doesn't call once you're grown-up and I didn't like to disillusion him.'

Heather had thanked him profusely and invited him in for a drink. He refused, explaining that he was on his way to a party, but he then astounded her by inviting them all round on Boxing Day morning, an invitation which she accepted with alacrity

Now, as the unwrapping ceremony continued, she saw Barnaby pick up the parcel with the holly on it. Once it was opened he gave a scream of delight. 'Look, Mummy! It's a china Rusty.' And it was: a beautiful red-coated spaniel with an appealing look in its eyes. 'Good old Father Christmas, he must have known about Rusty.' Cradling the figure tenderly in his hands he ran off to his room and placed it carefully on his shelf of treasures.

Rowena had now come to her parcel from Guy, and Heather was intrigued, wondering what he had thought of that would be suitable for a small girl he scarcely knew. Rowena opened the box and carefully put her fingers into the shredded paper protecting the ornament. As she drew it out she gave a gasp of pleasure. It was a beautiful, long-haired ballerina, arms outstretched, her pink tutu swirling around her. 'How did he know?' whispered Rowena. 'How did Father Christmas know that I want to be a dancer?'

'How indeed?' thought Heather. Even she hadn't known that her daughter was in the least interested in dancing, and with a pang of conscience she wondered what else Rowena kept hidden from her.

The day was bright and cold, and shortly after Christmas lunch a few snowflakes began to fall. This made the children's day as perfect as possible, and they played with their toys, watched television, ate too much, and finally at eight o'clock went happily to bed.

It was only when Heather bent to kiss Rowena goodnight that Brian's name was mentioned. 'Do you think Daddy could see us today? Do you, Mummy?'

'I believe so, darling.'

'Bridget at school said that heaven didn't exist. She said that once a person died that was the end. I don't believe her. The Bible says that you go to God after you die.'

'That's right, and I'm sure it's true. I'm also sure that Daddy would have been pleased to see you both enjoying yourselves today.'

'Mmmm. I kept thinking about him a lot. Did you?'

'Of course I did.'

'Mummy?'

Heather could sense that once again Rowena wanted to talk about Brian, but she wasn't yet ready to listen. 'What?' she asked, her voice making it plain that a prolonged heart-to-heart wasn't wanted.

Rowena's eyes grew shadowed. 'Nothing. I like my ballerina, she's my favourite present.'

'Good! Now sleep well. Tomorrow morning we're going next door: imagine that, two women in the all-male domain!'

Her daughter yawned. 'I'm not very keen on going. He's a policeman, he might know about you-know-what.'

'Of course he won't! It will be a nice change for us all. Goodnight, darling.'

Once she was alone, with the children silent in their bedrooms, it was impossible for Heather to stop her pent-up grief from overwhelming her. Brian had been marvellous at Christmas time, always full of ideas for games so that the television was rarely used. Often they would go for a walk after their lunch, Heather and Brian hand-in-hand as the children ran ahead.

She could picture the scenes, remember the sound of his voice, but to her distress suddenly – six months after his death – she could only visualise him as he was at the end. A shrunken, pain-racked man with fear lurking in his eyes. No other picture of him came to mind. She fetched some photos and studied them, but even then her brain refused to retain the image.

She thought of Roger's matter-of-fact statement that she would marry again. It was ridiculous. There would never be another Brian to offer her the tenderness, security and caring she yearned for.

In other words, she scolded herself, you want to opt out again. You don't want to live a life of your own, you want to be put on a pedestal and worshipped. It was both unrealistic and feeble, and whilst the realisation hurt it was, she thought, at least a sign that she was progressing. Recognising her problem was the first step to curing it.

She resolved that in the New Year she would quite definitely make a more determined effort to discover a way of life that was both within her capabilities and also fulfilling. At twenty-nine she was finally realising that she must learn to stand on her own feet. It was quite a satisfying feeling, but with dismay she realised that, had Brian lived, she would never have recognised the shallowness of her previous privileged existence. She would have continued in her gilded cage, happy, certainly, but never knowing her own potential.

Now that she was a single parent, the head of her own household, it was time she began to act like it. There would be no more looking back, and no more unwanted blind dates. She would be more positive, going out to meet the world instead of waiting for other people to bring it to her. Next year it would all be different.

The following morning certainly wasn't any different. The children squabbled over the breakfast table; Rowena wanted to wear her party frock to Guy's, and Barnaby wanted Heather to construct an intricate metal monster that had been in his stocking.

'Rowena, you can't wear your frock, it's far too thin. Wear your new jumper and skirt. Barnaby, take the robot next door with you and see if Guy can help, but before that eat your breakfast. For heaven's sake, don't start playing up the minute you're awake.'

'I don't want any toast,' said Rowena sulkily, and went upstairs to change.

Barnaby pushed his cereal round in a bath of milk. 'My shreddies have gone all soggy!'

'I'm not surprised; you put about half a pint of milk on them.'

'Didn't!'

'Barnaby!'

'Sorry. Do I have to eat it all?'

'As far as I'm concerned, you can starve. Go and put on your brown trousers and tan jersey, please.'

'The jersey tickles me.'

'Then put a short sleeved shirt under it, but *go and change*.'

They were ready by eleven and Heather gave the

children one final check over. Her eyes came to rest on a lovely butterfly slide in Rowena's hair. 'Where did you get that, Rowena?'

'Janice gave it to me.'

'Why?'

'She's had her hair cut and doesn't need it any more.'

Heather's instinct told her that Rowena was lying, but she had neither the time nor the inclination to press the matter further. She shrugged. 'Oh, come on! I've had quite enough trouble this morning already.'

'If you tell,' whispered Rowena to Barnaby as they went down the path, 'I shall break your china dog.'

His eyes filled with tears. 'I won't tell, I promise.'

'You'd better not!' The front door opened. 'Hello, Mr Harrison,' gushed Rowena. 'Happy Christmas!'

His eyes travelled over the group until they came to rest on Heather. Unaccountably she felt herself blushing, and quickly pushed the children indoors.

Guy looked at her pallid face, her overweight figure that even the expensive cashmere sweater and pleated wool skirt couldn't conceal, and mentally compared her with the slender, delicately beautiful girl she had been on her arrival. Slowly he gave her one of his infrequent smiles, the sort that was usually reserved for Barnaby. It made her feel a peculiar stirring of excitement, a sudden sharp awareness of Guy as a man as well as a neighbour. She stared at him, and for a fleeting moment they were both loath to look away.

Guy broke the spell first. 'How about a little something to keep out the cold?' he queried.

'Like a fur coat?' responded Rowena pertly.

'That's right. How clever of you to guess! I've bought your mother a fur coat for Christmas.'

'You haven't?' Her eyes widened in astonishment and she looked at her mother enviously.

'No, I haven't! That's a pretty slide. Where did you get it?'

She looked at him defiantly. 'Janice gave it to me. She's my best friend at school.'

He smiled. 'I see. Is that Janice Piper?'

'I don't know.'

'If it is, I know her family quite well. I must tell them how generous their daughter is. Heather, don't stand in the kitchen all morning, come through into the other room.'

Rowena was flushed and Barnaby avoided her eyes. 'It might not have been Janice,' she said nonchalantly.

Guy poured the children some lemon and lime. 'Really? How many friends do you have? It must be a lot if you can't remember who gave you such a lovely Christmas present.'

'Perhaps it was Liz. You won't know Liz.'

'Why's that?'

She gave a dismissive shrug. 'Just because.'

Heather was beginning to relax as she looked around her, and was scarcely listening to the conversation until she recognised the note of defiance entering Rowena's voice. 'What are you talking about, Rowena?'

'We were discussing her school friends. Incidentally, I saw you all in Woolworths last Saturday.'

'We didn't see you. It was so crowded I was grateful to get out alive! I lost the children for a time. I think they were attracted by all the sweets and toys on display!'

'Perhaps. You weren't at the sweet counter when I saw you, Rowena. You were at the bottom end of the shop.' Rowena was now suspiciously close to tears and Guy let the subject drop, hoping that he had frightened her enough to stop it happening again.

He handed the children their drinks. 'Right; now, here's a packet of crisps each, you can take your nourishment up to the back bedroom. I've set up a game there which I hope you'll enjoy. It should be better than our conversation; when I was young I hated grown-up conversations.'

'What sort of game?' asked Barnaby eagerly.

'Football. You turn the rods to make the men kick. I expect you've seen it in amusement arcades.'

'I've seen it in shops, but we've never been to an amusement arcade. My Daddy didn't like them.'

'Who does it belong to?' asked Rowena.

'Me.' There was something final about his voice that prevented further questions and they went carefully out of the room.

Heather sighed with relief. 'Peace! What bliss! I don't like the long, quiet evenings, but I rather enjoy a civilised silence in the day, even if it's only for a short time.'

He handed her a brandy and soda. 'How did yesterday go?'

'It was bearable. I got rather bogged down in morbid thoughts for some of the evening, but I think I managed to pull myself out of them pretty well. I tried to look at life more positively.'

'You're a believer in the power of positive thinking, are you?'

She laughed. 'I've got to be. What's the use of looking back and thinking "if only". It doesn't achieve anything.'

'Had any more nights on the town?'

'Certainly not, my one outing was quite enough! I found myself sadly out of touch with the new sexual code. I shan't repeat the experiment.'

'It must be difficult for a woman on her own. I can go out to the pub for a drink, sit by myself and no one will give me a second glance. You can't do that!'

'Probably that's lucky, since I can't afford to! Seriously, I'm turning over a new leaf next year. I'm already going to typing lessons and doing quite well. Once I'm proficient enough I shall look for another job.'

'I admire the way you've stuck to your present one.'

'Thank you, but it's only through necessity.'

'So the coming year will be one for self-improvement?'

'It may sound funny to you, but I really do have to make

the effort. I've got to learn to live a life of my own, find my own talents and develop them. I'm nearly thirty, Guy. If I don't manage it now I never will.'

He looked at her eager but heartstoppingly vulnerable features and felt a tremendous anger at her parents and her husband. Her deficiencies in housewifery weren't her fault, and he liked the fact that she didn't flutter, flirt and feign unintelligence as his wife had done. That was the sort of femininity he despised. Heather's femininity was inherent and required no artificial trimmings. He hoped that in learning to become her own woman she didn't change this deeply feminine core of her personality.

'What is it?'

He realised that he'd been staring at her while his mind raced. 'Nothing,' he said quickly. 'I wondered why you thought I found your plans funny. I don't. I greatly admire the way you're coping.'

'I'm not very good with the children.'

He smiled gently but didn't contradict her. 'Why is that, do you suppose? Were they closer to their father?'

'I think so. Nannies and au-pairs filled the maternal role.'

'Do you encourage them to talk about him?'

Heather's eyes shifted away from his. 'No,' she said shortly. 'I think I could use another drink.'

He knew when to let well alone, and as they drank they chatted about general things. Guy was amusing in a quiet way, his dry wit catching Heather by surprise at first, but once she was used to him she found him witty and very sharp in his observations of people and patterns of behaviour.

'I suppose it's your job that makes you study everyone so minutely. If you were a woman you'd be called inquisitive!'

'I'm afraid it is a weakness! I do it a lot more now that I'm on my own. A secret vice really.'

'You were married once?'

'Yes. I married at nineteen, my wife – Briony – was eighteen. We were both far too young and quickly drifted apart. She's now happy with a sheep farmer in Australia and I'm firmly wedded to my work.'

'There weren't any children?'

'We had a son. I haven't seen him for over five years. Australia's a long way to travel for weekend access. He was seven when he went; I send him birthday presents and so on but he never acknowledges them. I doubt if he'd know me any more. Briony keeps on at me to let Greg – the Australian sheepfarmer – adopt Tom, but so far I've refused to consider it. Mind you, perhaps she's right and I ought to let him go for his own sake.'

Impulsively Heather leant forward in her chair. 'No! Don't think like that. How would you have felt at twelve years of age if your father had signed you over to another man? You're his father, and you always will be.'

His eyes were an even darker blue than usual as he listened to the first impassioned speech he had ever heard from her. 'That's how I feel,' he said softly, 'it's nice to have it confirmed. Now I shall stick to my principles with renewed heart!'

The brandies and relaxed air of intimacy all combined to make Heather long to confide in Guy about Rowena. Surely he must have come into contact with such cases in his work. She swallowed hard. 'Guy, I'm having trouble with Rowena.' He sat perfectly still, listening intently. 'She's started . . .'

'Mummy! I beat Rowena every time! It's a super game, but she won't play any more. Will you play with me, Guy? Just once.'

Guy stood up. 'Sure. We'll carry on this conversation some other time, Heather. Ah! Here's Rowena, gracious as ever in defeat!'

Rowena scowled at him. 'It's a stupid game. My goalkeeper wouldn't work properly. Barnaby had the best end.'

'I didn't. We took it in turns. It was you, your fingers were all fumbly.'

'Don't quarrel,' said Heather gently. 'Rowena, we'll watch the men play, shall we?'

'Barnaby isn't a man, he's only a silly little boy! I want to go home. I'm bored.'

'I want to stay!' shouted Barnaby. 'You always spoil things. You're a horrid, moaning, cissy girl.'

'And you're a revolting, dirty, smelly boy! You cheated too.'

'Didn't.'

'You did. Cheat!'

'Liar!'

'Cheat!'

'Thief!' yelled Barnaby, stamping his foot in fury. There was a sudden silence. Horrified, Barnaby stood quite still, his hand pressed over his mouth.

Rowena looked round the room. The adults were exchanging a brief glance of complicity, or so she thought, and she snatched the keys from the table beside her. 'I'm going home,' she shouted as she ran off. 'I hate you all!' The back door slammed shut behind her.

Heather rose to her feet but Guy put a hand on her shoulder. 'Let her go. She needs time on her own. Come and watch Barnaby thrash me at football.'

'But . . .'

'Let her regain face. She won't want you there yet. Come on, if you're good we might let you have a turn!'

At one o'clock, all flushed and laughing, the three of them finally finished playing and reluctantly Heather pointed out that they had to go home. She was amazed at how the time had flown.

'I'd invite you to lunch,' said Guy regretfully, 'but I've already invited someone for the afternoon. Perhaps another time?'

Heather's stomach lurched, but for once with pleasure not fear. She liked Guy Harrison; liked his easy manner, his willingness to play games with Barnaby, and above all the sense of safety and security that he gave her. No, she told herself firmly, don't start that again. Remember your resolutions. Besides, he probably only thinks of us as pleasant neighbours, nothing more.

'Perhaps,' she responded casually, and missed the fleeting look of disappointment in his eyes.

'Yes, please!' shouted Barnaby.

Guy ruffled his hair. 'Right, be good and we'll see what we can arrange. Thanks for coming.'

'It's been lovely,' said Heather warmly, and he believed her. For a short space of time she had regained some colour and lost the tension lines round her mouth and the harassed expression that could so often be found in her eyes these days.

'I hope Rowena's recovered,' he added as they walked away. When he closed the door behind them he knew that if he wasn't careful he was going to get too involved with the family next door. Never again, he vowed, remembering the pain of Briony's desertion, but this time the words carried less conviction than usual.

Rowena was sitting watching television when they got in. She didn't bother to look up. 'I'm starving,' she said aggressively. 'What's for lunch?'

'Cold turkey and pickles. Lay the table for me, please.'

'Let Barnaby do it, he's so clever at everything.' Barnaby glanced at his mother and went to the cutlery drawer.

'Turn that thing off please, Rowena,' said Heather sharply. 'I've had quite enough noise from you for one day.'

'I don't care. I shall run away if you don't stop being horrid to me.'

'There's a case under your bed,' Heather responded with some asperity. 'Have you got time to eat before you go?'

'You don't care if I go away or not, do you? You're a

horrible, horrible mother. I really shall go, you know. I might ever fall in a river and drown. What would you think then?'

'That it was a great pity you didn't learn to swim while we had our own pool. Now, please stop the dramatics and come and eat your lunch.' Rowena dragged her feet and scraped the heel of one shoe on the kitchen tiles, leaving a scratch mark.

'Rowena! Behave yourself or I'll give you a smack. It's Christmas time, surely you can try and make an effort?' There was no reply, and feeling that she had handled it all very badly Heather and the children ate a silent lunch.

After the meal Heather and Barnaby settled down to watch 'Mother Goose' on the television while Rowena went upstairs to read her Girl's Own annual. After a short time she came down, smiling broadly, and walked over to Barnaby, holding out a small package.

'Here's something I promised you,' she said sweetly, sitting down beside her mother. Barnaby, surprised but pleased, undid it carefully. Rowena's eyes were fixed firmly on the television, but Heather watched with interest as Barnaby opened the small box inside the wrapping paper. He looked inside, and then his whole face crumpled and he began to sob, the tears coming so fast that he couldn't breathe properly and was gasping for air between his cries of grief.

Snatching the box from his trembling hands, Heather gazed down at the smashed remains of his treasured china spaniel. Scarcely able to credit that any child could be capable of such cruelty she gave a gasp of horror and turned towards Rowena, but Rowena's gaze was fixed firmly on the flickering screen.

As Barnaby howled and screamed, sobbing as though he would never stop, Rowena sat unperturbed until Heather gave her a stinging slap on her legs before pulling her to her feet and then smacking her hard on her bottom.

'You wicked girl! How could you be so spiteful,

Rowena? You're a wicked, wicked child!'

Her daughter wriggled in her grip. 'It's his fault. I warned him,' she shouted, beginning to cry himself.

'Warned him about what?'

'Telling on me.'

'I didn't tell!' hiccuped Barnaby. 'I didn't!'

'You called me a thief in front of your precious Guy.'

'Well you are,' he retorted defiantly, the tears still streaming down his face, his voice thick and pain-filled. 'You've broken Rusty now, so I'll tell all. You stole your slide from Woolworths, and pencils, and rubbers and sweets. You're a nasty girl and I hope they put you in prison.'

'Cry baby! It was only a china dog. It wasn't real. I wouldn't have hurt the real Rusty, but you won't have him ever again, will you?'

'Stop it!' screamed Heather. 'Stop this at once. I can't think properly. Is what Barnaby says true, Rowena?'

'You said so. You said there wasn't room here for a dog.'

'About stealing your slide,' yelled Heather, shaking Rowena furiously. 'Did you steal things from Woolworths?'

'Yes I did! And I'm glad! I hope that stops smarmy-boots next door from playing with Barnaby. He's a policeman so he won't be your friend now I'm a thief, Barnaby!'

Barnaby looked in disbelief from his hysterical sister to his broken dog and then back to Rowena. 'He was my favourite present,' he said quietly, 'and Guy's my favourite friend.'

'*Was* your friend. He won't be now.'

Heather couldn't bear any more and without thinking she smacked her daughter sharply round the face. At once Rowena dissolved into tears, throwing herself on the floor, kicking and screaming as she beat the carpet with clenched fists. For a moment Barnaby watched and then he fled, fled to the only person he could trust, the only person who would understand.

He burst into Guy's kitchen without knocking, tears still running from his eyes and the shattered dog clutched tightly to his chest. 'Rowena's broken Rusty. She said I . . .'

He tailed off. Guy Harrison was standing in the middle of the room with his arms round a tall, slim young woman with dark, curly hair. He had been kissing her, but at the sound of the distraught child he had quickly broken the embrace and turned towards the boy. Even so he wasn't quick enough.

For Barnaby it seemed like the end of the world. Here was his friend, in a house meant to exclude women, and he not only had a lady in it, he was kissing her. This was the final betrayal. He began to back away from the couple, stifling his sobs. You couldn't trust anyone any more, he thought. Not even Guy. He was lost in a topsy-turvy world where nothing was as it seemed, and there was no security in his life.

Guy walked quietly towards him. 'What's up, old chap? What's in the box!' Barnaby didn't answer, he simply turned and bolted out of the door. Guy turned to the young woman. 'I'm sorry, Priscilla, but there's trouble next door. I'd better go and see what's happened.'

'The young widow is in distress, I presume? By all means, Guy. I never realised that your cool exterior hid such a heart of gold. How fortunate that the lady isn't middle-aged and plain. You won't mind if I don't wait?' To his surprise he found that he didn't mind in the least.

'Do what you like,' he called over his shoulder before running round to Heather's house. Priscilla picked up her fur coat, draped it round her shoulders and walked briskly out to her sports car. She wasn't upset. There were plenty of other young men, and all far more infatuated than Guy. Mentally she crossed him off her list and swung the car round before departing with a squeal of tyres.

Guy caught up with Barnaby just as he was tugging at the back door. He picked him up and held him close, feeling the rapid beating of the boy's heart and the tremors that ran through the slight body. Without loosening his grip he made his way into the house.

Rowena was still having her tantrum on the lounge floor. Every time that Heather approached her she would lash out with a foot, once or twice catching her mother on the shins. Guy gestured towards the kitchen and Heather followed him. She felt that he couldn't have come at a worse moment than this, when all her inadequacies as a mother were so totally exposed.

He closed the door between the two rooms. 'Leave her,' he said shortly. 'She'll soon stop without an audience.' Miserably Heather nodded. Slowly, piece by piece, Guy managed to extract the whole story from her, and while his hands were moving comfortingly over Barnaby his eyes offered Heather nothing but sympathy and compassion.

Eventually the wails from the other room ceased. Guy handed Barnaby back to his mother. 'Rowena needs a lot of help,' he whispered. 'I'll go and have a word with her.' Heather gave him a grateful nod as she cuddled her son closely.

He found Rowena standing stiffly by the settee, her arms rigidly at her sides. Sitting down he tried to put an arm round her waist but she wouldn't let him.

'Go away. I don't like you.'

'That's a pity, because I like you. Why don't you like me?'

'You're a policeman; and you're Barnaby's friend, but not mine.'

'I'd like to be a friend to all of you. Why don't you like policemen?'

She hung her head. 'You know why.'

'Because of the stealing?' She nodded. 'I don't think that anyone is going to be too hard on you about the stealing, Rowena. You couldn't help it, could you?'

Surprised, her head came up sharply, and for a moment he could see her mother's vulnerability in her eyes. 'How do you know that?'

'Because I think you're feeling very lonely right now, and you probably took those things to give away to other girls so that you'd be their friend. Is that right?'

'Yes,' she whispered. 'I've stolen things at school too, only the headmistress told Mummy and so I stopped. I didn't mean to do it in Woolworths, but things looked so pretty and before Daddy died I used to go out and buy little presents for my friends. I only wanted things to be the same.'

'But I don't suppose it felt the same when you gave them to the other girls, did it?'

'No. I felt all horrid inside.'

He put a hand on her arm, and this time she didn't pull away. 'You're a very sad little girl at the moment, aren't you Rowena?'

She bit her lip, trying to keep the tears away, but they wouldn't be stopped. 'I want my Daddy!' she sobbed. 'I loved my Daddy and now I'll never see him again. Why did God let it happen?'

He had often asked himself the same question when he encountered tragedies in his working life, but he had never come up with an answer. 'I don't know,' he said honestly. 'What's important right now is to get you some help so that you can learn to cope with your father's death.'

She moved nearer to him until she was squeezed against his leg and he made room for her on the settee. He gave her a clean, blue handkerchief and she wiped her eyes, blew her nose and then handed it back. 'We're going to some meetings to help. Mrs Charles arranged it. I don't want to go because I don't like being asked questions.'

'Sometimes answering questions truthfully is the only way to find out what's going on in your head. Human beings are very complicated. Think of it as being like a car going in for its service.'

She giggled. 'Will they change my oil?'

'Let's hope not! I think you'll all get a lot of help from these meetings, but if you ever want to talk to me about anything you've only got to come round and see me.'

'Barnaby said it's a man's house.'

'Barnaby needs to think it is. That was my way of helping him. I'm telling you because I know you're old enough to be trusted not to tell him.'

She nodded gravely, proud of his trust. 'I would talk to Mummy,' she said, resting her head briefly on his shoulder, 'but Mummy's trying to cope too, and she can't talk about Daddy. As she's never had to be grown-up before it's very hard for her.' He gave Rowena a brief hug, surprised at the child's perspicacity.

He stayed with them for the rest of the afternoon, promised Barnaby that he'd search for a replacement china dog and even watched as Heather tucked the children into bed.

Alone together downstairs Heather felt awkward, but Guy quickly eased her discomfort. 'I'll have to go now. I'm on duty at eight. I don't suppose I'll get much free time in the next couple of weeks, but good luck with your typing, and I hope the family counselling helps you all.'

'Thank you for coming round and rescuing the afternoon for me. What about your visitor?'

'Priscilla is a very self-reliant young lady,' he said with a smile.

Unlike me, thought Heather opening the front door.

Guy stopped when he was level with her, turned and then gently lifted her chin with his fingers before placing a soft kiss on the corner of her mouth. 'You're doing very well, Heather. Don't give up.' She nodded mutely and watched him walk away. For a brief moment she had experienced a mad longing to hurl herself into his arms so that she could feel them round her, protecting her as he so often protected her son.

She had even believed that he was going to ask her out, and her acceptance was ready on her lips. His kiss had been so exquisitely light, controlled and caring, yet hinting at depths of passion beneath the surface; but he hadn't, the kiss had been nothing more than a seasonal gesture and she had allowed it to lead her into a ridiculously adolescent daydream.

Annoyed she gave herself a mental shake. This was to be her year. A year when she discovered exactly what her capabilities were and how she wanted to live her life. Romance, however tempting, was not on the agenda. She poured herself a glass of sherry and opened a new library book. When, now and again, her thoughts returned to the gentle kiss she resolutely moved them in a different direction.

That night she dreamt that she and Brian were in bed together, kissing and murmuring endearments. But as Brian bent to kiss her his features changed to Guy's and she awoke abruptly with her heart racing. Quickly she sat up, ashamed of her hot cheeks and the aching longing that she felt for the dream to continue. It was as though she had rejected Brian for another man and she despised herself. When she slept again the dream did not return.

All too soon the final few days of the holiday passed, and then it was back to work while Lynne had the children for the remaining days of the school vacation.

Chapter Eight

The January sales proved to be even worse than Heather had expected. On the opening day women were jostling for seats, demanding to see shoes from the window display, and then attempting to lower the price still further due to some minute flaw scarcely visible to Heather's eyes.

The entire week was like a nightmare, and even in her sleep she found herself selling shoes to women who turned into Sheila, Lynne, and Amanda, all screaming at her that they'd been given the wrong shoes.

She stumbled through each morning, not noticing that Rowena was scarcely eating, and only half-listening to complaints of various ailments ranging from headaches to twisted ankles, all intended as a means of avoiding school. She knew what the children were doing, but all that happened was an increased feeling of annoyance that they still seemed incapable of adapting to their new surroundings.

'Look,' she said sternly on one particularly bad morning, 'I don't like my work in the shop, but I have to go and that's all there is to it. It's the same for you two. You might not like school, but the law says you must attend, and you'll have to make the best of it. Now hurry up or I'll be late.'

'I hate you,' said Rowena. Heather had grown so used to this expression that it had long since ceased to trouble her. 'You'll be sorry one day.'

'I hate you too,' said Barnaby, and this was a surprise, even to Rowena who stared at him in astonishment. 'When you're not in the shop you're out typing or shut in your room sleeping.'

'I get very tired. I'm sorry, I know it's dreary for you, but things will improve when the better weather comes.'

'Why?' asked Rowena.

Unable to think of a quick answer Heather bent down to kiss them, but they both averted their faces and ran off. She was consumed by regret. They were moving away from her, not attempting to turn to her with their fears because she never had time to offer them the comfort they craved.

If the day started badly it finished even worse. The last customer of the day was interested in a pair of smart, woollen slippers that were on offer at half-price. 'They're for wearing round the house' she explained, her face as pale and drawn as Heather's. 'I look after my elderly mother who's bedridden, and I need something comfortable. These look lovely.'

'I know they look lovely, but to be honest people have complained that they pinch across the instep. I think you'd be better off with the more conventional type.' She brought out an assortment of colours and the woman bought a pair, thanked Heather profusely and left.

As soon as she'd gone Mrs Winter swooped. 'Are you out of your mind?' she exploded. 'The slippers that customer requested were far more expensive than the ones you sold her. The woollen ones are excellent value at half-price.'

'You know perfectly well that we've had loads of complaints, and that poor woman was going to spend every day wearing them.'

'That isn't our worry. I can't imagine what you were thinking of.'

'I was being honest, something you probably find hard to recognise.'

'Mrs Lorrimer! I think it's time that you and I discussed your position in this shop. I realise that you find such lowly work rather trying, but if there is one more incident like today's you won't have to worry because you will no longer work here. I hope I've made myself clear?'

Heather stared at the woman's mottled, angry face and her tight thin-lipped mouth, and for a brief moment contemplated telling her where she could put her slippers and her job: then she remembered the mortgage, and the imminent gas bill and bit back the retort. She lowered her head. 'I'm very sorry,' she mumbled.

'I should hope so. One other point. We do have certain standards to maintain here and it's becoming increasingly obvious that you are not paying enough attention to your personal appearance. Perhaps if you got up a little earlier . . .?'

This was too much for Heather. 'I already get up at six-thirty. I have my children to look after, the beds to make, packed lunches to prepare and . . .'

'Perhaps you should remember our policy concerning working mothers. There is no special allowance made for . . .'

'I know that!' shouted Heather. 'You've quoted it at me often enough.' She brushed past the surprised manageress and grabbed her coat and bag from the hook. Rita watched wide-eyed as Heather marched out of the shop, and she admired the older woman's nerve.

Once home Heather regarded her tight dress with distaste. She knew that Mrs Winter, however odious, did have a point. She was neglecting herself, and if she didn't start dieting soon none of her clothes would fit her. She had already gone from a small 10 to a generous 14, and at 5′3″ this was not attractive. She rested her head in her hands and wondered how much longer she could carry on.

'Mummy,' said Rowena, wandering in from the lounge, 'when you've stopped crying there's a letter for you.'

'I'm not crying, I'm just tired. Let me look.' She

glanced at the brown envelope and her spirits sank even lower. She knew what it was: their appointment for family counselling. That meant time off work, time that Mrs Winter wasn't likely to grant.

Heather had never deliberately lied before, but this time she would have to. She would get Lynne to ring the shop for her and say she was sick, otherwise she might lose her job.

A week later Heather, Rowena and Barnaby sat awkwardly on the green leather chairs with the wooden arms and studied the woman opposite them with varying degrees of suspicion. She was in her early thirties with a lot of eye make-up and wearing a bright, tight-fitting jersey dress.

She smiled cheerfully. 'I'm Dr Foster and you're the Lorrimer family, is that right?'

Rowena, taut with nerves, giggled and dug Barnaby in the ribs. He giggled back, trying to smother the sound with his hand.

'May we all share the joke?' the doctor asked pleasantly.

'No,' retorted Rowena defiantly. Heather kept silent.

'In that case let's talk about something different. How do you like your new school, Rowena?'

Rowena swung her legs and scuffed her shoes against the edge of the chair. 'It's all right.'

'Do you have a special friend there?'

'Yes.'

'Good. What's her name?'

'Can't remember.' Again she giggled. Heather didn't know whether she ought to tell her daughter off, thus demonstrating parental firmness, or leave her alone in case the doctor thought her interfering. She wished that she knew what responses were expected of her, instead of desperately wondering how a 'normal' mother would behave.

'What about you, Barnaby?' continued the doctor. 'Do

you like your new school?'

'Yes, thank you. My best friend's called Pigpen.' This provoked hysterical laughter from Rowena, but Barnaby remained straight-faced.

'Pigpen? Is that his nickname?'

'No, his real one.'

'Why is that, do you think?'

'Why's what?'

'I find it interesting that he's called Pigpen, and I wondered why.'

Barnaby shrugged. 'Because his parents chose it, I suppose.'

'They're fans of "Charlie Brown",' put in Heather, unable to sit silently while her children deliberately pretended to be both stupid and rude.

'It's quite all right, Mrs Lorrimer. I'll talk to you a little later.' Dr Foster smiled, but it was plain that interference was not welcome.

'Now, your daddy died last summer, is that right?' Both children nodded.

'How did that make you feel?'

'Sad,' said Rowena. 'Sad, and hollow inside.'

'And you, Barnaby?'

'Nothing. I just felt empty.'

'You must miss your old home and your friends. Have you any pets?'

'I've got a ballerina,' put in Rowena helpfully as Barnaby struggled for composure, 'and he's got a china dog.'

'A broken china dog,' he said angrily. 'Rowena broke it, but I've got all the pieces and Guy's going to try and get me a new one.'

'Who is Guy?'

The children looked at each other. 'Mummy's boyfriend,' said Rowena, and again they started their irritating giggling.

'He is *not* my boyfriend,' stated Heather. 'He's

simply . . . '

'We'll have our talk later, Mrs Lorrimer. Rowena, I understand that you've been in some trouble at school. Would you like to talk to me about it? On our own, if you wish.'

'No.'

'Would you like to paint me a picture then? A big, colourful one with lovely poster paints.'

Rowena shrugged. 'I don't mind.'

The doctor rang a bell and a smiling young girl in a checked overall led the children away to the painting room. The doctor then turned to Heather.

'Well, Mrs Lorrimer, these must have been worrying times for you.'

'Yes. It was difficult coping with the move and trying to bring the children up on my own, but when I found out about Rowena I simply couldn't believe it. It isn't the sort of thing I would ever have expected from her.'

'Has it occurred to you that perhaps some of Rowena's troubles stem from your own problems? I noticed that you were very quick to interrupt if you didn't like what the children were saying. Perhaps you're finding it difficult to let them stand on their own feet? It's a perfectly understandable reaction, especially as your husband was a good deal older than you and presumably must have provided both emotional and financial security.'

'I'm not finding it at all difficult, but they're only six and nine. I can't really wash my hands of them. They still need guidance and a secure home base.'

'It's interesting that you say six and nine when they're actually nearer seven and ten.'

Heather was running out of patience. 'I do know their ages. However, at this moment they are six and nine. In two months' time, if we're still seeing you, I shall call them seven and ten.'

The doctor smiled. 'You have a lot of resentment bottled up inside you. Did you realise that?'

'Resentment? What kind?'

'I hoped you'd be able to tell me.'

'I've no idea. I don't feel resentful.'

'Then you must be abnormally well-adjusted. Most women would feel some resentment at being forced to lower their standard of living so drastically, move away from all their friends and go out to work for the first time at the age of twenty-nine.'

'I'm thirty in three months,' said Heather maliciously.

Dr Foster ignored her. 'Your children mentioned a boyfriend . . .'

'He's our next-door neighbour who has been kind enough to take an interest in Barnaby. That's all there is to it. He's a good friend.'

'There's no need to be defensive. You're a very attractive young woman, there are bound to be boyfriends. What kind of a relationship did you and your late husband have?'

Heather glanced at her watch. It was already eleven o'clock. 'Does this really have any relevance to Rowena's problem?'

'It may well have. Was it a good marriage?'

'Perfect.'

'Come now, Mrs Lorrimer, no one's marriage is perfect. You must have had quarrels, disagreements, moments when you annoyed each other.'

'I'm sorry to disappoint you but we didn't. We had a wonderful marriage; he was everything to me, everything.' She was horrified to hear her voice breaking.

'Perhaps it was more a father/daughter relationship?'

'If so, it was highly incestuous.'

Dr Foster studied her for a moment. 'I think it's going to be quite a long time before we get to the root of your particular problems, Mrs Lorrimer. Is ten o'clock not a good time for you to attend? I notice that you keep glancing at your watch.'

'As a matter of fact, it isn't. Wednesday afternoons are

my only time off work.'

'Then let's say four o'clock on Wednesday fortnight, shall we?'

'Is this really necessary? Surely it's obvious that Rowena stole because she was feeling excluded by her classmates and wanted to get into their good books. She's finding it hard to adjust, and I'm sure she needs help, but I can't imagine why it has to involve Barnaby and me.'

'Because you are a family unit, none of you can remain unaffected by the behaviour and emotions of the others. Tell me, do you and the children talk about your late husband very much?'

'No.'

'Why not?'

'It's still too soon for me. I'd get upset.'

'People need a period of grieving before they can hope to start rebuilding their lives. If Rowena were able to discuss her father more she might not steal. The stealing is a cry for help. She needs to talk about him, but senses your inability to do so. This is her way of telling us all that she needs help.'

'I don't agree.'

Dr Foster smiled. 'I didn't suppose you would. I see from your notes that it's the change in social standards that seems to distress you the most. Would you call that an accurate statement?'

'No! It's Brian I miss, but I daren't face the truth.' She twisted her wedding ring round and round. 'If I do,' she whispered, 'if I let myself dwell on it, then I feel as though I'll go mad. I daren't think about it, can't you understand that? Without him I'm nothing, and if I force myself to face reality I . . . that is I might . . .'

'Yes?'

'I might not want to live myself,' she blurted out, then buried her face in her hands and sobbed like a small child.

The doctor let her cry until she had no tears left. 'I do understand,' she said gently, 'but at least you have the children. A childless widow has nothing. No incentive to carry on.'

Heather mopped her eyes. 'I know, but you see I'm not very maternal. I've always had help with the children and somehow I can't put myself in their place. Instead of reassuring them I snap and shout. I know it's wrong but I can't stop doing it.'

'You mustn't expect too much too soon; but please remember what I've said and try to let the children talk about their father. Will you try?'

'Yes,' murmured Heather.

'Excellent! Ah good! Here come the children.'

Rowena and Barnaby were both clutching large grey squares of paper. 'This is nice, Barnaby, very colourful. Is it your garden?'

'No, it's Woolworths, and that's Rowena stealing her slide in the bottom corner.'

'Pig!' shouted Rowena. The doctor ignored them both and moved on to Rowena's picture. 'You paint very well, Rowena. This is an excellent face, but it looks very angry. Who is it? Your mummy?'

Thank you, doctor, thought Heather.

'Actually no, it's you.'

'Is it? Then I must pin it up behind me for other people to look at. Thank you very much, Rowena.'

Heather got to her feet. 'Come along, we have to leave now, I'm late for work.'

'Is that it?' asked an astonished Barnaby.

'No, I'll see you all in two weeks' time. Goodbye for now.'

The children kept silent and Heather muttered her goodbye as she was half-way out of the room. Immediately they were in the corridor the children began to laugh. 'She must be potty!' giggled Rowena. 'I drew the ugliest face I could and she's going to hang it on her wall!'

'You were both very silly,' said Heather. 'You behaved like children at nursery school.'

'She didn't say much about my stealing, did she? I don't think she thought it was a very bad thing to do really.'

'I've no idea what she thinks, but I know that stealing's bad and so does your school, so don't go imagining that you can start stealing money again. Or anything else for that matter,' she added hastily.

For the next few weeks there was an uneasy truce between Heather and Mrs Winter. They spoke when they had to, but there were no more lectures. After the sale the shop was relatively quiet, and at last Heather felt that she was coming to grips with her work. Then disaster struck.

One Friday morning Barnaby complained of feeling unwell and Heather could see that he was flushed with fever. 'Is your throat sore?' she asked, wondering what on earth she was going to do with him.

'No, but I itch. I itch all over my back.' She pulled up his shirt and saw a crop of small spots, each with a tell-tale blister on the top. There was no doubt about it.

'Oh no!' she groaned. 'You've got chickenpox!'

'Is it bad? Will I die?'

'No, of course not! You'll be a bit uncomfortable for a few days, that's all. The trouble is, I can't get any time off work.'

Rowena slid off her chair. 'He might die left here on his own with a raging temperature.'

'I'm not going to leave him here alone. Kindly go upstairs and get dressed. You're late.'

'I expect I'll catch it.'

'I'm sure you will, now hurry up.'

Frantic with worry Heather rang Lynne. 'I'd like to help,' Lynne said slowly, 'but I haven't had it myself, and then there's Daisy to consider.'

'O God! I'm sorry, I never thought, I was so wrapped up in my own problem. Of course you can't come.'

'I could ask Mary. With her children at work she's always moaning about feeling bored. I'm sure she'd come.'

Much to Heather's amazement she did. She vaguely remembered meeting Mary at Sheila's house soon after her arrival, but there had been no contact since and she was overwhelmed at such kind-heartedness.

'Don't worry about anything,' Mary comforted her. 'He's safe with me. I've been through it all three times; there isn't much I haven't had to cope with!'

Thanking her profusely, Heather rushed off to work, ignoring Barnaby's tearful requests for her to stay. Even so she was late, but Mrs Winter settled for a pointed glance at her watch.

'They cut my bus out,' lied Heather smoothly, amazed at how quickly she was mastering the art of deceit.

Ten days later Rowena went down with it too. As in all things, she didn't do it by halves and was really ill. Her temperature soared and she moaned deliriously, so that a terrified Heather called the doctor in the middle of the night.

'A tepid bath and keep her uncovered,' said Dr Rawle patiently over the phone. 'It's a virus, there's nothing I can give you. Don't worry, there aren't any complications with chickenpox. She *will* get over it!'

As she tried to put a sobbing Rowena into the bath without touching any of her large, angry-looking blisters the tears were running down Heather's face as well. Then, not daring to dab her dry, she laid the child on top of a cotton sheet and persuaded her to sip a soluble aspirin through a straw.

Without Mary, Heather would have lost her job, but at last both children were recovered and life returned to normal for a time. Unfortunately, because they were thoroughly run down, the children then picked up every virus that was going round, plus a particularly violent stomach bug that meant Heather was up changing sheets for one entire night.

Again Mary came to the house, and Heather struggled

through her day's work trying to keep her eyes open and gradually feeling less and less well herself. Straight after the children's tea the stomach virus struck with ferocity and she spent most of the night in the bathroom. In the morning the children made their own breakfast and got ready for school without any assistance from their mother. Indeed, they seemed to enjoy the opportunity to show their independence, and Heather wondered if Dr Foster could possibly have had a point when she blamed Heather for not letting them grow up.

After they'd left she dragged herself to the phone and rang the shop. Mrs Winter was not convinced, and demanded a doctor's certificate as proof. The fact that Heather didn't have anyone to take it to the shop was disregarded. She had to see a certificate, it was in the staff rule book.

'Bloody staff rule book!' Heather swore and slammed down the phone. Immediately she contacted Dr Rawle, who was unable to come out, but explained that it was a forty-eight-hour bug and a diet of boiled water was all the treatment Heather needed. After a great deal of cajoling she reluctantly agreed to leave a sick certificate at the surgery without examining Heather, but she sounded very annoyed and far from her usual sympathetic self.

Groaning, Heather crept back upstairs and lay on her bed shivering and dozing for the entire day.

When the children arrived home they clattered up to her bedroom and stared at her in surprise. 'Mummy! You're not still in bed!' exclaimed Rowena indignantly.

'I'm sorry, darling, but I feel terrible. I'll come down in my dressing gown for a time if you like, then I'll go back to bed.'

With her head pounding she made it to the kitchen where she warmed some soup and cut a few sandwiches, trying to ignore her heaving stomach. As soon as the children had finished they ran outside to play. Heather took one look at the sticky remains of the chocolate mousse on the plates and began to retch. Finally she leant against the sink, her forehead damp with perspiration.

All at once the room began to spin round her, there was a rushing sound in her ears and then she was falling into a black tunnel. As she fell she was vaguely aware of the sound of breaking china, and then there was nothing.

When she opened her eyes again she was lying on the kitchen tiles and there was blood trickling from a cut on her left cheek. Still shivering violently she managed to pull herself upright until she could lean against the cupboard beneath the sink. Then, to her horror, she was violently sick all over the floor and again her head began to swim.

All at once Barnaby came running in. 'Mummy, can I have a lolly?'

'I'm sorry, Barnaby, I'm not well. Would you see if Sheila's in?'

'Why are there bits of china on the floor?'

'I knocked a plate off the draining board. Please, Barnaby, fetch Sheila. Tell her I'm not well.'

'OK. Then can I have a lolly?' Heather began to retch and he ran off, only to return within moments. 'She's out. Shall I try Lynne?' She nodded, too weak to make the effort needed for speech.

As Heather waited for him to return she began to feel a little better, and slowly and cautiously got to her feet. She decided to try and reach a chair but the room began to swim again and she cried out, although she knew there was no one there. Again darkness descended, but as she started to fall she suddenly felt strong arms reaching round her, half-carrying her out of the kitchen and laying her carefully on the settee. Her teeth chattering, Heather looked up into Guy Harrison's face.

'For Christ's sake! You look ghastly. What's wrong?'

'Only a tummy bug, but it's made me as weak as a kitten.'

'I'm calling a doctor.'

'There's no point. I tried this morning. Dr Rawle says it

will pass in forty-eight hours, and she's left me a sick certificate at the surgery. Would you tell Mrs Winter for me? She seems to think that I'm faking it.'

'Bloody stupid woman! This is all so unnecessary. Why didn't you ring me? Tell me what was happening?'

'I didn't think. I'm so hot, Guy,' and she began to move her head restlessly, closing her eyes and murmuring incoherently to herself. He quickly picked up the telephone.

When she came back to consciousness Heather was in her own bed, covered by one cool sheet and with her nightdress changed.

'Feeling better?'

'Lynne! For an awful moment I thought that Guy had done all this!'

'He wanted to, but I protected your maidenly modesty! By the time Barnaby had fetched me the doctor was on her way and Guy was ranting on about your stupidity and demanding to know why you'd let yourself get so run down. I told him about everyone being what they ate, but he wasn't over-impressed. He doesn't know that you live on chocolate and crisps all the week.'

'What did the doctor say?'

'That you had a severe attack of gastro-enteritis and must stay in bed for at least three days. She's left you some pills and potions and is calling back tomorrow. Guy came on rather strong with her. He seemed to think she didn't pay enough attention when you called her this morning.'

'I wasn't so bad then. It was only when I got up that I really felt terrible. What time is it?'

'Nine-thirty. The children are in their beds, the kitchen's been cleaned up and there's nothing left for you to worry about.'

'Where's Guy now?'

'Champing at the bit in the lounge. I'll send him up and then you get some rest. I'll look after things for the next few days. If I spend the night on the sofa I'm on the spot for the morning rush.'

'No, Lynne, really . . .'

'Yes, Heather, really! You can have Daisy for a month when I meet my millionaire who wants to whisk me off to the Canary Islands!'

When Lynne left Heather wished that Guy wasn't coming to see her in her present condition, but as soon as he put his head round the door she forgot all that and merely felt pleased to see him.

'You're a fine one!' he said in mock-anger. 'Couldn't you have got some help before the dramatic collapse? Or were you working up to the big scene?'

'You've got it in one. I'm a frustrated actress at heart!'

'Seriously, Heather, you should have told someone.'

'At our counselling session this week Dr Foster told me that I was still far too immature and must stop relying on other people. Because Rowena senses my inability to fulfill the role of a mature adult she can't unburden herself to me, and that's why she's turned to stealing. It's all my fault, and I felt that this time I must cope on my own. If I don't start growing up what will become of Rowena?' Tears of weakness filled her eyes.

'Did Rowena tell the psychiatrist this?'

'Hardly! Rowena doesn't tell her anything remotely resembling the truth. She and Barnaby just fool around, then go and do some painting while I'm put under the spotlight. Apparently my marriage was bad for me, and Brian and I weren't well-suited as I – in my youthful stupidity – had thought. In fact he prevented me from growing up, and for his own selfish reasons too. That really hurt, you know.'

'Bloody stupid woman! I think you ought to stop going to see her. I can't imagine who's benefiting. Still, we'll cross that bridge later. Right now you need plenty of sleep and no worrying. I'll call in on the dragon tomorrow and verify your illness.'

'Guy, why can't I cope? Other women do. Lynne and

Sheila manage extremely well.'

'How many single mothers do you know who nurse two children through chickenpox, flu, head colds and tummy upsets, hold down a job that they hate and learn to type in their spare time?'

'You make me sound almost capable!'

'And so you are. Now go to sleep!' He smiled affectionately and she relaxed, closed her eyes and was asleep before he was downstairs.

It was ten days before she was fit, and by then her skirts hung loosely on her, although she thought it was a rather drastic way to diet. However, from now on, she'd eat more carefully and hopefully the surplus weight caused by her old lazy eating habits wouldn't return.

On her last evening at home Guy called round. He studied her carefully. 'You look much better!' he said with satisfaction, 'Almost human in fact!'

'You flatter me, sir!'

'Seriously, Heather, how's the typing coming along?'

'Very well. I've finished my lessons and passed Stage II RSA. So you see, I'm a clever human!'

'Look, I hope you won't be offended but I've put your name forward for a typist/clerical position that's come up at work. They need a conscientious person with a tidy mind, and I think that's you down to a "T". Furthermore, having met Mrs Winter, I can't see you surviving at the shop much longer.'

'When does the job start? What must I do to apply?'

'Such enthusiasm! It doesn't start until next month, March 4th to be precise, and as I've put in a good word for you there's only the formality of an interview to be gone through. Providing you don't turn up looking like a punk I would say the job's yours.'

'What about a typing test? I'll be a mass of nerves.'

'Nonsense! Positive thinking, remember?'

'What do I do if the children fall ill again?'

'If Mary can't help you can take holiday. They're quite

flexible about that sort of thing as there are several married women working at the station.'

Heather's face was already brightening at the prospect of leaving Porters. 'It's tremendously kind of you, Guy. I don't know how to thank you.'

'If you get the job and do it well that will be sufficient thanks.' She gave him a dazzling smile, and he looked at her thoughtfully. There were small lines at the corners of her eyes, and dark smudges beneath them. She was, in reality, far less attractive than the first time he'd seen her, yet all at once he wanted to reach out and touch her. He wanted to know how she would feel in his arms, how she would respond to his kisses, but he didn't move.

Heather was too vulnerable. She would build any romance, however light, into something more permanent and in the light of his recent news from Australia he reluctantly decided that he was better off with casual affairs where both parties knew the rules and no one got hurt.

Heather stood quite still beneath his scrutiny. She wished that he was standing closer, so that she could put a hand on his arm or brush against him as though by accident. She couldn't understand her sudden overwhelming desire to make physical contact with him. If he had taken one step towards her then she would have gone into his arms but unfortunately he didn't.

'Well, thank you again,' she said breathlessly.

'Don't say that until you've tried the job! Ring the station tomorrow to fix up the interview, will you?'

'Of course.'

After he'd gone she realised with excessive pleasure that if she did get the job then she would see far more of Guy Harrison, and the thought elated her.

The interview went well right from the start. Once Heather had demonstrated her ability to copy-type a letter the rest of the discussion was almost a formality, and the senior secretary who was conducting the test became quite friendly.

'Detective Inspector Harrison has given you a glowing, personal testimonial, so we don't really need any other references. In fact, if you think you'd like the job, then consider it yours.'

Heather was stunned. 'What about the other applicants?'

'There aren't any. All the typists here are crowded into one room. Personal temperament is almost as important as typing skills, and far more difficult to assess at an interview. When we were told that you'd certainly fit in well, we decided not to advertise the post until we'd seen you. We've made one or two bad mistakes in the past and didn't want to do the same again. It's such a waste of valuable time.'

Heather, digesting the news that her months of purgatory under Mrs Winter were over, beamed with pleasure. 'I'd love the job,' she said confidently.

'Haven't you any questions?'

'Not really. I'm just thrilled to be given such an opportunity.'

'That's pleasant. When I last held interviews I hardly had time to ask questions myself the candidates were so busy enquiring about salary increases, paid holidays and sick leave. So, we're mutually satisfied. Are you a neighbour of the Inspector's?'

'Yes, I live next door.'

'Lucky you! There isn't an eligible girl in the station who wouldn't give her right arm to change places with you!'

'Really?'

'Yes, really, and some ineligible ones too!'

'He's more friendly with my son than with me. I don't see a lot of him myself.'

'And if you do you're not telling. Quite right!'

'It's true,' smiled Heather, wishing briefly that it wasn't.

'Fine. We'll see you on March 4th at nine-fifteen. I look forward to it.'

'So do I,' said Heather fervently, and left the building walking on air.

That evening she went to Lynne's and told her the good news. She was as thrilled as Heather. 'That's fabulous! Just what you need. I'm glad I suggested those typing lessons. What will you do with your spare evenings now?'

'Sleep!'

'Don't be silly. I think you ought to try an Open University course. It *is* hard work, but tremendously rewarding, and it keeps the old brain cells ticking over.'

'I couldn't, Lynne. I'm not bright enough.'

'Rubbish! I've got all the old papers from when I started. Sociology is very useful; it opens doors to welfare work, social services, that kind of thing. Go on, take them; you've nothing to lose.'

'Except my money!'

'I'm sure the police will pay you well enough. You're coming out of the poverty trap now, so go on climbing.'

'Oh well,' conceded Heather, 'give them to me. I'll have a look, but that's all I'm promising.'

'I hope you won't mind me saying this, Heather . . .'

'Which means I definitely will!'

'No, it doesn't! It's only that now you've got yourself this job – which is fantastic – I hope you'll begin to realise firstly how lucky you are, and I mean lucky, because think of all the unemployed at the moment, and secondly, that almost anything is possible if you work at it. OK, this job fell into your lap, but you needn't stay in it for ever. An Open University course *plus* typing skills really does offer you broader horizons. Life's just beginning for you, Heather. I suppose that's really what I'm trying to say, but I can sense that you're seeing this as a very pleasant end to your troubles, not a fresh start.'

Heather was silent for a moment. 'You've taken me by surprise,' she confessed with a laugh, 'but you're right. That was exactly how I was thinking.'

'Yes, because you've always been so negative, but I thought you'd left that behind you this year. What happened to the "positive thinking" resolution?'

'This is about as positive as I intended to get!'

'Heather, you should always have a goal in mind, something to strive for. I do; I'm forever planning ahead!'

'You're right, and I admire you tremendously, but I don't have your energy. I get incredibly tired these days, and the children drive me mad in the evenings. I can't imagine taking up anything else.'

'It's stress that's making you tired. Look, borrow this. It's a super book about yoga and meditation . . .' She saw Heather's face. 'Come on, what have you got to lose? Try half an hour a day and I guarantee that in two weeks you'll feel a new woman.'

'All right, but I was always hopeless at PE.'

'Anyone can do yoga, you don't have to stand on your head or anything. Oh yes, and borrow this too.'

'What is it?' Heather was highly suspicious.

'It's about the food we eat these days. Just read it and see what you think.'

'You're not a Christian Scientist or an Evangelist, are you, Lynne?'

'No! I'm not a suitable candidate for religion. I just want to take the best care possible of my body and mind, then if I crack up it's all down to me!'

'All right, but I'll be hard to convince.'

'Your kind make the best converts! Have you told Guy about the job?'

'He's not home yet, but my next port of call is Sheila's.'

Sheila, too, was thrilled for her friend. 'What bliss when you come to write your resignation letter. I bet you've started composing it in your head already!'

Heather laughed. 'As a matter of fact I have. However, I'm going to tone it down before I actually commit the words to paper!'

She told the children over tea, but they were too wrapped up in their own grievances over school to muster much enthusiasm.

'Perhaps you'll be nicer now,' remarked Rowena. Heather sighed. The family counselling wasn't having any appreciable effect on her daughter, who was becoming more and more impertinent, and she wondered if she should take Guy's advice and simply miss her next appointment.

'Will you be working with Guy?' asked Barnaby.

'Not with him, but in the same building. I'm going round to tell him later on.'

'He's out.'

She felt bitterly disappointed. 'Do you know where?'

'He's taking Priscilla to a show. He told me that girlfriends like an airing now and again.'

If she hadn't been so upset she would have laughed. 'Lucky Priscilla,' she managed to say lightly.

Barnaby scowled. 'She's a pain. All woman are a pain. I don't know why he goes in for all that sloppy kissing stuff. It's horrible!'

Heather tried to suppress a vision of Guy holding a pliant Priscilla in his arms and kissing her. 'Is she pretty, Barnaby?'

'I don't know! She's got long, red nails and her hair's curly and down to her shoulders. She wears lots of make-up and perfume. The perfume's nice.'

Heather wished that she hadn't asked.

'I'm going to watch the Tom and Jerry cartoon,' he added, slipping down from the table.

'So am I,' said Rowena quickly.

'No you're not, my girl. Homework first, and don't tell me that you haven't any because I shan't believe you.'

'I haven't any.'

'Bring me your satchel.'

Rowena collected it from the hall. 'Here you are. See, nothing in it!'

Heather looked, and there was no sign of a schoolbook. 'What's this?' she asked sharply, holding up a silver propelling pencil.

'That belongs to Janice. I forgot to give it back.'

'Well, give it back tomorrow, please. It's far too good to be lent.'

'Can I watch the cartoon now?'

'Go on then,' she sighed. Her previous euphoria had gone, mainly, she admitted, because Guy wasn't around to be told the news, but also because he was out with the glamorous Priscilla. Out having fun while she was sitting in a grey jumper and skirt with finger nails broken down to the quick. She looked at her hands in disgust, remembering how *her* nails had once been long and painted, and *her* hair softly permed. It seemed a lifetime ago.

Plunging her hands into the washing-up water she vowed to buy herself some rubber gloves, and also a new shampoo to bring out the highlights in her naturally fair hair. The image of Priscilla that Barnaby had conjured up was a sharp reminder of how badly she had let herself go. If Lynne was going to work on her mind and diet then she would do the same for her body.

Later that night she wrote her letter of resignation, and there was nothing to mar that moment of pleasure. Then she began to read Lynne's book on yoga, and was soon deeply engrossed.

Her resignation was received with obvious relief tempered by curiosity as to where Heather was going, but she refused to say, mentioning only that it was office work.

'I trust that you'll fit in better there,' Mrs Winter said coldly. 'If you hadn't left we would undoubtedly have had to dispense with your services before long. You have no ability in dealing with the general public.'

'How fortunate that I beat you to it,' responded

Heather sweetly and Rita giggled.

'She'd never have sacked you,' said the other girl when they were alone. 'She knows damn well most girls won't put up with her. I'm only staying until Ryan and I have enough money to put down a deposit on a house, then I'm looking elsewhere. I'll miss you, but I wish you luck.'

On her final day in the shop Rita bought two cream cakes for their afternoon tea break, but Mrs Winter never made any mention of the fact that Heather was going, and as she left the shop the woman never even troubled to say goodbye.

How she must have loathed me, Heather reflected as she climbed onto her usual bus for the last time. It didn't matter any more, and that was marvellous. No more days ruined by silent disapproval, her hands clammy under the eagle eyes of her superior. I'm free, she thought, and beamed at the astonished bus conductor.

When she got off the bus she gave him another smile and said a cheery goodnight. From now on, she vowed, there would be more smiles and laughter in her life.

Chapter Nine

Heather waited nervously for the bus which would take her to her new job. All the previous night she had lain awake, wondering what it would be like, and it was difficult to eat even a slice of toast before leaving home.

She had found time to glance at her horoscope which said that Saturn moving into a favourable position meant this was the perfect time to attempt new undertakings, and she hoped that this was true. She had been tempted to take two tranquillisers instead of the prescribed one, but instead she had used a technique from Lynne's book to slow down her breathing, and much to her surprise this had worked well, steadying both her stomach and her trembling hands.

In the event all her fears were groundless. The other typists greeted her warmly and gave her all the assistance she needed. At the end of her first day she was tired but also elated. The absence of Mrs Winter had been bliss, and she still found it difficult to remember that now she could talk as she worked.

There had been no sign of Guy, but as she was leaving one of the girls remarked to her friend that he was on night duty. It was quite a disappointment. She had wanted him to see how well she was coping and give her another of those brief smiles that made her feel – however foolishly – that she was special to him. It was, she decided, a harmless pretence.

The days passed and she became acquainted with

several of the policemen by sight. She sat quietly watching as the other women laughed and joked with them, flirting light-heartedly with their particular favourites, but she gradually realised that none of the men took very much notice of *her* as a woman, and she was piqued by this lack of attention.

Slowly she became more and more aware of her appearance. She noticed the way the other women dressed, and decided to discard her rather formal clothes and adopt the casual mix-and-match style that was now popular. One of the women, Charlotte, offered Heather the chance to join her mail order catalogue, and this allowed her to build up a new wardrobe whilst spreading the payments. Both the children noticed the difference, but neither of them passed any favourable remarks.

'You look silly and girlish in that,' Rowena stated on the morning that her mother wore a red brushed cotton skirt and a red and white sweater. 'Are you trying to catch a man?'

'Certainly not, and kindly stop being so rude.'

'I only wondered.'

'I can't think what put the idea into your head.'

'Guy says that all women try to catch themselves a man. He and Priscilla rowed about it.'

'Really!' said Heather calmly, but her heart leapt with ridiculous joy. Priscilla had sounded a formidable opponent. Here she pulled herself up sharply. An opponent in what? Surely *she* wasn't trying to trap Guy? All that she wanted was to see him from time to time and continue as his friend. Then she smiled at her feeble attempts at self-justification.

'I don't like your clothes much either,' said Barnaby. 'Daddy didn't like bright colours, and neither do I.'

'Well I do, and I'm the one who's wearing them.'

'You look like mutton dressed up as lamb,' said Rowena rudely, pushing her way out of the kitchen.

Heather chased after her and administered a slap on

her bottom. 'I'm tired of your insolence,' she shouted, 'and I don't want to hear any more of it again.'

Rowena slammed the bathroom door shut and locked it. 'The truth always hurts!' she yelled from her position of safety, and Heather – realising how foolish she'd seem having a slanging match with her daughter through a closed bathroom door – went away. She had hoped that both children would like the fact that there was now a little more money and that she was more cheerful and relaxed, but they seemed resentful of her happiness and jealous of her new friends.

The following Sunday, as she was washing-up, she saw a tall, leggy blonde with an ankle-length fur coat and suede boots saunter up Guy's back path, and soon they emerged hand-in-hand and walked to his car. She bit hard on her bottom lip. What had she expected? That he'd suddenly become a recluse? Office gossip was often about Inspector Harrison's numerous conquests. How could she have been stupid enough to think that he'd be romantically interested in a tired, rather dull thirty-year-old with two children when he could have the pick of every eligible girl in the area?

'Fool,' she said aloud. 'He was only being kind, forget him.' Yet there had been that one kiss, and surely she hadn't imagined the look in his eyes when he left her house that night? Apparently she had.

'He's not for you, my girl,' she continued. 'Accept it and get on with your life.'

Amazingly she found that she could. As the days passed she picked up both physically and mentally, and she had to admit that a lot of this was due to the yoga, meditation and better eating habits prescribed by Lynne. The family now ate far more fresh fruit and vegetables, and she virtually cut out cakes and biscuits from her shopping list. Spring was approaching and she felt almost optimistic. She could do her new job well, she was now getting the occasional whistle from lorry drivers and workmen on building sites – a great morale booster, however chauvinistic – and she began to feel that she was in control of her life at last.

Another of the typists recommended her hair stylist to Heather, and so one Saturday she left the children with Sheila and went into Croydon to see what he could do. When she came out she scarcely recognised her reflection in a shop window. The man had cut and layered her hair so that it clung closely to her head with a feathered fringe and the sides that curved in to her cheeks.

Sheila was astounded. 'What a difference!' she exclaimed. 'You look like Rowena's sister, it's positively indecent! Barnaby, Rowena, come and look at your mother.'

The children stared in surprise. 'What's happened to it?' asked Barnaby.

'It's been re-styled. Do you like it?'

He shook his head. 'You don't look like a mummy any more. You look more like a hedgehog.'

Rowena giggled. 'You don't, Mummy, it's nice. Can I have mine cut the same?'

'It wouldn't be possible, darling. Your hair is so lovely and thick with a natural curl. It's only because mine is fine that I've had it done like this. It will be easier to manage.'

'Oh well, I still like it.'

'Thank you. Come on then, Guy's calling for Barnaby in half an hour.'

Guy noticed the difference at once. 'What's all this then? Thinking of taking up photographic modelling?'

'Hardly!'

'You look very nice, tremendous in fact.' Heather blushed.

'Come on,' said Barnaby, impatiently tugging at Guy's arm.

'Hang on for a moment, young man. I hear you're doing very well at work,' he continued to Heather. 'Your diligence has impressed everyone.'

'I'm glad. It's super there, and I didn't want to let you down.'

His eyes travelled over her from head to foot, almost as though he were seeing her for the first time. 'You could never do that,' he said softly. Quickly she busied herself with Barnaby's buttons, hoping Guy wouldn't notice her heightened colour.

'That was nice of him,' said Rowena when the pair had left, 'especially as he's not very happy these days.'

'Why's that?'

'I can't remember. Something to do with his son.'

When Guy and Barnaby returned she noticed the shadows beneath Guy's blue eyes and the tight mouth with its give-away lines of tension. 'How did it go? Did your team win?'

'Yep! They played really well. Can Guy have some tea, Mum?'

'If he likes, but perhaps he's had enough of you for one day!'

'No,' Guy smiled, 'I'd love to stay.'

After they'd eaten and the children were watching television, he helped her with the drying-up and she was suddenly taken back in time to the days when Brian had stood laughing as she attempted to load the dishwasher, and he had teased her that it would be quicker to do them by hand. Suddenly Guy spoke, chasing away her thoughts.

'Heather, have you got the time and patience to listen to a problem I've got at the moment?'

'Of course. It's nice to be the one listening for a change!'

'It's about my son, Tom. He wants to come back here and live with me.'

'Why?'

'Apparently he and Greg can't get along any more. Briony says that it's six of one and half a dozen of the other, but basically it would appear to be in Tom's best interest to get away. There are two problems though.

One, he's twelve years old and we don't know each other at all. Two, even if we get along well, how do I cope with my long, unsociable hours?'

She was silent, turning it all over in her mind. 'There's nothing to be done about the first problem. That's a matter of patience on your part and willingness to adapt on his, plus a measure of good luck. As to the second, well, he's twelve years old – not exactly a baby – and I'm sure I could help out over meals and so on. I'm always in during the evenings if I'm needed.'

Guy shook his head. 'It isn't fair. Look at you! You're just getting yourself straightened out at last and I come along and try to dump this on you.'

'I'm grateful. It isn't very nice always being the one on the receiving end of assistance, you know.'

'In that case I'll tell Briony I'm willing to give it a try.'

'It's got to be more than a try. He can't come on a trial basis. There isn't any security in that, and he might behave very well at first if he thought that would ensure he could stay, and then change when you'd given your unqualified acceptance. Think how desperate he must feel being willing to come all this way to a father he scarcely knows.'

'The trouble is I'm not sure it *is* his idea. I've only heard all this from Briony. Suppose she's trying to get rid of him?'

'Would she do that? To her own son?'

'She might. She's very self-centred, and if he's making waves she might very well unload him like this.'

'In which case your welcome is all the more important.'

He put out a hand and placed it on top of hers. 'I'm very grateful. I wish I'd come to you before.'

A tremor ran through her but she kept her voice steady. 'You've listened to me enough; besides, what are friends for?'

'And I'm a friend.'

She coloured slightly. 'I hope so.'

'So do I.' There was a moment's silence. 'I'd better be off,' he said quickly.

Slowly, Spring began in earnest and Heather's spirits continued to lift. Life at the station not only provided a pleasant working environment, it also forced her to realise that compared with many other people she was very fortunate.

From time to time she was the unwilling spectator of a bereaved parent's grief, or an elderly person's stunned disbelief after a casual, profitless mugging. Even worse were the parents who had been summoned to the station after their children had been caught causing malicious damage to buildings or stealing items from general stores. Their faces always had a look of frozen disbelief, and Heather's heart would go out to them.

The counselling sessions with Dr Foster continued but, whilst Heather could now accept a great many of the doctor's comments about her own behaviour, Rowena made no appreciable progress. The stealing stopped, but more to please Guy than for any other reason, and the doctor's questions, painting therapy and apparently unconnected conversations left the child untouched and at times openly contemptuous.

One Saturday, in the middle of April, Amanda rang up. 'Heather! I feel so guilty about the Christmas debacle. It was very thoughtless of us. We've still got Rusty in case you were worried.'

'Good. How are you both?'

'Wonderful. We spent January and February in the Canaries. It was fabulous, you'd have loved it!'

'I'm sure I would,' responded Heather, wondering how her friend could be so tactless.

'The thing is, darling, we're out your way tomorrow and wondered if we could call in after lunch.'

She had already planned to take Rowena and Barnaby to the swimming pool, and she didn't look forward to listening while Amanda and Clive reminisced over lazy weeks in the sun and showed endless photographs. Just the same, she was about to say yes when her newly-acquired confidence stopped her. 'I'm sorry, Amanda,' she said firmly, 'but tomorrow's out of the question. How about next week?'

'Oh no, that's impossible. We've got sixteen people to dinner next Saturday evening, and a brunch at your old house the next day. The new owners are very sociable. They've made some fantastic alterations too.'

'Good for them. Well, I'm sorry, but there it is,' said Heather briskly. 'Give me a ring when you're next free and we'll try and fix up a meeting then.'

'All right, if you really can't change your plans.'

'I can't. Just as you can't change yours.'

'You're all well, are you? Children fully integrated into school and so on?'

'Sorry, Amanda, that's the doorbell. Bye!' She slammed the receiver back hard. Trust Amanda to disturb her just as she was beginning to forget the old life. On a whim she decided to ring Yvonne. She at least would understand why Amanda had annoyed her so much. Yvonne, however, was little comfort.

'Heather! Good grief, I thought you'd vanished from the face of the earth.'

'Yes, I'm sorry but I've been so busy that I . . . '

'Guess what? I'm going to get married again. He's really fabulous and so rich it's incredible! His name's Kevin, he's a second-hand car dealer.'

Heather could well imagine the kind of cars he dealt with. 'That's lovely,' she said with as much enthusiasm as she could muster. 'How does Rupert feel about him?'

'Well, actually he's not too keen. Kevin's sixty, you see, and I think that Rupert finds him boring. Still, he'll be off to boarding school after the wedding. That should sort him out and it will be bliss not to scrimp and save any more.'

'Yes,' said Heather slowly, 'I hope you'll be very

happy.'

'Happy?' For a moment there was a hint of the old Yvonne in the voice. 'Well, I don't know about that, Heather; but now I'm older I realise you can't have everything. Better an old man's darling etcetera!'

'Good luck,' said Heather and hung up. Strangely enough she didn't feel in the least envious, in fact she felt rather sad. Sad not only for Yvonne, but also for poor Rupert who had been spoilt to death for two years and was now being bundled away like surplus baggage. It was a kind of solution, but no longer one that she would find acceptable.

Slowly she walked over to the lounge window and watched her children playing out the front. Barnaby was right in the thick of things, but Rowena hovered on the fringe of a group of girls, her expression uncertain.

When she called them in for lunch she looked to see whether the daffodils that she had planted in November were appearing yet. Everyone else seemed to have a splendid display but her small patch of earth beneath the window was depressingly bare, except for weeds.

'Is Barnaby going out with Guy this afternoon?' asked Rowena, eating her beefburger with enjoyment. 'Is he? Because if he is, can we go shopping?'

'No he isn't, and I can't afford to go into Croydon this week. I've spent all my money.'

'All of it?' the children shouted in unison. 'What about our birthdays?'

'Well, perhaps I've got a few pennies put by for them!' Rowena was going to be ten on the 29th of April and Barnaby seven on the 30th.

'What will we do for our treat?' Barnaby wanted to know. 'Can we go to the pictures?'

'We'll have to wait and see. Remember we're going swimming tomorrow, so this afternoon you'll have to amuse yourselves.'

'I know,' shouted Rowena gleefully 'we'll play at

visiting Dr Foster!' Every mention of the name brought fresh bursts of giggles and Heather wished either the nursery rhyme or their psychiatrist, preferably the latter, had never been invented.

In the evening Guy came round. 'Sorry to disturb you,' he apologised, 'but I thought I'd let you know that Tom is on his way. I collect him tomorrow morning at the airport. I wondered if you'd like to come with me. I thought the children would enjoy the planes.'

'Yes, please!' shouted Barnaby.

Heather shook her head. 'I don't think Tom will want a party of strangers round him when he lands, do you Guy?'

Guy flushed. 'I suppose not. *I* was really wanting some moral support.'

'What's moral support? Is it money?'

'It's all right, Rowena, you can go and play Cluedo with Barnaby while we talk.'

'He's no good at it. He thought the spanner was the murderer last time!'

'Go on!' laughed Heather. 'He's got to learn.'

Once she'd gone Guy sat down. 'I'm hellishly nervous about this, Heather. I won't know what to say to the boy. In his one letter he sounded like an old man of ninety.'

'Just behave naturally, and give it time. Don't rush him.'

'What are you doing in the afternoon?'

'Swimming with the children.'

'How about coming round to tea after? Please, I need some help with this.'

Against her better judgement she agreed. When he left he kissed her cheek. 'What was that for?' she asked in surprise.

'Because I felt like it. You're very tempting in your jeans and jersey. I'm beginning to like the new look, and so are some of my colleagues. It's fortunate you can't hear the things they say. Your ears would be burning!'

'Fibber!' she laughed.

They all greatly enjoyed the swimming. Rowena kept assuring her mother that she really had swum a width, and it wasn't *her* feet Heather had seen touching the bottom half a dozen times during the journey. Laughing, Heather towelled Rowena's strong, curly hair and then made her pull her anorak hood over her head to keep out the chill wind.

'I do miss the car,' said Barnaby as they waited for a bus. 'Don't you miss it, Mummy?'

'Of course I do. I miss Daddy too.'

Rowena glanced at her in surprise. 'So do I,' she said quickly. 'In the pool I kept seeing men who looked like him. I knew they weren't, but just for a moment I'd forget and my tummy would go all funny.'

'I do that in the street,' confessed Heather, startled at her sudden ability to discuss Brian with the children. 'I expect it will stop one day.'

'It's sad-making though, isn't it?'

'Yes, I'm afraid it is. Oh look! Here's the bus.' They climbed on and Rowena sat very close to her mother all the way back.

'I wonder what Tom's like?' mused Barnaby as they were changing at home.

'Probably very shy and nervous. Remember, he hasn't seen his daddy for several years. He'll have an Australian accent too, because that's where he's lived ever since he was five.'

'Will we understand what he's saying?' enquired Rowena with interest.

'Yes, silly! It's English, but the vowel sounds are different.'

'What are vowel sounds?' asked Barnaby.

'You'll both have to wait and see.'

Guy welcomed them all with exceptional warmth, pulling a face at Heather when the children weren't looking.

'Where is he?' asked Rowena, staring round the lounge

as though expecting to find him lurking behind a chair.

'In his room. He's tired after his long flight.'

'Didn't he use an aeroplane?' asked Barnaby, and they both started their infuriating giggling.

'Trouble?' queried Heather softly.

'Yep. First of all he wouldn't say a word. When he did finally speak it was an endless flow of criticisms of the countryside, my driving and anything else he could think of until we reached home. Then I showed him his room, he walked in, closed the door and hasn't reappeared. That was two hours ago.'

'Does he know you've got visitors coming?'

'Yes, but he didn't seem in the least interested. I can't see much of Briony in him any more. When he was small he was the spitting image of her, but now he's all legs and black hair.'

Heather decided to change the subject. 'Rowena can swim.'

'That's great!'

'It would be, if it didn't necessitate her feet sprinting along the pool bottom while she makes token swimming gestures with her arms!'

He laughed. 'I'd have come to meet you if Tom hadn't stayed in his room. Did you have to wait long for a bus?'

'Not really. Besides, the sun does have a little warmth in it at last.'

'Talking of sun and spring, I must congratulate you on your daffodils. They're a very rare species, and a great credit to your gardening skill.'

'Probably the first disappearing ones!'

'Nonsense, I saw them this morning. Come on, I'll show you.' The children followed them out and Guy pointed to their strip of earth. 'Behold! The new, pygmy daffodil carefully nurtured by Mrs Lorrimer of Croydon!'

She stared in disbelief. It was true that they had appeared, but only the flowers. There was virtually no stem at all, just yellow flowers poking through the soil.

'What on earth's wrong with them? The market trader didn't say they were special.'

Guy was creased up with laughter, wiping his eyes with a handkerchief and trying to control himself. 'You ninny!' he said affectionately, 'you planted them upside down!'

'I didn't know there was a top and bottom to bulbs. I put the point in first. I thought that was there to make it easier when planting.'

'Didn't you see any roots, woman? I can't believe it! I simply can't . . .' He was overcome with mirth and turned away, struggling for composure. His laugh was so infectious that both the children joined in, but Heather's humiliation prevented her from seeing anything amusing about the situation and she walked back into Guy's hall and promptly collided with a tall slender boy standing at the bottom of the stairs.

'I'm sorry. They're all laughing at me out there and I hurried in without looking. You must be Tom. I'm Heather Lorrimer, and I live next door.'

Politely he held out a hand. 'How do you do? Why are they laughing at you?'

'I planted my daffodil bulbs upside down!'

'I hate being laughed at. Greg – my step-father – was always laughing at me because I'm not very sporty.'

'I don't like it either. I came in because I couldn't laugh at myself. I was more likely to burst into tears. Silly, isn't it!'

'Are your children sporty?' he queried, following her into the lounge.

'Not in the least. We spent an hour at the swimming pool today, but I think it's fair to say no progress was made. Barnaby whizzes around with armbands on and Rowena cheats!'

He stared at her with the same startlingly blue eyes as his father, and it was plain that in a few years time he was going to be equally devastating.

'You've met, I take it?' asked Guy, wiping his eyes. The

two children looked at their mother and the boy standing next to her. Barnaby's expression was hostile; he didn't like his mother's look of concern when she glanced at the older boy, but Rowena smiled and fiddled with her hair.

'Tom, these are Heather's two children Barnaby and Rowena.' Tom nodded. 'Say hello,' prompted Guy irritably.

'Hi!' responded his son, hands firmly in the pockets of his jeans.

'He isn't foreign at all,' said Rowena indignantly. 'He talks English.' Tom blushed furiously and Rowena smiled her sweetest smile at him. Why was it, wondered Heather, that her daughter could always be relied upon to turn every occasion into an awkward one with the minimum of effort.

'I did not say he was foreign. I was telling them, Tom, that you'd have an Australian accent; apparently they didn't understand.'

'Come on,' interrupted Guy. 'Let's have tea.'

During the entire visit it was painfully obvious that Guy and his son were ill at ease with each other. When they left Guy caught hold of Heather's arm. 'Thank you for coming. I feel so . . . I don't know . . . out of touch, I suppose.'

'I've enjoyed it. Tell him he's always welcome when I'm home. He's bound to miss his mother badly, and I might provide some womanly compassion when he needs it.'

'One night I'll take you out to dinner without any children around and we'll really make an evening of it. What do you say?'

She wanted to accept immediately, the thought of an evening out with him gave her a tingling feeling of excitement she'd never experienced before, but at the same time her stomach fluttered warningly. Calm down, she told herself, breathe slowly and steadily. 'We'll see,' she said aloud. 'I'm not one for gadding about at night.'

'And I'm not one to give up easily! Goodnight, and thanks again.'

'Tom was nice,' said Rowena sleepily as she was tucked into bed. 'I think I'll marry him when I'm grown-up. Why don't you marry Guy? We'd all have super fun, and he's got a car. No more waiting around for buses!'

'You marry for love, child, not motor cars! Where's your sense of romance?'

'It's true,' said Rowena closing her eyes, and Heather wondered what she was referring to.

The children's birthdays came and went. Heather took them to the pictures, and they didn't seem to miss the joint parties with film shows and conjurors from the old days. Heather realised that at last life in Berkshire was becoming less and less real to them. They now looked forward instead of back, and she hoped that her increased patience with them these days had helped contribute towards this. It was the meditation which had enabled her to put her problems into perspective, and she had a lot to thank Lynne for.

By May her life was going well. She frequently saw Guy at work, but he only ever gave her a polite nod. The general feeling in the office was that although highly attractive and eligible he froze off all overtures by his air of remoteness.

'I bet he's a super lover,' sighed Charlotte, just after he'd left the room. 'What do you think, Heather?'

They all turned to look at her and she went pink. 'I've no idea,' she stammered. 'I've never thought about him in that way.'

There was a chorus of laughter. The amusement was good-natured, but Heather felt abnormal. She had never thought of Brian in that way, and to do so about Guy seemed a betrayal of her love for her dead husband.

Slowly her yoga and meditation continued to improve her overall health and Dr Rawle, delighted with her progress, cut her tablets right down to one at night. She had terrible moments of grief and despair still, greater than ever at times, but the doctor explained that this was a healthy sign and cautioned her not to try and suppress her emotions.

Tom was a frequent visitor when his father was on night duty. He had passed an entrance exam for one of the area's private schools and was doing well there. Sometimes he did his homework on Heather's kitchen table and worked silently, at other times he talked to her about Australia and his life there.

'My mother doesn't write much,' he said one night. 'She promised to write every fortnight, but she doesn't, and all her letters are full of news about Greg and Sam. She never says she misses me.'

'She's probably afraid of making you homesick.'

'It isn't that,' he said flatly. 'She made me come here, and she didn't care if I was homesick or not. She said a boy's place was with his father. She should have thought about that before she took me to Australia, shouldn't she?'

'Who's Sam?'

'My half-brother. He's five and very good at ball games. He's sporty – just what Greg wanted.'

'I didn't know you had a half-brother.'

'It's meant to be a secret. You won't tell Dad, will you?'

'Not if you don't want me to.'

'He'd be cross because he'd think Mummy lost interest in me after Sam came along, and when Daddy's cross he can be quite frightening.'

'Did you like Sam?'

'Oh yes! He's all chubby and cheerful. I miss Sam more than Mum really. Is that wrong?'

'Not at all.'

'Well, I've sort of got you in Mum's place, but there isn't anyone Sam's age, so perhaps that's why.'

'Perhaps,' agreed Heather, longing to put her arms round him as she would Barnaby, but Tom was twelve and would be embarrassed. Instead she cut him a big slice of chocolate cake and gave him a glass of milk. 'There you are. We must put some weight on you now you're here.'

'Great!'

The following Sunday morning he came in as she was preparing lunch. He looked rather pale and held a letter in his hand. 'I've had a letter from Mum,' he blurted out. 'She's going to have another baby.'

Heather glanced at his worried expression. 'Is she pleased?' she asked casually.

'I think so. She wants a girl this time.'

'But the letter's upset you, has it?'

'Well, in a way. You see, she seems to forget to talk about me. I sent her my first term's report – it was really good, Dad said – but she doesn't even mention it. She doesn't ask what I want for my birthday next month either. She can't have forgotten that, can she?'

Heather sighed inwardly. The fear of rejection never seemed to leave Tom's eyes, and he was always certain that he didn't come up to people's expectations.

'I'm sure she hasn't. She's probably going to surprise you.'

He nibbled on a piece of raw carrot. 'I'm glad you live here. You don't shout at your children much, do you?'

'Not now, but I used to.'

'Do you hit them?'

'I smack them, but they don't take any notice. I don't think I'm strong enough even to make their legs sting!'

He turned away, busying himself with some shredded cabbage. 'Greg used to hit me,' he said casually, 'with his belt too. That hurt. Do you think Dad would hit me with a belt?'

'Certainly not! I've never seen him lose his temper with anyone, and I'm quite sure that a quick smack would be the most he'd ever give a child. Does he know about your step-father?'

'No. You won't tell him, will you? I mean, I think he

feels a bit strange because he doesn't know me well, and I don't want things from the past to clutter us up even more. Do you understand that?' he asked anxiously.

She bent down and kissed the top of his head. 'Yes, I understand very well. Come along, let's see what Barnaby and Rowena are up to out the front.'

That night, after the children were in bed, Heather sat and thought about their conversation. She felt that Guy ought to know, because it explained why his son was so slow in emerging from his shell, but she was reluctant to break her promise because if Tom ever found out he might cease to confide in her at all. She was still pondering the problem when Guy knocked on the back door. She was surprised to see him. For weeks now there had only been the occasional fleeting glimpse at the station, and she had begun to wonder if he was deliberately avoiding her.

'I thought I'd better let you know I was off to work,' he said. 'Tom will ring you if he needs to, but I'll be back in time to see him off to school.'

'Fine.' She expected him to turn away but he remained standing there, shifting his weight from one foot to the other.

'I hope it's all right by you, really I should have asked you first but . . . '

'What are you talking about?'

'I've booked us a table at Mario's for next Saturday at nine,' he said in a rush. 'Lynne will babysit and Tom can stay with her until we get back. If I don't see you before, I'll be round at eight. That will give us time for a drink first.'

'But I . . . '

'I know, I promised weeks ago. Unfortunately I've been tied up on a tricky case, but that will be over by then.' Heather felt flustered as the office gossip came flooding back.

'It *is* all right, isn't it?' he repeated. 'You aren't going out with anyone else that night?'

'Like who?' she laughed.

'Constable Short for one. He never stops talking about you.'

'Well, I hate to say this but I don't even know who he is!'

'That's fine by me.'

'You know, meals out aren't my . . . '

'It will do us both good. See you!' With a quick smile he went. I will not worry, resolved Heather. It's only an evening out with a friend. I don't think twice about eating at his house, so what's the big difference?

The difference was that this time there wouldn't be any children to occupy their attention and keep things impersonal. She was quite sure that he wouldn't attempt to make a heavy pass at her, but could imagine a lingering goodnight kiss, at which thought she gave a shiver of pleasure. She pictured his face close to hers, his blue eyes soft with affection as he bent to kiss her. She remembered how Brian would hold her close, his arms wrapped protectively round her, and all at once realised how much she missed the physical contact of married life. The quick kiss in passing, the casual arm round the waist. The absence of such affection left a big gap in her life, a gap that she was only now willing to acknowledge.

Then, as though determined to ruin the evening for herself before it began, she thought of Guy's girlfriends. Priscilla with the long nails, and the leggy blonde, and she knew that they wouldn't be content with lingering kisses. Undoubtedly they had experienced a far more intimate relationship with him.

For the very first time she wondered what it would be like in the arms of a really masterful and passionate man. Exciting obviously, but possibly dangerous as well. I'd like to know, she thought. I'd like to experience something different. Immediately she remembered Brian and felt like a traitor. Silently apologising to her dead husband, she made her way to bed.

That night she dreamt that she and Brian were living in Appletree Close and that she was cradled in her husband's arms in the living-room when Guy walked in. He stood watching for a moment before reaching out, pushing Brian to one side and taking Heather in his arms, trapping her in a grip of iron. She struggled silently, twisting and turning, but eventually his mouth imprisoned hers and she began to respond. As she did so his arms fastened round her neck, and to her horror she began to choke and gasp for air.

'Mummy! Mummy, wake up. The alarm's gone off.' She struggled up from the depths of sleep to find Barnaby with his arms round her neck trying to shake her awake.

'All right, darling, I'll get up now.'

'Mummy, I feel sick!' shouted Rowena, and the dream was lost in the usual morning rush and the struggle to get the children off to school.

She didn't mention her dinner date at work because she knew that Guy wouldn't want anyone at the station to know. It would be awkward if there was any serious involvement between them she realised, and wondered whether Guy had considered that.

On the Friday when she got home the children were chattering excitedly about their holiday. 'What holiday?' she asked.

Rowena sighed. 'It's Whitsun next week, we don't go to school. I brought a note home last week.'

'Why didn't you remind me?'

'Why did you forget?'

'Because I'm busy. Because I have to spend all day working in an office and . . . ' because I'm too wrapped up in myself at the moment, a small voice told her. She took a deep breath. 'Could you manage alone, Rowena, if I paid you some pocket money?'

'No!' Rowena began to grizzle. 'Barnaby won't do as I tell him. He's horrible, he . . . '

'All right, forget it. I'll have to ask Lynne.'

'I want YOU here!' shrieked Rowena, stamping her foot. 'It's meant to be a holiday, and that beastly baby spoils our games. I don't want to be alone at Lynne's. I don't like Whitsun, that's when Daddy died.'

Heather closed her eyes. How could she have forgotten? Was it really only a year since that last meeting in the hospital room? It seemed a lifetime ago, and certainly she was no longer the same woman as the one who had sat weeping in the hospital corridor. She recalled the horror of his death in the midst of so many perfect, laughter-filled days of their lives. She recalled the children splashing in the pool as Brian collapsed at her feet on the patio.

A year; one single year, and yet she could scarcely remember the woman she was then. The struggle for survival, the amount of adaptation required of them all, the enormous changes in their lives, everything had built up to such an extent that as time passed she had less and less time for looking back and remembering.

Her loss was still as great; his memory was still bitter-sweet, and yet she knew that the reserves of courage and self-assurance she had been forced to dredge up would never have been utilised had Brian lived.

Neither would there have been women like Sheila and Lynne in her life. All her women friends had been wives of Brian's contemporaries. They, like the Heather of old, were only required to be decorative and competent hostesses in return for which they spent their lives in pampered isolation. She knew that she could never live like that again.

Even her children, despite Rowena's stealing and Barnaby's nervous habits, had become more real to her. She hadn't felt like a mother until Brian died. Her children had been nothing more than attractive toys to be played with when she wanted, but always there was someone to take them away when she grew bored. At least now motherhood was a reality, with increased pleasure but also increased pain.

She was still deep in thought when Tom came in. 'Dad

says, what are you doing about next week's holiday?'

'She didn't know there was one,' said Rowena, coming sulkily back into the kitchen. 'She doesn't think about us any more, only her new job.'

Tom glanced at Heather who was glaring at her rebellious daughter. 'My Aunty Grace is coming each day; not that I need someone around, but Dad said that she's quite happy to look after Barnaby and Rowena as well.'

'At least your dad takes the trouble to make sure you're properly cared for,' said Rowena.

'Your mum's at home much more than my Dad,' he retaliated. 'I think you're luckier than me.'

'So do I,' said Barnaby as he wandered in. 'Your dad's always taking ladies out and kissing them. Our Mummy never goes out kissing.'

'Barnaby!' remonstrated Heather, smiling despite herself, but Tom was red with annoyance.

'My Dad does not go out kissing all the time. He wouldn't do that. He isn't sloppy.'

'He is too. I saw him kissing that Priscilla twice. Once in the house and once outside the front in the car. I watched from my bedroom window, they were there ages.'

'Thank your father, Tom,' said Heather quickly. 'I'll be extremely grateful.' Tom nodded and left.

Heather pulled a face. So much for her mood of self-congratulation. Without Guy her children would have been left to their own devices for a week.

Annoyed at her own stupidity she decided to use her annoyance to good purpose by clearing out the cupboard under the stairs which was used as a general rubbish dump for the entire family. At eight o'clock, tired and with an aching back, she was finished. As she straightened she put a hand to her spine and groaned.

'Is it rheumatism, Mummy? Old people do get rheumatism, it was on television the other day,' said Rowena brightly.

'I can always rely on you for the well-chosen word. No,

it isn't rheumatism – yet.'

'You have to use a stick or a cage thing that's pushed in front of you when you walk. Janice's Nana is crippled with it. Her fingers are all swollen.'

'I take it that you and Janice are still friends?'

'Oh yes! For ever and ever.'

'Good.'

Once the children were in bed Rowena wouldn't lie down. She insisted on reading aloud, which aggravated Barnaby who could hear every word and wanted to sleep.

'Do be quiet!' he shouted at her.

'I can't. I'm excited. Next week I'll see lots of Tom. I've got a crush on him.'

'What's a crush?'

'It's like loving, but even more. Guy's got a crush on Mummy!' They both shrieked with mirth.

'Stop it!' Heather shouted from the foot of the stairs. 'Don't be so stupid. Keep your stupidity for your schoolfriends please, Rowena. Now, go to sleep.'

'Boy,' called Barnaby in a penetrating whisper. 'Why was she so ratty?'

'Because it's true,' whispered his sister.

'Go to sleep!' shouted Heather, and slammed the lounge door shut.

Chapter Ten

Saturday was dry but dull and the children – over-tired from the previous night – were fractious, teasing each other from the moment they got up. In her pre-yoga days Heather's head would have been pounding by midday, but she was amazed at the difference in her now. She was even able to rationalise their behaviour and then take positive steps to quieten them down.

'This afternoon,' she announced over lunch, 'you can both do the story with illustrations that Dr Foster wants for our next counselling session.'

'It's stupid!' moaned Rowena, kicking out at Barnaby beneath the table but connecting with her mother's leg.

Heather caught her daughter's eyes. 'Behave!'

She began to grizzle. 'I didn't mean to kick you, I meant to kick Barnaby.' Her brother pulled a face and kicked heftily back at her. He was more accurate, and there was a dull thud followed by her high-pitched screams.

'Right, that's enough. There'll be no dessert. You can go to your rooms and start writing now.'

'But, Mum . . . ' moaned Rowena.

'No "buts", just do as I say.' Considering that their essays were meant to describe their feelings about the rest of the family, thought Heather humorously, they were likely to be rather hostile and biased.

At six in the evening they were watching TV while Heather went for a bath before looking carefully through her wardrobe. She picked out a deep pink cotton shift and a slender gold chain belt together with a pair of gold sling-back sandals and a cream and gold handbag. She thought that the whole outfit should look smart but not over-dressy.

As the children washed and cleaned their teeth she began to apply her make-up. She hadn't taken so much care over her appearance for a long time, and thoroughly enjoyed it. When she had finished and changed she went into Rowena's room. 'There! How do I look?'

Rowena wrinkled up her nose. 'Silly! Like a Barbie doll.'

Taken aback, Heather re-checked her appearance in the mirror. Perhaps she'd overdone the gold, or possibly the pink dress was now too girlish for her. If so, she'd better hurry and decide what was more suitable.

Barnaby peeped round the door. 'You look gorgeous, Mum. Like one of Charlie's Angels.' She hoped that was a compliment.

'Cooee!' called Lynne. 'I'm here, complete with Daisy and a good book.' Heather hurried down to greet her. Lynne took a step back in mock-surprise. 'My word! You've pulled out all the stops tonight. Lucky Guy.'

'Rowena says I look like a Barbie doll!'

'She's jealous. She doesn't want you to go out, she told me that quite firmly the other day.'

'Why?'

'Because you've devoted all your spare time to your children lately, and now they expect your complete attention day and night. This will do you all good, and with any luck Guy will ask you out again. I must say you're looking far fitter.'

'It's that fibre, fruit and vegetable book. It's given me loads more energy although I don't follow it to the letter, the children wouldn't stand for that!'

'Mummy!' called Barnaby. 'Come and say goodbye.'

Rowena feigned sleep as her mother kissed her, but Barnaby hugged her tightly. 'You smell delicious, just like fruit pastilles. Will Guy kiss you?'

'What a funny question! I don't think so, why?'

'Well, he does seem to like kissing, and on TV the men always kiss pretty girls.'

'I'm not a girl any more, I'm a woman. It makes a difference!'

Guy was waiting in the lounge when she went down. He was immaculate in a beige suit, chocolate brown shirt and beige tie. Once again Heather realised what an exceptionally attractive man he was. His eyes swept over her and he smiled. 'You look sensational! I'll have trouble keeping the wolves at bay!'

'I doubt that!'

'Right, Tom, see you later. We'd better be on our way.'

All at once Heather's mouth went dry. She hoped that her tongue wouldn't remain stuck to the roof of her mouth for the entire evening.

'Cheer up!' he joked in the car. 'Didn't your mother tell you you'd always be safe with a policeman?'

'She didn't say anything about when I grew up!' They both laughed. He leant across her to fasten her seat belt and his hair brushed her face for a second; she felt half-excited and half-frightened by the sensations this aroused in her, but he seemed oblivious of her confusion and they set off in companionable silence.

Mario's was a highly popular restaurant which had only recently opened. Even so it was plain that Guy was a regular customer. The waiter greeted him warmly and showed him to his 'usual' seat, discreetly tucked away in a corner of the dimly-lit room. In the middle of the table was a small candle inside an orange glass bowl. It flickered slightly as they sat down, casting strange shadows over their faces. For a moment Guy looked a complete stranger and Heather felt a second's panic before the shadows moved and he became familiar again.

'Do you come here a lot, Guy?'

'I don't have a standing reservation for my assortment

of girlfriends, if that's what you mean!'

'I didn't mean that at all. Your girlfriends are your own affair.'

He laughed. 'A somewhat unfortunate, if apposite, way of putting it.'

Before she could think of a reply the waiter handed them their menus and she cast her eyes down the list, horrified by the prices. She finally settled for the seafood cocktail followed by trout and almonds, reasoning that Guy had known the prices before he booked the table.

'There,' he said with a smile after the waiter had taken their orders, 'you made that decision quickly enough. This positive thinking is paying off, I take it?'

'Yes, I think so, but it isn't easy. Until last year I never had to make one single decision of any consequence and I've found it hard to learn.'

'You chose a husband,' he pointed out.

Heather was silent. 'Yes,' she said slowly, 'but somehow even that seemed to be predestined. Everyone took it for granted that we were going to marry, although my parents were worried over the age-gap, and I can't remember consciously sitting down and wondering whether I should or shouldn't make the trip up the aisle. That sounds bad, doesn't it?'

'It sounds as though you were fortunate that it turned out so well. Brian must have loved you very much.'

'Why do you say that?'

'Not many men have the time or the patience to make all the decisions concerning family life.'

'Yes,' she said softly. 'Brian loved me very much.'

'And your parents?'

She hesitated. 'Materially speaking they spoilt me, but not emotionally. They were fairly old when I was born and both were fully engrossed in their careers. At first they probably hoped that their life could remain the same after my arrival, but of course it couldn't. I always felt guilty for spoiling things for them.'

'That's dreadful!'

'I was probably over-sensitive. Perhaps they just weren't demonstrative people. Besides, they were too old to give me any sort of physical rough and tumble.'

Guy pushed his empty paté plate to one side. 'You say that, and yet you repeated the pattern by marrying a man who was over forty and proceeding to have two children by him. If you didn't like your own childhood, why did you choose the same kind for your own children?'

She leant across the table, her face animated. 'Brian wasn't a bit like my father. I was young too, which made it quite different. My mother was forty when I was born and my father forty-five; Brian was forty-three when Rowena arrived and I was twenty.'

'Forty-three isn't exactly young to start a family.'

'He already had a teenage son called Aidan, and he'd wanted a larger family but it didn't happen. He was delighted with his second family. Anyway, I loved him. I wanted to be his wife, and at the time we married I wasn't thinking about children, only my love for Brian.'

'What became of Aidan?'

'He was killed when a lorry hit his motorbike.'

'That must have been hard on Brian.'

'It made our two children all the more precious.'

'I suppose it's true that no one looks ahead to children when they marry. I didn't study Briony as a prospective mother, which is fortunate because I'd have been horribly wrong!'

'What did you think?'

He paused, his head down as he cut his steak carefully. 'I thought that she was a very attractive, high-spirited girl with a marvellous sense of humour who would never bore me.'

'And?'

'She never did bore me, I bored her instead. Well, perhaps to be more accurate, the demands of my job bored her. We were always having to cancel social engagements, and once I moved into CID it got worse. Finally she found someone who could be relied upon to be there when needed.'

'In Australia!'

'She met him here. He was working his passage round the world before settling down and taking over his father's sheep farm. His trip ended abruptly in England. He found Briony as fascinating as I did, and he had the advantage of plenty of free time. End of fairy-tale marriage that never was. Yours was one long period of bliss, I take it?'

'Why do you say it like that? As though it's wrong to be happily married? Dr Foster is always trying to make me tell her about any arguments or quarrels Brian and I had; she won't believe that there weren't any. The odd exchange of words naturally, but nothing more.'

'I suppose I'm jealous.'

'You were unlucky, that's all.'

'I'm not jealous because my marriage failed,' he said, his eyes on her face, 'I'm jealous of Brian.'

Heather's heart gave a leap of joy. He does care, she thought, he really does care. 'That's silly,' she said slowly, 'he's dead and you're alive. How can you be jealous?'

'Easily, mainly because he so obviously made you happy. I've never seen you as sparkling as you are tonight, talking about him.'

She flushed. 'You shouldn't be jealous. I'm ashamed to say that until Rowena reminded me I'd forgotten that it was exactly a year ago that Brian died. It wasn't because I'd ceased to think about him – I still miss him every day – and it wasn't because I'd deliberately blotted the date out of my mind. I forgot purely and simply because I was too busy, and I feel utterly ashamed.'

'He wouldn't see it like that,' said Guy confidently. 'If he was the kind of man you say he was, he'd be happy to know how well you were coping, even if it did stop you remembering the anniversary of his death. When I think back to the way you were when you arrived next door, all helpless and bewildered, and then look at you tonight I find the change unbelievable. You should be proud of yourself, Heather. I didn't think you had it in you to succeed. I marked you down as a poor little rich girl who would quickly look round for another wealthy protector.'

Heather flinched.

'I know,' he said quickly, 'I sound a real swine, don't I? But that's what I thought. Mind you, my feelings now, as I'm sure you know, are quite different.'

Heather's heart was racing, and all at once she found that her appetite had deserted her. 'Why did you go out of your way to help Barnaby?' she asked, trying to change the subject before she made the mistake of responding to what was probably a practised technique.

'I thought that Rowena looked a tough little girl and would cope all right, but somehow Barnaby seemed frail, and very lost. Perhaps it wasn't only that either, perhaps he filled a gap for me too. A gap that Tom had left behind. Certainly Barnaby helped me as much as I helped him.'

They both declined the sweet trolley and ordered coffee. Guy asked Heather's permission to light a cigar and she laughed. 'I didn't have you marked down as a cigar smoker, more as an anti-smoking campaigner!'

'I rarely have one – only on special occasions.'

'And this is a special occasion?'

'It is for me.'

Heather's hands trembled and she clasped them in her lap, hidden from Guy's watchful gaze. She felt excited and elated sitting opposite him. He was a man any woman would be proud to be seen with. Even more exciting was the way he was talking, showing that he cared enough about her to be jealous of Brian. At the thought a frisson of excitement went through her.

This was something entirely new. A feeling she had never experienced during her courtship with Brian. That had been safe and reassuring. This evening out was stimulating and exciting, but it didn't feel in the least safe.

She was like a swimmer standing with one foot in the edge of the water and the other firmly on the sand, not knowing whether to go ahead and take the plunge or draw back before she was too committed. It would be easy to start getting emotionally involved with Guy, but if she did then there was no doubt that her life would become far more complicated.

She found too that she was reluctant to relinquish any of her hard-fought control over her own destiny. Coward, she chided herself. You can't shut yourself away from men for ever. Try. If he really does want to start taking you out, accept. Find out what it is that the other women talk about. See if there *is* something you've been missing all these years. But if there was, she realised, then it negated her marriage, her commitment to Brian, all her previous life-style, and she couldn't bear that.

'What are you thinking about?' he queried, leaning over the table towards her. 'You look very solemn.'

'Do I? I was only thinking about how wrong you were when you summed up Rowena.'

He pulled a face. 'I thought this was to be our evening out. I hadn't planned to spend it talking about the children all the time.'

'I'm sorry. I suppose they're constantly on my mind. Barnaby's easy to understand, because he's so loving and open, but Rowena bottles everything up, and I've found it hard to understand her. Even at our clinic sessions she lies non-stop. After she goes off to do her painting I tell Dr Foster, but she only says, "How very interesting. Why's that, do you suppose?" as though I'm the expert!'

'Has the stealing stopped?'

'Yes. That stopped as soon as Mrs Charles caught her.'

'So what does Dr Foster say now?'

Heather sipped at her coffee. 'The same thing every time. It's packaged slightly differently but the message is always clear enough. There's nothing wrong with Rowena; it's me. I have to grow up before Rowena can feel safe enough to entrust me with her fears. I've been the little girl for too long and I'm not willing to relinquish the role. Once I do then Rowena will sense it and turn to me for comfort. But, Guy, I honestly do feel that I have grown up, yet Rowena's no different.'

'You most certainly have. I, for one, don't think of you as a little girl!'

'I wish you'd tell Dr Foster that. According to her, even my gasto-enteritis was psychosomatic. I felt I couldn't cope any more, and so I collapsed, forcing other people – i.e. you and Lynne – to take over.'

'Did she really say that?' Guy sounded both incredulous and angry.

'Yes, those were her exact words.'

'The woman's plainly an idiot. The sooner you stop seeing her the better. She's not helping Rowena and she's certainly not helping you any more. When are you due to go again?'

'Next Thursday.'

'Cancel it.'

'Guy, you've said that before but I have to go. Besides, some of the things she's said have been true. I may not have liked hearing them, but that doesn't mean they were invalid.'

'Look, just because the woman was right early on doesn't mean that she's infallible. Maybe she was good for you at one stage in your life, but she certainly isn't any more. You tell me that you've finally grown-up, well prove it. You don't need a psychiatric prop – which is all she is – and Rowena isn't improving, so break away. You know in your heart it's right. Let's see you act on your own initiative for once.'

'Is it that important?' she asked softly.

'It is to me, Heather. I want to know that I'm taking out a confident young woman. I'm too old for female versions of Peter Pan.'

She was flustered and took refuge in humour. 'You

make me sound like a dog you have to exercise!'

He smiled. 'Now I know where Rowena gets that clever-clever act from, and I thought you were a romantic person!'

'I was, but I've learned that it's unrealistic.'

'I think there is a time and place for a touch of romance.'

'Like tonight?' she asked, her breathing uneven.

'Like tonight,' he agreed, and his eyes glittered in the candlelight.

'Sometimes you frighten me,' she said quietly.

'Me? What do I do that frightens you?'

'Nothing, at least not in the way I made it sound. It's just that when I'm with you I'm frightened of what I may discover about myself. Myself, and the way I used to live.'

'Meaning?'

She looked troubled. 'I'm afraid of discovering that some of the things I previously believed weren't true.'

'No one remains the same, Heather. Events, people, time, they all combine to change us. Because Briony left me it doesn't mean that once, for a short period, we didn't truly love each other. If I ever fall in love again I don't suppose it will be in the same, intense, unrealistic way because I'm no longer a young and impulsive man. That doesn't make my feelings for her when we married any the less genuine. There are many different kinds of love, Heather.'

'I suppose there must be. I used to think that there was just one person for each of us; someone we were predestined to meet, who would fulfill our needs and enable us to live happily ever after.'

'You say "our" needs, but I take it you mean the woman's?'

'Yes.'

'Men have emotional needs too. Marriage is a partnership, not a one-sided contract.'

'I know that now, which does prove that I'm a little

more mature these days.'

'Exactly! Now, drink up your coffee and we'll get back. Tom will be exhausted.'

'It's been a wonderful evening,' she said on the drive home. 'I really appreciate all the things you do for us. There must be times when you wish I'd never bought the house next to yours.'

He gave her a quick glance. 'Only at the beginning. Never after that, as I'm sure you know.'

When they walked into the house Lynne looked up from her crochet work and noticed Heather's sparkling eyes and heightened colour. 'Have a good time?'

'Lovely, thanks. I expect you're tired, Tom.'

'A bit. Hi, Dad! Can I have the door key? I'll be getting off to bed.'

Guy tossed it to his son. 'Here you are. I won't be too late.'

'Goodnight then. Thanks for the evening, Lynne.'

She grinned. 'My pleasure. I hope I've converted you!'

'And what, may I ask, does that mean?' queried Guy.

'I've been trying to wean him off the fried breakfasts and red meat that the pair of you apparently enjoy every day. I've given him some leaflets on the dangers of excess animal fats, and the importance of fibre in our diet.'

'Sounds like a fun evening! I enjoyed my T-bone steak, french fries and fully caffeinated coffee very much, so please don't start telling me about damage to my heart. I'm too full to cope!'

'I know the unconvertible when I meet them. Mind you, I've succeeded with Heather and see how fantastic she's looking. Come on Daisy, home to bed with a good book, or a friend who's read one!'

'That baby is the most placid I've come across,' remarked Heather after Lynne had left. 'I've hardly ever heard her cry.'

'Too full of fibre to utter a sound, I imagine!'

She laughed. 'I hadn't thought of that. Would you like a

brandy before you go?'

'Sounds perfect.' He put his glass on the coffee table and then settled himself on the sofa next to Heather. She felt nervous and on edge. When he put an arm casually along the back of the sofa she jumped and his eyes were thoughtful but he didn't remove his arm. Instead he gently removed her glass with his free hand and turned her face towards him.

'You look beautiful tonight, Heather. I felt that every man in the restaurant must envy me.'

'Don't be silly! Your other girlfriends are beautiful. I'm reasonably attractive when I take a lot of trouble.'

'*You're* beautiful,' he repeated and put his lips on hers. His mouth was soft and tender, and she relaxed against him. 'I've wanted to do that all the evening,' he whispered as they drew apart.

Heather's lips were tingling and there was a strange aching feeling in the pit of her stomach. She looked at him with wide, startled eyes. Now he drew her close to his body and his arms tightened round her as he bent to kiss again, only this time his lips were firmer, more demanding, and his hands were moving insistently over her back, fingers searching for a zip that he could undo.

She was so caught up in the sensations his kisses were arousing that it was only when his fingers finally made contact with her bare flesh that she realised what was happening. She gave a gasp and struggled to free herself; immediately he released her and lifted his mouth from hers.

Alarmed by her immediate response to his lovemaking she stood up and straightened her clothing, her breathing rapid and shallow. Guy studied her carefully, his face an impassive mask. 'Don't you think Tom will be wondering where you are?' she murmered, acutely aware of her tousled appearance.

'He knows where I am.'

'But he's expecting you back; you said you wouldn't be late.'

'So I did,' he said lazily, and got reluctantly to his feet.

For a moment they stood face to face. He put a hand to her face and stroked one smooth cheek. 'Now you look even more desirable,' he commented, then he took his hand away.

'I'm taking Tom to a cricket match tomorrow. Would you all like to come?'

She was too confused by her emotions, too intensely aware of his overwhelmingly masculine presence to feel confident of managing a normal family outing with him. 'I can't,' she said quickly. 'I've promised Lynne I'll see her about an Open University course.'

'I see.'

'Barnaby and Rowena would love to come, I'm sure.'

'I'm sure they would too. But you can't be persuaded to join us?'

'No, really, I . . . '

His eyes became cool and remote. 'I understand. Don't worry, I've never forced my company on a woman yet and I don't intend to start now. I'll collect the children at eleven.'

She walked with him to the front door. 'It really was a marvellous evening,' she said. 'I can't remember when I last enjoyed myself so much.'

'Good. Well, I'd better get back then. As you so rightly said, Tom will be waiting. Goodnight, Heather.'

He left her without even the briefest of kisses and she knew, knew with complete certainty, that she had ruined everything because of her own stupidity.

When Guy called for the children next morning he was cool and over-polite towards Heather.

'I don't suppose you feel much like playing cricket after last night,' she joked. 'Or do wine and brandy improve your co-ordination?'

'I feel fine, thank you. Come on you two, Tom's waiting.'

She kissed the children, chilled by the rebuff, and waved out of the window until they had gone. For a moment she hesitated, then picking up her cardigan, she ran to Lynne's house, desperately hoping she would be in.

'Hello there! I didn't expect to see you today. Where's lover-boy?' she laughed.

'He's not my lover, and it isn't funny,' said Heather, pushing past her friend. 'The evening was ruined after you left, Lynne, ruined!'

'Steady on. Too much drama's bad for Daisy's disposition! Sit there, I'll put the kettle on.' While she waited Heather reflected miserably on the previous evening. 'Right,' said Lynne cheerfully, bringing in two mugs of tea. 'Now then, tell me all about it. You both looked pretty happy when I left.'

'We were, that's what makes it so awful. Lynne, he isn't at all like I thought.'

'In what way?'

Heather coloured. 'He was . . . Well, we were kissing, you know, and it was nice. It's been a long time since I've had any affection, and . . . '

'Affection? You're not a pet cat!'

'If you don't want to hear . . . '

'Sorry! Go on.'

'As I said, it was lovely. I was enjoying it, and then . . . then he started trying to undo the zip at the back of my dress. I couldn't believe it. What sort of a woman does he think I am?'

'A perfectly normal one, I imagine.'

'You mean all women sleep with men on their first date?' Heather asked, acidly.

Lynne burst out laughing, but stopped abruptly as Heather's face crumpled and she began to cry. She put an arm round her friend's shaking shoulders. 'Heather, he wasn't trying to get you into bed, he was only trying to be a little more physical than lingering kisses. Nice as they are, what comes after is usually better!'

'In other words he wanted to maul me about.'

'For God's sake, Heather, grow up! When a man makes love to you he is not mauling you around. He's paying you a compliment. You're a widow with two children, not a green girl. Think back to your early days with Brian. There must have been some sort of physical contact before you married.'

'Not a lot. He respected me, and understood how I felt. Of course we held hands and kissed, but that was all.'

'Wow! The earth really moved for you, didn't it! Was there something wrong with him? Health-wise I mean.'

'No!'

'Then it was you. You say he understood how you felt. Well, how did you feel?'

Heather shrugged. 'You know.'

'I'm sorry but I don't. I'm a very physical person. I like touching and being touched. When I'm in love I enjoy the man making love to me. I feel marvellous, as though I could take on the world.'

'I don't like losing control of myself,' said Heather slowly. 'When we were first married sex was pleasant, comfortable . . .'

'Sounds like Darby and Joan.'

'I enjoyed it,' she said defiantly. 'Then, after a time, Brian became more assertive, and I didn't like that. I hated not knowing what I was doing, feeling myself losing awareness of what was happening. I told Brian, and he stopped at once. From then on it was always quiet, soothing. He was a very kind man.'

'He was a bloody fool!' said Lynne sharply. 'I'm sorry, Heather, but he was. Just as you were starting to discover what being a woman really meant he let you revert to being a child again. Apart from this peaceful sex life it couldn't have been much different from living with your father.'

'But I didn't like it the other way.'

'You did! Your body did, but your innate inhibitions – probably due to your old-fashioned childhood – came to the surface and you ran away from it all. Christ, Heather, there's a whole new world waiting for you, and you've got a fantastic bloke like Guy willing to show you. I'd change places with you any day.'

For a moment Heather was silent. 'You mean, he wasn't being unreasonable? He didn't intend going all the way?'

'That's a very old-fashioned expression but no, he didn't intend that. Sex on the sofa with the children upstairs would hardly be Guy's scene!'

'So I was stupid.'

'Silly certainly, and he must be thoroughly confused. You looked like a woman who was falling in love when you walked in last night.'

'Rubbish!'

'Is it? Don't you think about him a lot? Hope to see him at work? Long for even a small glimpse of him at home?'

'Yes, but . . . '

'Then I'm right. Fortunately he's equally keen on you.'

'He *isn't*. He goes out with elegant women, all tall, slender, and without any children underfoot.'

'That doesn't mean he's in love with them. If there was anyone special he wouldn't take so much trouble over you.'

'Perhaps you're right,' Heather said hopefully.

'I am, and the sooner you apologise to him and explain, the better. He'll understand, he seems pretty sensitive – for a man!'

Heather sank back in the armchair. 'I will,' she vowed fiercely. 'I'll tell him when he brings the children home.'

'Good. And once you're going out regularly ask him to find me a friend!'

'I thought you enjoyed your independence?'

'I do, but the occasional night out wouldn't come amiss. Daisy's not too hot on doling out compliments!'

When she got home Heather felt far better for the talk. From lunch-time on she spent most of the afternoon standing hidden behind her bedroom curtains waiting for Guy's car to appear. At last, at seven o'clock, it drew up outside her house and she watched as Barnaby and Rowena climbed out. Quickly she ran out, determined to speak to Guy before her courage failed. He was sitting behind the steering wheel with Tom at his side, and showed no sign of noticing Heather's presence. It was Tom who wound down his window.

'Did you have a good time?' Heather asked him, her eyes flicking towards his father.

'Yes thanks. Dad made fifty-eight not out.'

'Well done, Guy.'

He turned an unsmiling face towards her. 'It wasn't difficult, their best bowler was injured.'

'Guy, about last night . . . '

'It's all right, I got the message quite clearly. Now if you don't mind I'd like to go on in and get changed.'

'But you don't understand.'

'Oh yes I do, Heather. I definitely do. So long, children.'

'Bye,' they chorused, and rushed indoors, leaving Heather staring after the car, biting on her bottom lip in frustration.

Later that evening she saw Priscilla arrive, her hair piled on top of her head and her dress clinging to every perfect curve. Heather disliked her so much that it was like a physical pain, and she disliked her even more when she and Guy left together twenty minutes later, Guy's arm casually round Priscilla's waist.

Chapter Eleven

The next few weeks were agony for Heather. She didn't know when she felt worse; the times that she didn't see Guy for day after endless day either at work or home, or the times when she did and he either walked briskly through the office without sparing her a glance, or greeted her coldly whenever their children brought them into contact.

'I'm getting fed up with Priscilla,' said Tom one Saturday. 'She's getting very bossy. She told Dad that I stayed up too late, and said "The 'A' Team" was too violent!'

'What did your dad say?' asked Rowena.

'He just laughed and said that ours was a man's house and if she didn't like it she'd better stay away. She went kind of quiet after that.' Silently Heather applauded Guy, but her pleasure was short-lived.

'We're going to her parents' house for tea tomorrow. I've got to wear a *shirt*,' he added in horror.

'I think you look nice in your summer shirts,' said Rowena.

'You would, you're another stupid girl!'

All that evening the news niggled away at Heather. It looked as though Guy was being taken to meet Priscilla's parents for approval, which probably meant that he had marriage on his mind. She imagined him married, living next door with Priscilla so that every time Heather stepped into her garden she might come face-to-face with one of them, or even both, hand-in-hand and blissfully happy.

In bed she decided that she would never be able to stand such a situation, she would have to move. Then reality intruded, reminding her that she couldn't afford a move, and the children were only just settling down in their new school. If Guy and Priscilla married she would have to accept it. This was so horrible to contemplate that it took a long, concentrated period of meditation before she was able to sleep.

The next week everyone at work began talking about the police dance in the middle of August, and speculating on who would attend, and – even more important – with whom.

'You should see the Chief Constable's wife,' laughed Charlotte. 'She's frightful, all frizzy blue perm and long frocks!' Everyone giggled. 'It's perfectly true,' she assured a doubtful-looking Heather, 'you wait and see.'

'I don't think I'll be coming. I haven't anyone to bring, and it wouldn't be much fun on my own.' The others exchanged quick glances and then got on with their typing.

At lunch-time Heather was eating her sandwiches when she suddenly realised that everyone else had gone out and she was alone in the room with Police Constable Short, who was diligently searching through the same filing drawer time after time.

'Can I help?' she enquired.

'It's all right, I'm just . . . Mrs Lorrimer . . . '

'Heather, please!'

'Heather, I wondered if you'd like to come to the dance with me. It's usually a tremendous evening and I'd very much like to take you.'

She stared at him in astonishment, and then remembered Guy making some comment about the fair-haired young man. 'I'm sorry,' she said gently, 'but I'm not a great one for socialising, but I do really appreciate you asking me.'

'Well, perhaps a drink one evening? Any evening. I know you've got children to consider.'

She shook her head. 'No, thank you.' His face clouded with disappointment, and she wished that she could forget Guy's dark hair and blue eyes, the strength of his arms and the way his eyes crinkled up when he smiled, and instead be interested in Constable Short. However, she couldn't, and it was kinder to let him know at once. Quietly he slipped out of the room.

When they were all going home Heather could tell that the women were waiting to hear what had happened during the lunch-break. 'Darren Short invited me to the dance today,' she said casually, 'but I said no. It was kind of him to ask me, wasn't it?'

'Why did you refuse?' queried Charlotte in surprise.

'Because I don't particularly like him.'

'You don't even know him!'

'And I don't want to!' snapped Heather, fed up with their attempts at matchmaking. 'I'll pick my own men, thank you very much.' There was an awkward silence as she hurried out of the cloakroom.

That Thursday evening Tom was doing his algebra homework on Heather's kitchen table. After forty minutes he sighed. 'It's no good: I can't understand the question let alone find the answer. I'll ask Dad in the morning.'

'How was Sunday tea?' Heather asked casually.

'We didn't go. There was some trouble on and Dad had to work. Priscilla was raging mad. She yelled and screamed at him until he told her to . . . well, go away. We haven't seen her since, and Dad doesn't think we will. I'm glad; she was like a witch with her long nails and ghastly hair!'

'She was very attractive,' said Heather, determined to be fair.

'I think you're much prettier.'

'Thank you, Tom,' she responded, wishing that his father felt the same.

The following weekend, Heather decided to tackle the back garden. As pushing the lawnmower was hard work, she paused for a break half-way.

'No machete needed this summer!' a voice called from behind her. She spun round and found Guy watching her.

'No,' she laughed.

'How's work?'

'Fine.'

'Children behaving?'

'As far as I know.'

'I hear you've turned down the love-sick Darren Short.'

Heather moved towards the wire fencing separating their gardens. She couldn't understand why he was being so friendly all at once. 'Yes, I did. Who told you?'

'Gossip travels fast in the station, as you should know. May I ask why you rejected him?' His voice was light, almost teasing, and she found that her legs felt weak and her pulse was racing.

'If you must know it was because I don't have any particular feelings for him. He isn't my type.'

'Isn't he? Well, who is?'

She gave a small smile. 'That's my secret.'

'If I asked you to the dance would you come with me? Or aren't I your type either?'

'You'd have to ask to find out.' She was enjoying this verbal flirtation. It was a new experience for her but she was astonished to find that she knew instinctively how to play the game.

'Very well then; will you come to the dance with me?'

'Do you really want me to?'

'Obviously, otherwise I wouldn't have asked.'

'Then I'd be delighted to come.'

He gave a smile of pure pleasure.

'About our last evening,' she began hesitantly.

'It's all right, I understand. I frightened you off, and I'm very sorry.'

'But who . . . ?'

'Let's just say a mutual friend told me, and I'm very glad she did.'

'You mean Lynne?'

'Mummy!' shouted Barnaby, tearing out of the back door. 'May I have an ice cream? The van's just coming down the road.'

She glanced at Guy. 'I'll have to go in and find some change, but I look forward to the dance.'

'So do I,' he said softly.

'I'm so glad!' said Lynne when Heather told her the news. 'It was all quite ridiculous. The pair of you made a mountain out of a molehill. I think Guy's male ego was somewhat bruised.'

'He wouldn't let me explain, and in the end the situation became impossible. We were almost avoiding each other. Oh, Lynne! I'm so excited. What shall I wear? Do you think it's long dresses or not?'

'You'd better ask at work.'

Three days later she did just that. Everyone stopped typing and Charlotte stared at her in frank surprise. 'I didn't think you wanted to come? You said it wasn't your sort of thing.'

'Well I've changed my mind; it's a woman's prerogative, isn't it?'

They laughed. 'Sure, well you *can* wear a long dress, but mostly it's cocktail-type clothes. I bet Darren's pleased.'

'I'm not going with him,' said Heather reluctantly.

'Who are you going with? A boyfriend from your past or something?'

'Actually, I'm going with Guy Harrison.'

There was a moment of stunned surprise as all the women looked at each other. 'Good for you,' said

Charlotte faintly, and no one spoke again for the rest of the morning.

'Do you think it's too low in the front?' asked Heather anxiously as she paraded before Lynne and Sheila in her living-room.

'It's lower still at the back!' laughed Lynne.

'I know, but that doesn't matter so much. It's the front I'm worried about.'

'It's stunning,' said Sheila firmly. 'Personally I think you're far too good to be wasted on a policeman, but there it is. You're over twenty-one, and I don't suppose you want to hear why I think this is a mistake?'

'Of course she doesn't, you misery! You do realise, Heather, that you won't be able to wear much underneath the dress?'

'I've got a black strapless bra that I thought would be all right.'

'It's the right colour certainly,' said Lynne, once again eyeing the clinging black satin dress that had sparkling sequins round the tight-fitting waist and hem, 'but is it backless as well?'

'No.'

'Then forget it. It's all right. You're perfectly respectable, or respectable enough. At least it isn't conventional. I quite expected your "little black number" to have a puritan collar and cuffs!'

'I hope Guy likes it. I've never worn anything like this before, but somehow I thought it would help me live up to Priscilla and the other blonde girl that calls in from time to time.'

'Big Priscilla would have over-filled that dress. As I've never seen the blonde I can't comment on her, but the important thing is to be yourself, not someone you think Guy wants you to be.'

Five hours later Heather was sitting in Guy's car, a black lace shawl across her arms for later in the evening.

'You look . . . amazing,' said Guy as he carefully closed the passenger door. 'I doubt if anyone will recognise you as the diligent typist who never stops to smile at the men as they pass through.'

'Well, that's work, and this is pleasure.'

'It most certainly is!'

Heather was amazed at the amount of attention she received from men she scarcely knew during the course of the evening. Even the Chief Constable beamed paternally at her, and demanded the honour of the opening dance after the meal. He was a big man but light on his feet, and Heather – who loved dancing – thoroughly enjoyed herself. After he had returned her to Guy's side she was radiant. 'He's a super dancer!' she enthused. 'I'd never realised what a friendly man he is either. The other girls said he was stand-offish.'

'So he is, usually. Mind you, he's the right height to take full advantage of your dress.' He sounded annoyed and refused to meet Heather's eyes.

'I thought you liked the dress.'

'I do, but only for me. I don't care to see other men peering down the top of it.'

'He didn't! We were talking quite a bit, that's why he looked down on me.'

'Yes, and bananas have zips on them! I wasn't born yesterday. Come on, this time it's my turn.'

His obvious jealousy gave her a thrill of pleasure. Lynne had been right: if he didn't care then he wouldn't be annoyed.

At four a.m., exhausted but happy, they arrived back at Appletree Close. Guy drove the car to the back of his own house and turned off the engine. 'Lynne's staying overnight, isn't she?'

'Yes. Where's Tom?'

'At my mother's. Do you want to come in for a coffee?' He was watching her carefully as he spoke, and she hoped he couldn't sense the sudden delight that flooded through her.

'Thank you,' she responded quickly, and got out of the car.

Once in his living-room he turned on the stereo and made some filter coffee. He put the coffee down on the nearest table and then took hold of Heather's hands and pulled her onto the sofa. Taking her face between his hands he kissed her slowly and deliberately, his obvious passion scarcely restrained. This time she responded with equal fervour, and then his lips were all over her face, neck and the delicate hollow at the base of her cleavage. His small, butterfly kisses sent tingles of pleasure through her and she moved instinctively closer to him and clasped her arms round his neck. With a smothered groan he began to move his hands confidently over her body. Her head whirled as sensations coursed through her body, sensations so pleasurable she could hardly bear them, and then, abruptly, he pushed her gently but firmly away from him.

'I think we'd better drink that coffee,' he said curtly, and stood up.

'What is it? Did I do something wrong?'

'No my dear Heather, you did everything right. That's what's wrong. We've both had a lot to drink, and now is neither the time nor the place to get carried away. If we continue like that I can't be held responsible for my actions!' and though he laughed there was suppressed anger in his voice.

Quickly Heather stood up. 'I'd better go, or I won't be able to get up in the morning.'

He stood in front of her and tilted her chin. 'You're very beautiful in that black creation. Beautiful and far too tempting.'

She smiled. 'I now know you too well to worry. I trust you completely, Guy.'

'Perhaps you shouldn't: I'm only human, remember!

Go on then, home before my good resolutions falter!' At the door he gave her the lightest of kisses, a mere brushing of lips. 'Sleep well,' he whispered, but she was far too excited to sleep.

Over breakfast Lynne grinned at her friend. 'No need to ask how it went. You look like a cat that's been at the cream!'

'It was tremendous. You were right. It was stupid of me to be frightened of Guy. I've never had such a wonderful evening.' As soon as the words were spoken she felt a rush of guilt over Brian, but Lynne didn't seem shocked.

'I'm glad. You deserve a few breaks at last. Are you going to tackle that Open University course next September?'

'Yes, I'm looking forward to it. Do you know, these days I've actually got surplus energy, and all thanks to you.'

'Nonsense! I made suggestions, but it was you who had to carry them out. It must have taken quite a lot of will-power at first.'

'Yes,' admitted Heather. 'I suppose it did.'

No sooner had Lynne left than Sheila came round to find out what had gone on. 'Was your policeman bowled over by the dress?'

'Yep! It was super, we had a great time.'

'You really are keen on him, aren't you?'

'Yes, it's unbelievable but I am. He's completely different from Brian, far more abrasive and less patient, but when I'm not with him everything seems pointless and dull.'

'Sounds like love!'

'Does it? Perhaps it is.'

Sheila sat down by the kitchen table, her face sour. 'God, Heather, how could you? With *him* of all people.'

'What do you mean? When I first came here you said you fancied him yourself.'

Sheila looked apologetic. 'Did I? Well, I'm feeling rather jaundiced about the police right now. They picked

Scott up last week for siphoning petrol from cars on the estate. He's already been in trouble twice; once for shoplifting and once for throwing stones through glass windows of houses that were nearly completed. Now he's got to go to court again.'

'I had no idea,' said Heather quietly. 'I am sorry. You must feel dreadful.'

Sheila lifted her head. 'I don't need sympathy from you. After all, Scott isn't the only child to go round shoplifting, is he? It's just unfortunate that I don't have a policeman for a boyfriend.'

'What on earth are you talking about? Rowena did steal money from school, but I told you about that ages ago. It wasn't shoplifting, although it was equally wrong.'

'What about Woolworths?'

Heather looked blank. 'What do you mean?'

'Come off it! Even Barnaby knows that Rowena goes round pinching things from Woolworths whenever she gets the chance.'

'She does not! It did happen, but that was months ago. She doesn't do it any more.'

'Doesn't she? I should ask your friend Guy if you don't believe me. Barnaby says Guy knows all about it. Now, if you don't mind, I've a lot of baking to do.'

'I didn't ask you to come,' Heather pointed out as Sheila left.

After tea, while Barnaby watched television, Rowena sat at the kitchen table crayoning. Heather hesitated, not wanting to disturb the happy atmosphere of the day. Then she looked more closely at her daughter and realised that the crayons were brand new. A plastic case full of long, coloured crayons with the price tag still on them.

'Where did you get those crayons, Rowena?' she asked sharply. Rowena kept her head down and didn't answer.

'Rowena, answer me, please.'

'Janice gave them to me,' she mumbled.

Heather walked straight to the telephone. 'What's her

number?'

'I don't know.'

It was nearly the end of the summer holidays, and highly unlikely that Janice had had the opportunity to give Rowena anything, but she intended to make quite sure. 'All right, where does she live? What's her surname?'

'I don't know! I don't know!'

'Rowena, you must know her surname. What do they call her on the register?'

Rowena was scarlet in the face. 'I can't remember.'

'If you don't remember, I shall ring up your teacher and ask her for Janice's address. I can easily make up a reason for doing so.'

'No, don't, Mummy! Please don't.'

'Then you tell me.'

'I can't.'

'Of course you can. Her name, please, Rowena.'

'She hasn't got one!' shouted Rowena. 'There *is* no Janice. I haven't got any special friend. I haven't got any friends at all. I made her up so that you didn't know. Now you've spoilt it! I hate you for bringing us here and making me go to that horrid school.'

Heather was stupefied by shock. 'Darling, I had no idea you were so lonely. Please, tell me where you got the crayons and then once that's sorted out we'll talk about your school.'

For a moment Rowena stared defiantly at her mother, then the tears began to form in her eyes and she wiped them away with the back of her hand. 'I took them,' she whimpered.

'When?'

'On Saturday, when we all went into Croydon. You were busy looking at the school blouses and I saw these and just took them. I'm sorry, Mummy.'

'How often have you "just taken" things from shops lately?'

Rowena was crying in earnest now. 'Often, well, quite

often. I don't mean to, Mummy. I can't seem to stop myself. I won't go to prison, will I? I don't want to go to prison.' She was sobbing loudly but Heather, infuriated by the fact that Sheila had known while she, the child's own mother, had not, was far from sympathetic.

'You deserve to,' she said angrily. 'What an example to set Barnaby. And suppose Guy found out? What do you think he would do if he knew?'

'Lock me up?' Her crying doubled in intensity. 'Don't tell him, Mummy. I don't want to be locked up. I want my Daddy. Please, don't tell him. I wish my Daddy was here.'

'I'm very glad he isn't. He'd have been horrified, and so am I. I'm going to put Barnaby to bed and then you can show me every single thing you've taken and we'll go into town next weekend so that you can give them back yourself.'

'No!' screamed Rowena. 'I won't. They'll take me to court. I'll be taken away from you and Barnaby. Mummy, don't make me take them back, please.'

Heather, remembering the stunned faces of disbelieving parents at the police station, and her private belief that they must have neglected their children in some way, was angrier than she had ever been in her life.

'It's too late for all this crying. You should have thought about the consequences before you did it. I thought this was behind us. I can't understand you at all.'

'I was lonely,' sobbed Rowena, but Heather was already walking away. All the time she was putting Barnaby to bed she could hear Rowena sobbing. Although horrified by the revelation of the child's solitude, her overwhelming emotion was one of anger that a daughter of hers could be so dishonest and deceitful for such a length of time.

'Why's Rowena crying?' asked Barnaby, pulling on his pyjamas. 'Is it about Woolworths?'

Heather stared at him. 'If you knew, why didn't you tell me about it?'

'I wanted to, but she made me promise not to. I did sort of tell by mistake once, and that's why she broke my china Rusty. She said that if I told again she'd throw Marmaduke over the garden wall.'

'But you told Sheila, didn't you?'

'No! I only told Scott.'

'That's even worse! Why didn't anyone tell me? We should have kept going to that clinic, however much we hated it. I wouldn't have stopped if I'd known that she was stealing again.'

Still simmering with fury she kissed him goodnight and hurried down the stairs to a strangely quiet kitchen. Once there she stared around the room. The crayons were still on the table and Rowena's chair had been pushed back, but there was no sign of the child herself.

'Rowena! Come along, I'm not going to search high and low for you. Come out at once.'

There was no answer. With steadily increasing fear Heather searched the back garden, the living room and even the bathroom. Her heart thumping behind her rib cage, she told Barnaby to stay in bed and then set off round the estate, searching in every possible hiding place. She hunted and called, but it was useless. Rowena had vanished.

Chapter Twelve

Thirty minutes later Heather returned to the house, desperately hoping that Rowena would be back in the kitchen, but only Barnaby was there, standing desolately in his pyjamas and crying quietly to himself. The sound of Guy's car drawing up sent Heather flying out to meet him.

He smiled broadly as he greeted her. 'My goodness! The enthusiasm of the woman. That's the kind of welcome I like!'

'Rowena's run off,' Heather blurted out, and his smile vanished.

'When? How long ago?'

'About forty minutes.'

'What happened?'

'Sheila told me that Rowena was shoplifting again. I didn't believe her until I saw Rowena using a brand new set of crayons. She tried to lie her way out of it, but in the end confessed and I lost my temper. I can't believe it! Sheila knew, Scott knew, Barnaby knew, I'm surprised that you didn't know, but *I* didn't have a clue. I've never been so humiliated.'

'As a matter of fact I knew too, but I'll talk to you about that later. The important thing is to find Rowena; not because of your injured pride but because she must be terrified out of her wits and might be anywhere at all. She's quite likely to go off with the first sympathetic person she meets, if you've given her the sort of tongue-lashing I suspect you have.'

'It's my fault, is it?' shouted Heather, oblivious of being outside where everyone in the close could hear her. '*I'm* responsible for her being a thief and a liar. There was never even a Janice. The girl didn't exist. What do you think of that?'

'I think it's very sad,' he said quietly, 'and so should you.'

'You're no different from Dr Foster,' cried Heather. 'In fact I can't imagine why you told me to stop seeing her, unless you felt that you could do the job as well yourself!'

He didn't even bother to answer, but took hold of her arm and steered her back into the house where Barnaby sat quietly, his fingers in his mouth.

'Have you rung the police, Heather?'

'No! I don't want them to know about the shoplifting.'

'What on earth does that matter? Surely what's important is that she's found, and as quickly as possible. I'll ring them.'

Heather sat quietly in a chair, shaking from head to foot and trying to stop herself picturing a stranger enticing Rowena into his car with sympathy and false promises.

Why, oh why, had she chosen that particular moment to lose her temper so completely? Why hadn't she realised that poor Rowena needed help and support, not punishment?

'You're sure about that?' Guy was saying urgently, and she lifted her head at the change in his voice. 'Where?' he continued. She stood up and reached for the phone. 'We'll go straight there,' he said and replaced the receiver. When he turned to Heather his expression was gentle. Putting his hands on her shoulders he held her firmly. 'You've got to be brave, Heather. Rowena's had an accident, she's being taken to the operating theatre now. Get Lynne to come and stay with Barnaby, then we'll go straight to her.'

'Where is she?' she whispered, her mouth so dry she could scarcely form the words. 'Is she badly hurt? How do you know it's Rowena?' She couldn't believe it, didn't want to believe it.

'They described her clothes; the pink dress with white flowers, and that teddy bear brooch she got in last year's crackers.'

'Is she badly hurt?'

'She is quite ill. There's concussion and a fracture of her left leg. They'll tell us the details at Croydon General Hospital.'

'What's happened?' asked Barnaby, his face paper-white.

Heather put her arms round him. 'Rowena's hurt her leg and had a bang on the head. Lynne's coming down to stay with you while Guy takes me to see her. You'll be all right, won't you?'

His lip quivered. 'I suppose so. Will she die?'

'Of course not! I'm just going to pack some things in a bag for her and I'll be back as soon as I can. She'll be fine in a little while.'

'Is it my fault? Because I told Scott?'

'No, Barnaby. It's my fault, because I lost my temper.' He looked relieved.

'I'll never forgive myself,' she told Guy on the journey. 'How could I be so insensitive?'

'Don't make things worse than they are. Only saints behave perfectly all the time, and I personally don't know any. Do you?'

'It isn't funny, I . . . '

'Relax. Stop punishing yourself and try to keep calm. Rowena's going to need all the help you can give her during the next few weeks.'

When they arrived at the children's ward the Sister quickly telephoned the news of their arrival to some other department before taking Heather and Guy into a small cubicle that served as her private room.

'Your daughter's in the theatre now, Mrs Lorrimer.

The operation is on the leg. It's a compound fracture, and it's going to be quite some time before she can come home again. She'll be in traction for several weeks until the bones have healed correctly.'

'Someone mentioned concussion,' said Heather nervously.

'Yes, there is a degree of concussion. She kept talking about shopping and a china dog, and didn't know her name or address. The X-rays revealed no fractures of the skull, but she will need careful watching for the next forty-eight hours.'

'Is there somewhere I can wait?'

'Certainly. We'd prefer it if you were here for the critical period. Have you any other children?'

'A boy of seven.'

'He can stay with me overnight,' put in Guy. 'You're needed here.' There was a tap on the door and a young policeman came hesitantly into the room. 'I want a word with Mrs Lorrimer when you've finished, Sister.'

'I think we're through, Constable.'

He waited until she'd left before advancing into the room. When he caught sight of Guy he hesitated. 'Carry on,' said Guy. 'I'm here as a friend, not on duty.'

'I see, sir. Mrs Lorrimer, how long had your daughter been gone before you reported her missing?'

'About half an hour.'

'Did she often wander off?'

'Of course not. We'd had a . . . a disagreement and Rowena was crying in the kitchen when I went up to put my son to bed. When I came back down she'd vanished.'

'And you spent the next twenty-five minutes searching for her yourself?'

'Yes. I live on the Heathfield estate, and I expected to find her there. I never imagined that she'd actually run away, right off the estate. How did the accident happen?'

'According to witnesses, your little girl dashed across the road without even a glance at the traffic. She was crying at the time.'

A lump formed in Heather's throat. 'You think that's likely, Mrs Lorrimer?' he pressed. She nodded, unable to answer him without breaking down completely.

Guy drew the policeman to one side and they talked quietly for several minutes. After that the constable put his notebook in his pocket and walked over to Heather. 'I'm sorry to question you at a time like this, but it's something that has to be done. I hope your little girl gets on all right.'

'Thank you,' she said softly. As soon as the door had closed behind him she began to cry.

'Stop it, Heather,' said Guy firmly. 'She'll be out of theatre soon, you've got to be strong for her sake.'

'I'm tired of being strong.'

'That sounds like the old Heather, not the new one.'

Unconsciously she straightened her back. He was right. This was her chance to prove to herself once and for all that she was capable of looking after her family on her own. 'Of course,' she said as she looked him straight in the eyes, 'you needn't worry, I shan't disgrace myself.'

He put an arm lightly round her shoulders. 'I never thought you would. Look, I think they're wheeling her back now.'

Together they stepped out into the corridor and sure enough, lying asleep on the trolley, was Rowena. Her hair was covered by a neat white cap and her face looked tiny without its usual surrounding mass of curls. For a moment Guy's arm tightened round Heather, and then he stepped back and watched her looking down on the still form of her daughter. Rowena murmured and moved slightly, and at the same time a nurse came down the corridor pushing a medicine trolley. All the sounds and smells became jumbled in Heather's head, and for a terrible moment she was back in Charing Cross Hospital where Brian lay dying.

She swayed on her feet, and at once Guy put his hand

under her left elbow. 'Don't worry, she'll soon be her old self again. You're not really alone, remember, you've got me. I'd stay too but I think I ought to get back to Barnaby. I'll pop in tomorrow morning on my way to work, all right?'

Numbly she nodded. She wanted to beg him to stay with her, but she knew that she mustn't. He was right. Barnaby needed him, and it was her place to stay with Rowena. It was the least she could do for her after that horrible scene in the kitchen.

During the night, as she sat at her daughter's bedside, she kept remembering Guy's words. 'You're not really alone, you've got me,' and she wondered if he meant for ever. She doubted it. He was probably referring to the present crisis, but it was nice to recall the words and the tender way in which they had been spoken.

At four o'clock in the morning Rowena opened her eyes and looked sleepily round. She was in a small room on her own and seemed puzzled by her surroundings. Her eyes fastened gratefully onto Heather's. 'Mummy? Where are we? What happened?'

Tears of relief pricked at the back of Heather's eyelids. 'You had an accident, darling. A car knocked you over. Do you remember?'

'No. I'm thirsty and my leg hurts. Can I have a drink?'

'I'll go and ask the nurse.'

'Am I in hospital?'

'Didn't I say? How silly of me! Yes, you're in hospital. You've had an operation on your left leg and it's all in plaster and up in a swing!'

Rowena smiled. 'I can see it. Will you ask for a drink? My tongue's dry.'

The night sister brought a small container of water and held it to Rowena's mouth. 'Only a sip, poppet. We don't want you being sick. You can have some more later. Are you in any pain?'

'My head aches and my knee hurts.'

'I'll fetch you some painkillers.'

As she went briskly out, her starched skirt rustling in the deep silence of the hospital night, Heather took hold of Rowena's right hand. She squeezed it lightly. 'What a fright you gave us!'

'Did I? Where was the car? Was it at the back of the house?'

'No. Don't worry about it.'

'Why can't I remember?' Rowena's eyes were huge with fright. 'Why don't you tell me? Is Barnaby hurt too?'

'Sshh! Of course not, he's fine. He's staying with Tom for the night.'

'Oh! *Why* don't I remember?'

'Because you banged your head and it gave you concussion. You will remember, later on.'

The sister returned, the pills were swallowed and Rowena slept restlessly for the remainder of the night.

For the next two days she was very ill. Her temperature refused to come down and she was fretting constantly for Barnaby and her father. She didn't seem to remember that Brian was dead, and when Heather gently reminded her she turned her face away and refused to listen.

Guy visited whenever he could, and he brought Heather clean nightdresses for Rowena and a notepad so that she could compile a shopping list. 'Sheila's going to do it for you. She seems to feel ridiculously guilty about all this, as though she's in some way to blame.' Heather could understand why, but she didn't tell Guy.

Then slowly, day by day, Rowena began to improve. After a week in isolation she was thought well enough to be put in the big ward, and here she began to make rapid strides in her recovery. Now Heather found herself redundant for a great deal of the time, and she decided to return home at night so that she could spend a few hours with Barnaby.

'Sure,' said Rowena casually when Heather told her what she proposed to do. 'I'll be fine. Can Barnaby come and see me or isn't he allowed?'

'I'll find out, but I think he's too young.'

'OK. Give him my love. Tell him I'm sorry about his china dog.'

'He knows that, darling. See you tomorrow.' Her last glimpse of Rowena showed her surrounded by a group of mobile children, all chattering brightly while her daughter queened it in splendour.

The weeks passed. Rowena grew bored and fractious. Heather was exhausted from working all day, seeing to Barnaby's tea, then catching a bus to the hospital for evening visiting and another one to get her home two hours later, but to her secret pride, she coped very well. Guy was away on a course in the week, and it was only at weekends that he was there and able to take her in the car. She didn't know which she appreciated the most, and told him as much, which made him laugh.

'I can't get conceited with you around me! I've a nasty suspicion it's the car that you really like!'

At last, at the end of November, the doctors decided that Rowena, once she'd mastered the art of crutches, could go home. She had been taking school lessons in hospital and her teacher had sent her essays to do and maths to work on. Even so it was like a holiday, and Rowena wasn't sorry to hear that she couldn't return to school until the New Year.

Barnaby was madly excited on the Saturday she was finally released from hospital. He was shaking all over and kept sniffing and coughing from the moment he got up. 'I'd forgotten how aggravating that habit was,' confided Heather to Guy as they set off. 'I hope he doesn't get addicted to it again.'

'You're all right, aren't you, Barnaby?' laughed Guy. Barnaby nodded, too excited even to speak. Tom had stayed at home, suddenly shy after not seeing Rowena for so long.

When she hobbled out of the entrance Barnaby hurled

himself at her, and Guy only just stopped him from sending his sister flying to the ground. 'Steady on! She'll be back inside again if you don't take care!' The two children climbed in the back and sat close together, whispering and giggling in their excitement.

It had been arranged that Mary, who had looked after the children during their bout of chickenpox, should look after Rowena while Heather was at work. She had come down and offered her services, and Heather was overwhelmed by such kindness.

'You must like young children,' she said gratefully.

Mary laughed. 'I don't mind them when they're on crutches. It's when they're dashing around the house that they drive me mad. Besides, I feel that this would never have happened if it hadn't been for us women talking too much.'

'What do you mean?'

'Well, we encouraged you to go out and meet people, and then when you did, and began seeing Guy Harrison, we started picking you to bits for no reason at all. I think it was because of Scott that Sheila went for you that day. It was stupid because Scott's always been a right pain, and Sheila knows that better than anyone, but for some reason she decided to blame the police and Guy's a policeman so bingo, she speaks out of turn and in the end it's poor Rowena – who's already having trouble – who suffers the most.'

'I didn't know you all discussed me. You've always been very kind. I'm grateful for the way you helped me to settle in and cope with a job despite school holidays. I couldn't have done it alone.'

Mary looked carefully at Heather. 'You're too nice, that's your trouble. I hope you and Guy work something out between you. You deserve a break, and he's really neat. I wouldn't say no myself if I were single and ten years younger!'

Heather blushed. 'That's what Lynne says, but he's a

good friend, that's all. There's nothing like that between us.'

'I know, and the moon's made of green cheese! It's all right, I don't blame you for keeping quiet about it. I still wish you luck.'

For the final three weeks Mary was as good as her word, and it meant that when Barnaby broke up Heather didn't have to take time off until the holiday period when she was entitled to five days. Guy was delighted to have the holiday off himself, although he was quite resigned to being called in should an emergency crop up.

At last the weeks of excited anticipation were over and it was Christmas Eve. When the children were finally asleep Heather put some of their gifts round the tree that Guy had provided and sorted the rest into their giant stockings. She felt excited herself, and realised that this year Christmas really would seem like Christmas again, with Guy and Tom spending their entire holiday with them. For a brief time they would seem like one big family, and for a moment Heather wondered what the position would be in another twelve months, but then pushed the thought aside. She wouldn't spoil the present by trying to look into the future. She would live from day to day and make the most of everything. She was glad that there was a hint of snow in the air; it completed her vision of a perfect Christmas.

Guy and Tom arrived at eleven-thirty. Tom had a small bunch of flowers for Rowena, and Guy handed Heather a beautiful pot of orange and white chrysanthemums.

'What about me?' asked Barnaby. 'Don't I get anything?'

Guy put his hand in his pocket and brought out a small box. 'Here you are. A do-it-yourself bonsai tree kit.'

'What's a bonsai tree?'

'A miniature one; you keep it indoors.'

Heather was standing with her head buried in the

flowers. 'They smell glorious. Thank you, Guy.'

'And me,' put in Tom. 'I helped choose it.'

'Then thank you, Tom!' For a moment the two adults looked at each other over their children's heads, and there was a tenderness in Guy's expression that she had never seen before.

The Christmas lunch turned out perfectly. Heather glanced round the table and thought how well Guy and Tom fitted into the family, as though they all belonged together. However, she knew that they didn't, and wished that she could freeze the moment and keep it somewhere, a reminder in the future of one of those few perfect days that occur in a lifetime.

'You're looking pensive, Heather,' remarked Guy.

'I'm overfull, that's all! Who got the lucky charm in their Christmas pudding?'

'I did,' said Guy.

'You mustn't tell us your wish,' Barnaby told him earnestly. 'If you do it doesn't come true. Daddy told me that and he was right. I wished for a motor bike, but I told a friend at school and I never got one.'

'In that case I most certainly won't tell!'

'What *did* you wish for?' asked Heather as they washed up.

'I can't tell you; you heard Barnaby!'

She giggled. 'He's not an adult, I am.'

'Indeed you are, and a most alluring one in that check dress. Not quite up to your black number, but I suppose a man can't have everything!'

'I'm glad you like it. Rowena said I looked like a fire-engine!'

'Nonsense, you should wear bright colours more, they suit you.' She felt him move closer to her and brush his lips against the top of her head. 'Where's the mistletoe?' he murmured.

'There isn't any, too expensive.'

'How unromantic! I would have brought some round

with me if I'd known.'

During the afternoon they played charades, card games and a new board game that Tom had been given for Christmas. When Barnaby won, despite not understanding how he'd managed it, his face glowed with pleasure.

'I won, Daddy! I won!' he shouted to Guy. A sudden silence filled the room and Barnaby blushed furiously. 'I'm sorry, I forgot. It's all been so nice that I was thinking you were my Daddy.'

'That's all right, Barnaby,' said Guy easily. 'I'm very flattered. Has anyone got the energy for a short walk before tea?'

They all went except for Heather who laid the table for yet another meal. She kept seeing her son's excited face, and hearing the words tumbling from his lips. She knew how much he'd like to have Guy for a father, but hoped that he didn't harbour any great hopes of it coming about. Marriage no longer held any great appeal for her, but she knew that she was happier when with Guy than at any other time. It was an arrangement that seemed to give them the best of both worlds.

After tea Tom and Barnaby went upstairs to play. Rowena, Guy and Heather sat quietly by the fire. Guy was reading a detective novel – which caused him a lot of unintentional amusement – and Heather was half-asleep.

Rowena suddenly sat up straight. 'Mummy, I want to talk to you.'

'What about, darling?'

'About stealing things from shops.'

Guy glanced up from his book and then continued to read. Heather turned to her daughter. 'What did you want to say?' she asked gently.

Rowena swallowed hard. 'I wanted you to know that although I did it once, you know, a long time ago, I stopped as soon as Guy found out. I didn't want to let him down. Then, when I heard that Guy and Tom were moving away it changed everything.

'Things have been so much better since we got to know them. You're all pink and laughing again, like you used to be; well, even nicer really because you're with us much more and I thought it was going to go on like that for ever. When I found out that it wasn't I just couldn't bear it.

'In Woolworths I thought, why should I care what Guy says? He isn't going to stay very long so I might as well take the things. Life was horrid again and I felt all knotted up inside, so I took the crayons and a few other things. I know it was still wrong, but that was why. I did have a reason.'

Heather went and put her arms round Rowena. 'Don't worry about it. It's over and done with. Next time you feel sad or hurt, please tell me and let me help you. Taking things doesn't make it better, does it?'

Rowena shook her head. 'Besides, Guy isn't going anywhere, are you, Guy?'

He put his book down on the arm of the chair. 'As a matter of fact, I am. I was going to tell you, but at a more appropriate time. I've been offered a promotion at Easter, which necessitates a move to Norfolk.'

'Norfolk!' She stared at him in shock and disbelief.

'Yes. It's quite a way, isn't it?'

Heather bit her bottom lip and took some deep breaths before standing up and moving briskly round the room. 'I'll just wash the cups up,' she murmured and hurried into the kitchen.

Rowena looked at Guy. 'I shouldn't have told, should I? Now she's unhappy too.'

He ran a hand through her hair. 'It's all right, Rapunzel, there's nothing to worry about.'

'Who's Rapunzel?'

'A princess who let down her long, golden hair to let a prince climb up into her bedroom, or something like that!'

She laughed. 'That's rude!' Guy grinned and followed Heather out.

She was carefully washing each cup and saucer and

took no notice of his arrival. He walked across the room and put his arms round her waist. 'I'm sorry. I should have told you earlier, but I . . . '

'It's all right,' her voice was low and calm. 'You aren't under any obligation to tell me anything. I should have realised that in your line of work you'd be called upon to move around the country. It was just rather a shock.'

'Do you know why I didn't tell you?'

'No, but I'm sure you had excellent reasons.'

'I was putting it off because I was afraid.'

'Afraid of what? That I'd become hysterical and burst into tears? Those days are gone, Guy.'

'I know they are, which is precisely why I didn't tell you. The truth is, I want you to come with me to Norfolk.'

'Come with you?'

'Yes. I want to marry you, Heather, and take you there as my wife.'

Her hands stopped turning the mop in the washing-up water and she stared out of the window into the dark garden with a strange hollow feeling in the pit of her stomach.

'Well? Haven't you anything to say?'

'I . . . I'm confused; you've taken me completely by surprise.'

'Surely not! You must know how I feel about you.'

'I know you like me, yes; but marriage, that's rather different, isn't it?'

'Yes, it's a commitment for life. A commitment that only adults are capable of making.'

She gave a gentle laugh. 'I think I'm a fully-fledged adult now, Guy. In fact, if you'd asked me a few months ago I'd have fallen into your arms weeping with happiness.'

'But not now?'

'No,' she said slowly. 'Not now.'

'What's changed? Have I done something wrong?'

'Of course not, but something has changed: me. I'm

used to being in control of my own home. I enjoy taking decisions and having the freedom to sit and read a book for a whole evening even if there's housework crying out to be done. I don't think I could give that up now.'

His face was sombre. 'Do you love me, Heather?'

'Yes, that's what makes this so hard. I do love you, and more intensely than I've ever loved before, but that doesn't change the other things.'

'I love you, and I want you as my wife. Doesn't that count for anything?'

'Of course it does.' She was almost crying now. 'Do you think this is easy for me? I'm only just beginning to realise how many things it's possible to do in life, and I can't turn the clock back and forget.'

'I wouldn't want you to.'

'Yes you would. The first time our commitments clashed I'd be expected to give mine up and play the supporting, wifely role. You know that's true.'

'It isn't. I don't want you devoting your life to me. Don't you realise that I wouldn't have wanted the old Heather for my wife? I liked the girl you were, but I've fallen in love with the woman you've become.' He tried to draw her to him but she resisted.

'What about the children?'

'I'm glad you mentioned them. I didn't want to use them, it seemed rather an unfair trick, but you know perfectly well that all our children would be thrilled to bits.'

For the first time she began to weaken. He could see it in her eyes and pressed home the advantage. 'I'm not suggesting the kind of marriage you used to have. Ours will be an equal partnership, with all major decisions taken jointly.'

'Completely equal?'

'Completely equal. You have my word on it. Please, Heather, say yes. I can't stand the thought of losing you now, when you've become so important to me.

'I have?' Slowly she was beginning to realise that perhaps, after all, it would be possible. She moved her body closer to his and he could see the tears sparkling on her lashes. 'I don't want to lose you either,' she whispered.

'Then you'll marry me?'

This time there was no hesitation. 'Yes, Guy, I'll marry you,' she answered and went freely into his arms.

'What's happening?' asked Rowena, standing in the doorway looking puzzled.

'We've decided to get married,' answered Guy, tenderly cradling Heather's head against his chest.

'Oh good! That means I can leave my horrid old school and you can mend my doll's pram too. Can I be a bridesmaid? I'd like to wear a peach-coloured dress.'

Heather gave a gurgle of laughter. 'She's a highly altruistic little girl, is Rowena!'

'Ugh!' shouted Barnaby, running into the room. 'There isn't any mistletoe out here, is there?'

'No, darling,' said Heather, drying her eyes on Guy's handkerchief. 'Guy and I are going to get married.'

'You don't have to kiss in front of everyone, do you? Where's the lemonade? Tom and I are thirsty. I've won two games and he's won five so far.'

'Another non-romantic!' laughed Guy, releasing Heather to find the lemonade.

'Here you are, passion-killer!' she joked as she filled two glasses.

'Thanks. When you get married there won't be any babies, will there?'

Heather and Guy glanced at one another. 'We'll have to wait and see,' said Heather softly, and she took hold of Guy's hand.

Also available from Woman's Weekly Fiction

Betty Paul

CONDITIONS OF LOVE

Overwhelmed by personal tragedy and the breakdown of her career as a singing star, Caroline retreats to a remote seaside hideaway. The last thing she needs is to meet a bedraggled and desolate young man, ten years her junior and even more in need of a helping hand than she.

Despite her own problems, Caroline cannot turn her back on her uninvited guest but Trevor has his pride. He will only accept help if he works for her in exchange. Delicate and discreet, the relationship between the stage star and the down and out starts off as strictly business and ends up so much more...

Further titles available from Woman's Weekly Fiction

While every effort is made to keep prices low, it is sometimes necessary to increase prices at short notice. Mandarin Paperbacks reserves the right to show new retail prices on covers which may differ from those previously advertised in the text or elsewhere.

The prices shown below were correct at the time of going to press.

	ISBN	Title	Author	Price
☐	1 86056 001 6	**I Can Only Dance With You**	Jan Webster	£1.99
☐	1 86056 090 3	**The Lost Years**	Diana Morgan	£1.99
☐	1 86056 075 X	**A Walk in the Wood**	Ann Gilbert	£1.99
☐	1 86056 095 4	**To Be a Fine Lady**	Delia Ellis	£1.99
☐	1 86056 011 3	**A Rose By Any Other Name**	Nina Lambert	£1.99
☐	1 86056 980 6	**Conditions of Love**	Betty Paul	£1.99
☐	1 86056 016 4	**September Fair**	Rose Boucheron	£1.99
☐	1 86056 071 7	**Change of Circumstances**	Margaret Bingley	£1.99

All these books are available at your bookshop or newsagent, or can be ordered direct from the address below. Just tick the titles you want and fill in the form below.

Cash Sales Department, PO Box 5, Rushden, Northants NN10 6YX.
Fax: 01933 414047 : Phone: 01933 414000.

Please send cheque, payable to 'Reed Book Services Ltd', or postal order for purchase price quoted and allow the following for postage and packing:

£1.00 for the first book: £1.50 for **two books or more per order.**

NAME (Block letters) ....

ADDRESS ....

.... Postcode..............................

☐ I enclose my remittance for £......................

☐ I wish to pay by Access/Visa Card Number ☐☐☐☐☐☐☐☐☐☐☐☐☐☐☐☐

Expiry Date ☐☐☐☐

☐ If you do not wish your name to be used by other carefully selected organisations for promotional purposes please tick this box.

Signature ....

Please quote our reference: 3 503 500 C

Orders are normally dispatched within five working days, but please allow up to twenty days for delivery.

Registered office: Michelin House, 81 Fulham Road, London SW3 6RB

Registered in England. No. 1974080